WHOSE MIDLIFE CRISIS IS IT ANYWAY?

GOOD TO THE LAST DEATH BOOK TWO

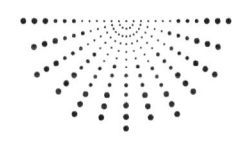

ROBYN PETERMAN

ROBYN PETERMAN

Copyright © 2020 by Robyn Peterman

All rights reserved.

No part of this book may be reproduced in any form or by any electronic or mechanical means, including information storage and retrieval systems, without written permission from the author, except for the use of brief quotations in a book review.

This book is a work of fiction. Names, characters, places, and incidents either are the product of the author's imagination or are used fictitiously. Any resemblance to actual persons, living or dead, businesses, companies, events, or locales is coincidental.

This book contains content that may not be suitable for young readers 17 and under.

Cover design by *JJ's Design & Creations*

Edited by *Kelli Collins*

PRAISE FOR ROBYN PETERMAN

"Daisy's life has been turned upside down, and we get to watch the aftermath. Prepare to root for a new heroine. You'll fall in love with this hilarious hoyden and all of the hot water she dives into. Head first! Masterful and heartwarming, don't let this one get away!"
—NY Times Bestselling Author Darynda Jones

"Brilliant and so relatable! I laughed, I cried, I swooned, and I sighed. Heavily. Robyn Peterman has her finger on the pulse of midlife madness, and I can't get enough."
— USA Today Bestselling Author, Renee George

"I'd read the phone book if Robyn Peterman wrote it! It's A Wonderful Midlife Crisis is a home run of hilarious, heartwarming paranormal fun. Midlife's a journey. Enjoy the ride. Crisis included… Read it!"
— Mandy M. Roth, NY Times & USA TODAY Bestselling Author

"Hilarious, heartbreaking, magical and addictive! No one can turn a midlife crisis upside down quite like Robyn Peterman. A stay-up-all-night novel that will have you begging for more."

— *Michelle M. Pillow, New York Times and USA Today Bestselling Author*

ACKNOWLEDGMENTS

This series has been in my head for two years. It took a call and a nudge from Shannon Mayer to make me pull the file out and finish book one. Now you're getting book two! Each word was a joy to write and I owe Shannon for yanking me into the Paranormal Women's Fiction group. Playing in a sandbox with strong talented women who have each other's backs is a rare and special experience.

As always, while writing is a solitary experience getting a book into the world is a group project.

The PWF 13 Gals — Thank you for a wild ride. You rock.

Renee — Thank you for all your support, your friendship, your formatting expertise and for being the best Cookie ever. You saved my butt on this one. Forever in your debt.

Wanda — Thank you for knowing what I mean even when I don't. LOL You are the best and this writing business wouldn't be any fun without you. You make the journey more fun.

Kelli — Thank you for saving me from scary grammar mistakes. You rock. And thank you for letting me be late. LOL

Nancy, Susan and Candace — Thank you for being kickass betas. You are all wonderful.

Jay — Thank you. Your cover captured what was in my mind perfectly.

Mom — Thank you for listening to me hash out the plot and for giving me brilliant ideas. You really need to write a book!

Mandy — You rock hard! So happy I can call you my friend.

Steve, Henry and Audrey — Thank you. The three of you are my world. Without you, none of this would make sense. I love you.

DEDICATION

This one is for the over-forty gals because we ROCK!

MORE IN THE GOOD TO THE LAST DEATH SERIES

ORDER BOOK THREE NOW!

Midlife's a bumpy journey. The ride is a freaking roller-coaster. The crisis is real.

With my life back to normal--*normal* being a very relative word--one would think I'd catch a break.

One would be very wrong.

With an Angel gunning for me and a Demon in my bed, life couldn't be more complicated. Not to mention, I'm going to have to make a rather *large* life choice.

Do I want to live forever?

Does anyone? Forever is a very long time.

Whatever. I'll think about it tomorrow... or next week... or next month. As long as I have my girlfriends, my dogs, a super-sized case of merlot and my deceased squatters, I'm good to go.

My midlife crisis. My rules. If it doesn't kill me dead first, I plan to have a most excellent midlife crisis.

BOOK DESCRIPTION

WHOSE MIDLIFE CRISIS IS IT ANYWAY?

Midlife's a journey. Enjoy the ride. Crisis included.

Never knew that life after death was far more dangerous than *real* life.

Never in my forty years did I think my new *normal* would be gluing body parts back onto ghosts and hosting a houseful of dead squatters. Thank God for superglue and a strong stomach.

Never thought I'd date the Grim Reaper and that I would be the one to blow it. I mean, how idiotic does one have to be to get dumped by a dude who lives in Hell?

Going about business as usual is not usual in any way. No one is who they seem to be… and to be honest, neither am I. What I'd known to be true has turned out to be myth. The

BOOK DESCRIPTION

Angels are frightening and the Demons are hot. Wait. I mean *not*. Who am I kidding? The Grim Reaper is very hot —like a freaking pre-menopausal hot flash hot.

Now I'm in a race against time and all sorts of unsavory supernatural horrors to save my deceased gay husband's afterlife. And that was a sentence I never thought would leave my lips.

Whatever. I'll yank up my big girl panties, stock up on wine and lean on my girlfriends as needed. As they say, when the going gets tough, the tough get inebriated… or something like that.

With everything to lose, I have no choice but to grow some lady balls. That I can do. I just hope balls will be enough.

I had planned to live midlife in peace, not in pieces.
    Good luck to me…

PROLOGUE

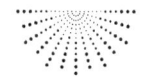

Heather stood in the doorway of my bedroom with an expression of shock on her face. She bent down and scooped up a handful of black crystals. They slipped through her fingers and floated back to the floor.

"Can you do anything for him?" I asked hoarsely.

I'd cried so hard my voice sounded like I'd swallowed shards of glass. It had taken Heather a half hour to get to the farmhouse. When she found me on the floor in the fetal position sobbing, she'd freaked out. Trying to explain to her what had happened was impossible. Instead, I took her to my bedroom and showed her Steve.

My best friend.

The man I'd been married to when he was alive.

The man who'd come back as a ghost to tell me he was gay, and to help me find someone to love me the way I deserved to be loved.

"Oh God," she gasped out as she approached the bed and

looked at him. She put her hand over her mouth and tried not to cry.

"I need your help."

"You stopped the darkness from taking him," Heather whispered, flabbergasted. "How?"

Gideon had asked the very same question. Had no one ever stopped the darkness?

"I quit my job," I said. "I'm no longer a Death Counselor."

"Yet you can still see Steve?" she asked.

My gut clenched in terror for a moment, and I thought I might throw up. Gram couldn't see the dead since she was no longer the Death Counselor.

My head whipped to the bed. Steve was there—I could see him. My cry of relief was primal and guttural. It sounded strange to my own ears. But strange had become par for the course. All that mattered was that I could see him. I wasn't sure what it meant as far as the rules went, but I didn't care. I was grateful that I still had the ability.

"Yes," I choked out. "I see him."

Heather eyed me for a long moment and shook her head. "Daisy, there is no one like you. No one."

"Not sure if that's good or bad," I replied, moving to Steve and sitting next to him.

He looked awful, but Heather didn't comment or act repulsed. That was a relief. Even though Heather was one of my dearest friends, I would have kicked her ass. Steve could hear us. He was in enough agony. He didn't need to be made aware of his revolting appearance.

"Can you help me send him into the light?" I asked.

Heather tilted her head and gave me an odd look. "Why would you think I could help you send Steve into the light?"

The cryptic games were wearing on me, but I played along. Maybe this was how it worked.

"You're the Angel of Mercy. You send people into the light."

Heather paled and sat down on a chair. "I'm not the Angel of Mercy."

"Yes, you are. You *have* to be," I insisted, glaring at her. "You can see the dead like I can and talk to them. You *are* the Angel of Mercy. Stop playing games. I need you to help me send Steve into the light. I'll give you anything you want. I just need your help."

"Oh God, Daisy." Heather's chin fell to her chest. "You have it all wrong."

"Have what wrong?" I asked as a feeling of dread washed over me.

"Every good story has a major plot twist," she said slowly, growing more agitated with each word.

"Go on," I said, not liking the direction of the conversation, but knowing I needed to hear it.

"The Grim Reaper—Gideon—sends souls in question into the light, and the Angel of Mercy sends them to the darkness—opposite of what you might assume," she explained. "It's been that way since the beginning of time. It's for balance and to eliminate conflict of interest."

"Don't," I said. "Do *not* screw with me."

Heather stood and began to pace the room. "I'm not," she whispered. "I would never do that to you."

The realization hit me like a ton of bricks. Gideon had

...lied to me. Steve had tried to tell me, and I didn't understand. I had been warned by the other ghosts that everything was not as it seemed. Gideon had not sent Steve into the darkness—and I was the biggest idiot alive.

I couldn't even comprehend what I'd done by sending Gideon away, and right now wasn't the time to rip myself a new one.

Had Heather done this to Steve?

That didn't seem right, but it was the only option left. My body trembled violently. I didn't know how much more I could take.

"Why?" I asked. "Why would you do this?"

Heather stopped in confusion and looked at me. "Daisy, I didn't do this."

Fury consumed me. It had happened. I witnessed it. I was there. Someone had to be responsible. If it wasn't Gideon and it wasn't Heather, who was it?

"Fine," I said harshly. "I'll play along. If you're not the Angel of Mercy, who in the hell is?"

"Clarissa," Heather replied. "Clarissa is the Angel of Mercy."

The need to scream or destroy something was overwhelming. Sitting still wasn't going to work. I'd implode.

Hopping off the bed, I stripped off my clothes and yanked on running gear.

Clarissa had warned me. She had warned me to my face and I didn't get it.

The bitch had destroyed me in every way possible, and I'd played right into her plans. I'd banished the man I was in love with and destroyed my best friend in the process.

"Correct me if I'm wrong," I ground out between clenched teeth, wanting to put my fist through the wall. "From their *titles*, I would think the Grim Reaper was the bad guy and the Angel of Mercy was the good one. Even with what you told me they do, this makes no sense. *Clarissa* is the damned definition of evil."

"Nothing is black or white," Heather said, running her hands through her hair and closing her eyes. "The simplest way to explain it is that Clarissa is a Heavenly Angel—so to speak—and Gideon is a Demon… or a fallen Angel. Bad people do good things and good people do bad things. Existence is a shade of gray. Living forever takes its toll on people."

"I'd hardly call them *people*. People don't live forever," I snapped.

Heather opened her eyes and leveled me with a stare. "What would you call me?"

Meeting her gaze, I was at a loss. I had no idea. My understanding of just about everything was completely screwed.

"Honestly, I don't know," I said emotionlessly. "I don't even know."

Turning my back on her, I walked over to Steve and gently tucked the covers around him. It made no difference. I was aware he felt no real physical pain, but it helped me. Quickly pulling a copy of my will from the safe under the bed, I thrust the papers into Heather's hands.

"Everything goes to Gram," I said. "Make sure it happens, please."

"What are you going to do?" Heather asked, alarmed.

"I fucked up, Heather."

Her expression would have made me laugh if the situation wasn't so dire. I never dropped the F-bomb. I'd never dropped one in my life. However, the F-bomb was merited now. Tons of F-bombs were merited.

"Talk to me. Please," she insisted.

"What are you?" I asked as I tied my tennis shoe and broke a lace in my rage.

"What do you mean?"

"I mean, *what are you?*" I snapped, getting frustrated and grabbing another pair of running shoes. "You're not the Grim Reaper and you're not the Angel of Mercy. What are you?"

Heather only paused for a moment. "I'm the Arbitrator. I'm the Arbitrator between Heaven and Hell."

"They exist?" I demanded. "Heaven and Hell are real? God and Satan are real?"

"Depends on your definition, but yes," she told me.

I didn't have time to even get into that right now. I had an Angel of Mercy to eliminate.

"Daisy," Heather said in a worried tone. "Tell me what you're planning to do."

"I'm going to kill Clarissa," I said so calmly, Heather blanched. "In the space of several hours, I've destroyed my entire life. And she warned me. The piece of shit warned me and I didn't listen."

"Daisy, that's not allowed," Heather said, putting her hand on my arm.

"She tried to send Steve to the darkness based on a lie

and her hatred of me," I hissed. "I should just forget about that?"

"No." Heather pressed her fingers to the bridge of her nose and sighed. "No, you shouldn't, but..."

I stopped for a moment and tried to make sense of my thoughts so I could make Heather understand why this was the only way. I knew Steve wouldn't get better. In my act of saving him, I might have very well sentenced him to a life of nothingness.

"Heather, I just banished Gideon from my life because I blamed him for what happened to Steve," I said flatly.

"Gideon didn't try to defend himself?" she questioned, startled.

I shook my head and laughed. It was a hollow, ugly laugh. "He tried. I wouldn't listen. Seems like that's a pattern for me lately. Hence, I systematically just decimated any chance of happiness I'll ever have. It's gone. I have myself to thank for that—not Clarissa. She started the ball rolling. I grabbed it and ran it in for a touchdown. However, she played with Steve's fate because she was jealous of Gideon and me. She'll pay for that. And for what she did, she dies."

"Sit down," Heather demanded. "Now."

"I'll give you five minutes," I said, still standing. "If you want to represent me in my murder trial, I'd appreciate it. You'll probably lose and that might not be good for business. I'll understand if you don't want me for a client. However, I *am* going to kill her and it's completely premeditated."

Heather's laugh was so shocking, I almost smiled. But smiling wasn't in my repertoire right now.

"Let me start by saying I would love for Clarissa to be eliminated from this world. However, it's not an option. She can't be killed."

"Are you serious?" I shouted.

"I am," Heather said. "Here's the real question. Do you want Steve to stay in this state forever?"

I paled and sat. "No."

"Fine," Heather said. "I'll represent you."

"I thought you said Clarissa couldn't die," I said, confused now.

"There are far worse things than death, Daisy," she said with the beginnings of a smile. "Far, far worse."

"Clarissa's decision was wrong. Steve didn't commit suicide. Why can't it just be reversed?"

"Once a decree has been made, it stands," Heather said. "However, in this case…"

That was all I needed to hear. I was in. "Tell me what I have to do."

"You won't like it."

I sighed and pressed my lips together. The choices were not many. I was sure none of them were good, but at this point, it didn't matter. As long as Clarissa would pay for what she'd done and Steve wouldn't be left like a dead vegetable, I was game. Gideon was gone. Due to my stupid habit of assuming I knew what the hell was going on, Gideon and I probably couldn't be fixed. It would forever be the biggest mistake I'd made, and I had to live with it. However, I was never going to assume anything again. If that was my lesson, the price had been damned high.

"I don't care. I'll do it."

So, she told me. She told me in great detail what had to be done. It was far more horrifying than what I'd imagined. But Heather had given me something.

Heather had given me hope.

There was a blinding golden light at the end of a very dark tunnel.

And maybe if I came through it in one piece with a small bit of my sanity intact, I'd search for Gideon and apologize. I didn't think he would accept, but I would find him someday and tell him.

He deserved that.

I owed it to him… because I still loved him. Not that it would make a difference in the end, but I knew. And that would have to be good enough.

"When do we start?" I asked.

"We start now," she replied.

"Let's do it," I said.

Heather looked at me for a long moment, and then sighed. "Daisy, you can get your *happiness* back too. Love doesn't disappear that easily."

I smiled, but I doubted it. Heather hadn't been here when it went down between Gideon and me, but it was a nice thought—one I'd hold on to.

Forty was a shitty year, and it had barely started. Midlife had been one hell of a bumpy ride so far. I chose to believe midlife was a journey—not a destination. It was the only way I could go forward without breaking.

There was no other choice. My best friend's afterlife was on the line… and possibly my *happiness*.

May the best woman win.

CHAPTER ONE

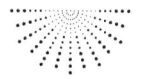

Three Days Later

"I found thirty-nine dang silver wisdom sparkles in my hair today," Jennifer griped as she tried like hell to frown but failed. "Looks like white pubes sprouting up out of my head. And wouldn't you just know, JoJo, my hairdresser, is on maternity leave."

"Wait," June said, perplexed as she rummaged through her large tote and pulled out a bright pink tin. "I thought JoJo was a man—a gay man."

"He is fabulously gay, but if that hottie was straight, he'd be husband number six. That boy wields a curling iron with skill—great with his hands if ya know what I mean," Jennifer said with a chuckle and a wink that came kind of close to looking like a wink. "Anyhoo, his Labradoodle, Barbra Streisand, is having puppies and he took two weeks off."

"Makes sense to me," June said with a laugh. "Probably helps that he owns the salon."

"Probably," Jennifer agreed with a sigh and tried to frown again.

Again, no luck.

Jennifer recently had so much Botox injected into her face that her facial expressions were not in working order.

"While I like the wisdom sparkle nickname, the pube part is a bit uncouth," June said with a shake of her head as she put the container of what I was pretty sure were cookies on the steps of my front porch.

"It's the truth," Jennifer shot back. "My face looks like a baby's ass and my hair looks like an old lady with her bush on her head instead of in her pants."

"You're not old. You're just gross," June admonished her with a smile. "And anyway, I read that sixty-five is the new forty-seven."

Jennifer laughed and pilfered a cookie from the tin. "You made that up."

"I most certainly did," June agreed. "However, I stand by it."

I stood on my front porch and tried to think of something to add to the conversation to be polite. Politeness was ingrained in my Southern DNA. Nothing came to mind. Today, even being Southern wasn't enough.

I adored June and Jennifer. They were my coworkers and two of my dearest buddies, along with Heather and Missy, who thankfully hadn't joined Jennifer and June in the surprise morning visit... or rather, ambush. I was in sweatpants, a crappy t-shirt with holes in it and paint-splattered running shoes. My coat covered the worst of it, but I was very aware I looked like hell warmed over. I felt like it too.

My world had imploded as of three days ago and I couldn't bring myself to tell my friends about it. Part of me was grateful they knew nothing about the physical existence of Angels, Demons, ghosts, Immortal Arbitrators and Death Counselors. The other part of me was devastated that I couldn't tell them the truth.

My life had become an unending horror movie.

"You could pluck the wisdom sparkles," June suggested, pulling her coat tighter around her body.

The cool November air felt like a sharp slap of reality in my face. I hadn't ventured outside in a few days. The need to run ten or a million miles pulled at me, but I wouldn't leave my farmhouse right now.

It wasn't safe.

I also couldn't invite my friends inside.

"You pluck one tinsel pube, five of the little bastards come back in its place," Jennifer announced, plopping her round little body down on my porch swing.

"I call bullshit on that," I said, surprising myself with the sound of my own voice. I hadn't spoken in a while.

"You're only forty, Daisy. Just you wait," Jennifer warned, trying to raise her brow at me.

She failed. She'd gotten a *double dose* of botulism shot into her head. Her eyebrows were going to be frozen on her wrinkle-free forehead for at least six months.

"Men look distinguished when they go gray," June said

with a sigh. "My Charlie is so handsome with his gray hair. Women just look old. Not fair."

"You're both beautiful," I said, mustering up a small smile.

June was an adorable and well-put-together fifty-seven-year-old. She was like a mom to us all—happily married to Charlie, who was a medical tech at our small-town hospital. She had four awesome kids and had won the *Marriage Goals Award* with Charlie. June was the only one in our posse who had gotten the happily ever after. The rest of us were a hot mess.

Jennifer—also adorable, just not as *put together* as June—was sixty-five and had sworn off men after her fifth divorce. She was short, round and obsessed with using her investments made off of her divorce settlements to *improve* her face. It was a given that the *wisdom sparkles* wouldn't work for her.

"We're concerned about you, Daisy," June said kindly. "Are you doing okay?"

There was no way to answer the question. I would never be okay again. And there was no way to make them understand.

"I'm fine," I heard myself say. "I'm just… I think I might need to be alone for a little while."

"That's understandable," June said with a nod. "We're here for you, sweetheart. Always."

I wasn't sure exactly what June thought was wrong with me, but my appearance and the fact that I hadn't been to work in days must have tipped them off that something wasn't right.

"That was kind of wussy," Jennifer commented to June.

June shrugged and gave Jennifer a look that I was sure she used on her own children when they were out of line. "I don't like to push. It's rude."

"I've got no problem with it. I have no filter whatsoever and I'm not nearly as tactful as June is," Jennifer stated.

"That's correct," June chimed in, supporting her buddy with the tiniest of eye rolls.

"Thank you," Jennifer replied, taking the compliment at face value.

A compliment was a compliment, no matter how insulting.

"My pleasure," June replied.

"So anyhoo, to get back to the matter at hand, I'd like to say that Gideon, while he has a fine ass, is a dick and a good-for-nothing jackhole," Jennifer said as her voice rose an octave, proving she was upset even though her face was incapable of conveying it. "The fact that he quit and took a job out of the country is bull crap. I hope he gets fired and that his nuts shrivel up and fall off."

"Where did you hear that?" I whispered. My broken heart was beating so loudly in my chest I was sure the gals could hear it. Jennifer had almost gotten a smile out of me with the shriveled nuts part, but I was still too raw.

"Heather told us," June said, taking my hand in hers and giving it a little squeeze. "Apparently, he didn't even give notice at the firm. Just up and left."

Normally, I craved June's motherly attention. Today it didn't help. Nothing helped… yet. Soon I would have to grow bigger lady balls and face life head-on, but right now, I was in a strange and secret limbo.

"It's all good," I lied. "And I'm the one who ended it, not Gideon. It wasn't his fault at all."

The last part was true, and his name on my lips was utter torture.

Jennifer eyed me for a long moment. I felt like a bug under a microscope. Also, I thought her face might have twitched despite all the Botox. I wasn't about to share the news. The silver wisdom sparkle pubes were all she could take.

"You've forced my hand, Daisy," Jennifer said, shaking her head.

"I have?" I asked, confused.

Jennifer rubbed her little hands together and grinned. At least I thought she grinned. Note to self… never get Botox.

"Jelly beans get their shine from shellac that's made from insect shit," she announced with glee.

Closing my eyes, I really tried not to smile. Smiling seemed so wrong with Steve in the state he was in, but Jennifer's knowledge of the ridiculous was enormous. When Steve was alive, he'd loved her outrageous humor. He'd be happy that I was enjoying it now.

Jennifer spent hours at the nursing home with my gram, entertaining her with a fount of useless and stomach-turning facts. I loved Jennifer for that but it was hard being on the receiving end when all I wanted to do was go back inside and cry.

"You lie," June gasped out, appalled. "I love jelly beans, especially the pink ones."

"You're eating poop," Jennifer said as June gagged. "Perfume musk comes from a sack in the front of a deer's pecker."

"Do you actually search for this kind of stuff?" I asked, realizing that maybe Jennifer's hilariously nasty and pointless skill with the absurd might be just what I needed right now.

"You bet I do," Jennifer said with a cackle as she swung on the porch swing with her feet barely touching the ground. "A pig's orgasm lasts for a half hour."

"Next time around, I'm coming back as a pig," June said with a chuckle as she seated herself on the top step.

"Last but not least—and this one actually pertains to the situation," Jennifer said as she stood up so whatever the hell she was about to say had more of an impact. "A male honey bee's ejaculation is so strong that it makes his junk explode and kills him."

Tilting my head to the side, I stared at my friend. "How exactly does that pertain?" I asked, kind of scared of what she might say. One never knew what would come out of Jennifer's mouth.

"I wish a honey bee's ejaculation on Gideon. You're too good for him. The son of a bitch is like my ex-husband," Jennifer muttered.

"Which one, dear?" June inquired.

"All of them," Jennifer snorted. "Not a single one was good enough for me. Took me till I was sixty-three to figure that shit out. However, the stock I bought with the divorce settlement checks is lovely. I tell you what, I'd like to give

Gideon a good knee to the balls and knock his nuts up into his esophagus."

"Well, he's gone," I said, wanting to wrap up the impromptu get together or, at the very least, change the subject. "Aren't you two supposed to be at work?"

"Nah," Jennifer said, swiping a few more cookies. "Heather's got some kind of urgent lawyer business and told us to take the next two weeks off. Closed down the entire office."

"With full pay," June piped in. "I don't feel quite right about that, but Heather insisted."

"Daisy, I can tell you want us to leave since you haven't invited us in and tried to feed us," Jennifer announced with a cookie in her mouth as an appalled June lightly punched her in the arm. "Being that you're as Southern as they come, I'd have to surmise that you really do want to be alone. Just remember we're a phone call away, my friend."

"Get your butt in the car," June said with a wink to me as she pulled Jennifer across my front yard. "Jennifer's way with words is slightly lacking."

"Thank you," Jennifer said.

June rolled her eyes for real and giggled. "However, she was right about us always being there for you. Call us any time of day or night, Daisy. I mean that."

I nodded and gave them what I hoped looked like a smile. It felt like a forced grimace, but they seemed satisfied and drove away slowly, waving until I couldn't see them anymore.

I knew exactly what Heather's urgent business was. She was gearing up to help me take on Clarissa and save Steve's soul from being damned to the darkness. Just as nothing was what it appeared to be, Heather was not simply one of my dearest friends and a lawyer who had hired us all from the old firm we'd recently quit.

No, Heather was much more.

And unfortunately, so was I.

CHAPTER TWO

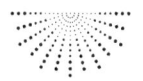

So far, midlife had been a shitty journey. The ride had been out of control, and the crisis was included—whether I'd ordered it or not.

"I can't help you," I whispered. "I'm so sorry."

She didn't acknowledge my words. I was unsure if she'd even heard me since I'd barely heard myself. My throat was raw from the recent crying jag I'd indulged in after June and Jennifer left. Of course, I'd eaten the entire tin of cookies June had made as well. It was not a good day so far. My voice sounded foreign to my own ears, and I was fairly sure I had chocolate chip cookie crumbs in my sweats.

Talking about Gideon wasn't something I had wanted to do. It was still too painful and entirely my fault that he'd disappeared—something I would regret until the day I died. I'd done it thinking I was avenging Steve. I'd been gravely mistaken.

Staring at the dead woman who sat on my couch felt like

a breath of forbidden fresh air. The others were gone, and I felt the loss like an open wound. The ghost sat quietly and stared at her hands. Every few minutes she would glance my way. She was either newly deceased, which I doubted due to her state of decomposition, or she hadn't heard the word on the street yet.

I'd quit my unpaid secret side job. I was no longer the Death Counselor. Never again would I glue body parts back onto semi-transparent ghosts or help the dead find closure so they could move forward to whatever the heck came next. My inner debate as to the *truth* of the afterlife still waged violently inside me.

Closing my eyes, I almost laughed. Almost. I still had six cases of superglue in the garage. I hadn't smiled for real in what felt like an eternity. It was inappropriately fitting that the first thought that made the corners of my lips turn up was the recent memory of reattaching arms, legs and jaws for my former dead roomies.

Did I want to quit? No.

I had to. There was no choice. I'd done it in a moment of desperation, but it had been the right choice. Steve was safe and Steve was here.

A month ago, I thought I'd lost my mind. I was wrong.

Three days ago, I'd almost destroyed my world. Correction. I did destroy my world and my happiness. I also came very close to destroying my best friend. As much as it shredded me, I was of no use to the sad specter sitting in my living room.

Knowing there was nothing I could do for the woman, I

felt like I'd lost my humanity—my mind would have been an easier loss to take.

"You're in the wrong place," I tried again, hoping she understood me. "I can't help you."

Her reaction was full of confusion.

Join the club…

"I mean, it *was* the right place," I said, realizing that I was confusing myself. "But it's not anymore."

The poor woman must think I'm nuts. She would be correct. I wasn't certifiable, but I was definitely missing a few screws.

"I had to stop," I told her, unsure if she could follow what I was saying.

Most of the dead understood English, but the young woman in my house could be an exception. I was surprised I could see her at all. I assumed that once I'd quit, I would lose the ability like Gram had. Thank God I could still see Steve.

"Sssiiiiiiinngea," she said. "Boooooooouuns."

Shaking my head, I tried once more. "I can't do anything for you. I wish I could, but I can't."

The woman appeared to have been young when she'd died—maybe mid to late twenties. She was lovely in a sad and decomposing kind of way. Most of the dead were a bluish-gray hue, but I could make out that her hair had been blonde by the few strands that still held color. It was difficult to tell her exact age. She was rough-looking—missing part of her head and a good deal of her jaw. For some bizarre reason, she was familiar to me.

Being compassionate had bitten me in the ass repeatedly. Why stop now?

"Do I know you?" I asked, realizing it was an unfair question since there was nothing I could do for her. Making her leave so she could find someone who could aid her was what I should do, but...

Who in the hell that could be was anyone's guess. The *gift* had been passed from my gram to my mother, and then to me. As far as I'd understood, we were the only line of Death Counselors. But since the dead hadn't come back, I took some comfort at the possibility that there were indeed more than just Gram and me in the world.

"Sssiiiiiiinngea booooooouuns," she repeated in a broken whisper.

"Let me explain," I said, unable to decipher her words. "I used to be the Death Counselor, but I messed up."

She waited and stared at me with sad, sunken eyes and a trembling body.

"*Messed up* is actually a mild term for it, but I'm not a big cusser. I mean, I do say shit and damn, but the F-bomb would have worked in my last statement, and I'm not really good with that one," I went on as if the conversation we were having was even remotely normal. "You don't really need to hear about my prowess or lack thereof with profanity. So anyway, my dead husband—Steve—came back to tell me he was gay and..."

What in the hell was I doing? The dead woman wasn't my therapist.

But wait... She needed to understand why I couldn't help her. The truth didn't always set you free. It was complicated and horrifying in my case, but if the travesty that was my life could convince the gal on my couch to seek help elsewhere, then so be it.

"I thought I'd gone insane," I told her, moving across the room and sitting next to her on the couch. "I didn't tell anyone that there were ghosts all over my house and following me to the grocery. I mean, who are you going to tell that to without them having you locked up in the loony bin? Right?"

The woman simply stared.

There seemed to be no judgment in her eyes, or more likely, she had no clue what I'd just said. It didn't matter. I'd finish what I'd started and, at the very least, she might think I was so unhinged she'd leave. I didn't want her here, but I didn't want to hurt her feelings either. She was dead, for the love of everything unholy. She'd already been through enough.

Plus, being Southern dictated my polite manners. Being Southern could seriously suck.

"So… umm… I figured out a way to communicate with my squatters," I continued. "It's called dead man mind-diving… or dead woman, to be nonsexist and fair. In a moment of absurdly inappropriate dead-humor, I thought about having a t-shirt made."

She didn't laugh.

I didn't blame her. My comedic skills were sorely lacking, and it was one of those jokes that you had to be there to get.

"Sorry about that. So, then I embarked upon a life of crime and committed a misdemeanor for my dead friend

Sam. I don't regret it at all. However, I'm not cut out for ten to twenty in the state pen. You feel me? I was completely relieved I could use a Ouija board to help the others. Mail fraud is the other illegal hobby I took up. I sent post-dated letters and cards to the loved ones of my dead guests so they wouldn't have unfinished business. Risky? Sure, but it was way easier than breaking and entering."

The woman politely nodded. She lost her head. Reaching forward, I caught it in my hands and handed it back to her.

Standing up, I sighed. "Hang on a sec. Stay here."

Sprinting to the garage, I convinced myself gluing her head back on didn't mean I was taking the job back. I couldn't. It would endanger one of the people I loved most in the world. However, sending the poor woman on her way knowing that her head was firmly attached was the right thing to do. It would suck all kinds of butt for her to wander around without a head.

As long as I didn't solve her problem, a little superglue surgery was fine.

"Can you hand me your head so I can glue it back on for you?" I asked as I sat down next to her again.

Not a sentence I thought I would ever speak.

She had propped it back up on her neck. With what I thought was a smile—it was hard to tell since most of her jaw was gone—she carefully handed me her head.

Turning it at an angle so her eyes weren't staring at me, which would have freaked me out, I used two full tubes of superglue. It was slightly excessive, but I wasn't in the business of gluing body parts on anymore. I didn't need to be careful about overuse. Plus, I had no clue how far she would have to travel for help. Extra glue could hopefully keep her head attached to her body for months if she was careful.

"For this to work, I need to hold it in place for two minutes," I explained, making eye contact again since her head was no longer in my lap. "But since it's your head, I'm gonna do it for three minutes. Cool?"

"Sssiiiiiiinngea booooooouuns," she told me.

"Umm... okay," I said, looking around for my dogs.

Donna the Destroyer wasn't actually a dog at all even though she resembled one. I'd found out she was a Hell Hound and could understand the dead better than I could. I'd barely blinked an eye at the news. Since I was hanging out with deceased people, gluing on appendages and living a life of crime, the fact that my puppy was a denizen of Hell was the least of my problems. Plus, I adored her.

Karen the Chair Eater could not see the dead. However, she could dig a hole in the yard the size of a refrigerator without an ounce of shame. She'd eaten all of my mums and had room-clearing gas for thirty-six hours. Again, I didn't bat an eye. I simply held my nose and loved her anyway.

The dogs were nowhere to be found.

"I don't understand you," I said apologetically.

"Sssiiiiiiinngea booooooouuns."

"Mmmkay," I said, glancing down at my phone to see if the three minutes were up.

There was no way I could hug her and go into her mind to talk to her. I'd figured out the system by trial and error with a little help from Donna the Destroyer. It hurt like a mother humper to mind dive, but it worked. The dead's voices were as clear as if they were still alive.

But I wasn't the Death Counselor anymore. I'd be risking Steve's afterlife if I did.

"Singea Bonus?" I tried. "Is that your name?" I'd never heard a name like that before, but if she was from another country, she could have an unusual name.

She tried to shake her head, but I had a darn good grip on it.

"Sssiiiiiiinngea boooooooouuns."

"Not your name?" I asked. "How about Sissy G. Boons?"

She reached up and gently touched my face. Her skin felt like dry paper. I was still amazed that the ghosts were somewhat corporeal even though I could see through parts of them.

"Naawwwooo," she said.

Breathing in through my nose and slowly out through my mouth, I fought back every instinct I had to help her. It wasn't in my nature to walk away… but I had to.

Standing up and moving to the other side of the room now that her head seemed like it wasn't going to tumble off of her neck again, I put some distance between us. If I hugged her so I could understand her, the darkness might come back for my dead, gay best friend and former husband. I'd stopped it from taking him by quitting. Taking the job back on wasn't possible. It was a risk I was unwilling to take no matter how much this woman moved me.

"Look," I said, hoping I sounded firmer than I felt. "I'm going to tell you my story in a nutshell, and then you have to leave."

"Sssiiiiiiinngea boooooooouuns."

"Right," I said, twisting my hair with my fingers and

forcing myself to take a seat across the room. "I already told you that I can see the dead. Well… actually, you could probably figure that out since we're having a conversation of sorts."

The woman stared at me and clasped her hands politely in her lap. She was quite easy to talk to and it felt kind of good to lay it all out on the table, so to speak.

"Here goes nothing. I turned forty. I had a mind-numbingly boring job as a paralegal. Turns out my bitchy, sex-obsessed, evil ex-boss Clarissa happens to be the Angel of Mercy. I seriously want to kill her for what she did, but apparently, you can't kill Immortal people. Who knew? That's incredibly unfair and total bullshit, but I'm getting ahead of myself. However, I would like to point out—probably more for myself than for you—that nothing is as it seems to be. Movies have very bad information in them about good and evil and I'm a freaking idiot for assuming so many things that were dead wrong. Oops, sorry about the dead thing. I should have just said wrong, not dead wrong. That was rude," I said apologetically.

She tilted her head slightly to the right and waited for me to keep spewing out my heinous life story. I was wildly relieved that it stayed on her neck and didn't fall to the floor and roll around. Superglue was some amazing stuff.

"Then the dead started showing up. I got a dog, and then I got another one. I committed a misdemeanor or two, and then found out from Gram that I was a Death Counselor. It would have been great to have known that shit a little earlier, but whatever. Then to make weird even weirder, Steve—my dead, gay husband—showed up to apologize. His unfinished business was to help me find a man who could love me the way I deserved to be loved. I forgave Steve because that's how I am and he's my best friend. I do have to add that I was kind of shocked that I didn't know my husband was gay. I didn't think I was *that* person. You know?"

I was also kind of shocked that the dead gal on my couch hadn't left the house screaming in terror. She was either brave or she didn't understand a word I was saying. Or she was possibly Southern, like me, and was too polite for her own good.

"In the past month, I've grown some fairly massive lady balls. I fell in love with the Grim Reaper and screwed that up to the point of no return. I didn't trust the right person and I might have damned Steve to the darkness. The only way to stop that from happening was to quit being the Death Counselor. Steve isn't supposed to go to the darkness. He's meant for the light."

"Yausssss," she said with a very careful nod.

My gaze jerked to hers and I stared with surprise. I thought she wanted my help. Was I wrong? Did she have a message about Steve? I was pretty sure she'd just agreed with my assessment that Steve was meant to go to the light.

"You know Steve?" I asked, feeling light-headed and shaky.

Never again was I going to assume that I knew what the hell was going on. It had almost ended me. Lately, my mind was filled with thoughts of ending *myself* after I made sure Steve was okay. My future without Gideon was so bleak it made me ill.

"Naawwwooo," she said.

"Wait," I said, squinting at the ghost. "When you said *yes*, did you mean that Steve is supposed to go into the *light*?"

"Naawwwooo."

"Is he supposed to go to the darkness?" I asked as my eyes narrowed dangerously.

I wasn't real sure how to fight a ghost, but if she had come to take Steve into the darkness, she was about to lose her head again, and I wouldn't give it back. Was she a bad dead guy… or girl? Were there dead politics I knew nothing about? The absurd possibilities were endless.

"Naawwwooo."

We were getting nowhere fast. My gut had led me vastly astray recently, but the woman on my couch didn't seem evil—just sad, lost and in need of help. I wasn't the one to do that. She needed to leave. Just her being here might make the others think it was okay to come back. As long as I wasn't the Death Counselor, Steve could stay on this plane until I destroyed the vicious Angel of Mercy and made things right. Of course, there was a fine chance that I would die in the process, but at this point, it might be a welcome escape.

Looking down at my hands, I felt like crying. I wanted to help her. It wasn't going to happen.

Closing my eyes, I tried one last time to make her understand. "I can't help you. You need to find someone who can. I'm sorry."

When I opened my eyes, she was gone.

CHAPTER THREE

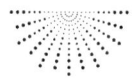

"Daisy, what are you doing?" Heather asked as she walked into my kitchen, took off her cashmere coat and busted me.

My head snapped up and I gave her a small guilty smile. My dogs were useless as far as watchdogs went. They were still sound asleep at my feet. I loved them anyway.

Heather looked exhausted. Normally, she was pulled together and very attractive. Her short pixie cut framed her lovely face and highlighted her big blue eyes. My friend was long, lean and strong. Not today. Today her eyes appeared dull and lifeless. She had the very same circles under hers that I sported underneath mine. Heather was dressed professionally in a beautifully cut business suit, but it was like putting a Band-Aid on a gunshot wound.

I hoped she had some news, or at the very least, a plan. If the news was bad, I wanted to avoid it for a few minutes. Pretending like things were normal—a bizarrely relative word right now—even for just a short time was a luxury. However, my friend had asked me a question and I was going to answer her.

"I'm eating French fries," I said, stating the obvious since it was pretty hard to deny. Of course, the pile of delivery bags littering the kitchen counter was also a good indicator as to what I'd been up to for the last few days.

Right after the dead woman disappeared, I decided to drown my sorrows in unhealthy calories. I had plans to run on the treadmill later since there was no way I would leave Steve alone at the house. Last night I'd logged twenty miles on the old machine without breaking a sweat. My dogs had seemed impressed. I probably should get my sweat glands checked. It was a strange new occurrence I couldn't explain, along with my vastly improved eyesight. Midlife changes were mysterious. So far, they weren't all that bad, but not sweating had to be unhealthy—kind of like my lunch. Whatever. It was on my very long to-do list. I had far bigger problems than not sweating and being able to see without glasses at the moment.

Heather sighed, sat down next to me and pilfered a few fries. "These are good," she said, chewing on one of the ass-extending potato sticks. "Where did you get them?"

"Billy's Burger House. They deliver and it's two-for-one day."

"Where's the other bag of fries?" Heather asked, giving me a lopsided grin.

"In my stomach," I replied. "Along with the cookies June brought over this morning. And I will add that those cookies were better than sex."

"Don't know what kind of sex you've been having," Heather said with a chuckle. "But cookies are *not* better than sex."

"The last sex I had—and I hesitate to label it as sex—was with Stan the Two-Minute Man."

"The one with the hairy back?" Heather asked, scrunching her nose in distaste.

"Yep," I said with a shudder as I drenched a fry in ketchup and popped it into my mouth.

"Then I retract my statement," Heather said, sounding like the lawyer she was. "These fries are definitely better than sex with Stan."

"Thank you for your support," I replied, wondering what her reaction would be if I pulled the ice cream cake out of the freezer that I'd had delivered from the Dairy Freeze yesterday.

"You're most welcome," Heather replied with a small grin. "You should think about becoming a lesbian. Much easier and way more fun."

A smile pulled at the corner of my mouth. "If I liked vaginas, I'd be there in a hot sec. Unfortunately, I'm fonder of the male anatomy."

Heather was an out-and-proud lesbian—an anomaly in our small Southern, God-fearing, Georgia town. For a while, Heather and my bestie from childhood, Missy, had seen each other. I didn't know the details of their breakup, but I suspected it had to do with Missy's hellfire-and-brimstone upbringing. It made me sad that two people who clearly had feelings for each other felt they couldn't be together because of the homophobic opinions of idiots who believed they were following the word of God.

I still wasn't certain if God existed, but if he did, I was pretty damn sure he wouldn't take issue with it. Good people were good people. Period. I would hope that character ranked higher than the gender of the person who you loved. The silver lining was that Missy and Heather were still friends. I would never be able to choose between them, and I was wildly relieved I didn't have to.

"Do you have news?" I asked as my stomach clenched.

Heather sighed and pressed the bridge of her nose. "First, tell me this. Can you still see Steve?"

I nodded. "I can."

"Has his condition changed at all?"

Heather had seen Steve in his coma-like state three days ago. I'd called her and she'd arrived shortly after I'd stopped the darkness from taking Steve by quitting my job as the Death Counselor.

Steve was in the bedroom we'd shared before he'd died in a car accident over a year ago. He'd come back to apologize for ruining my life. He hadn't ruined my life. Our lack of intimacy had messed with my head for years, but that was on me as well. He was and would always be someone I loved with all of my heart.

Now he was upstairs lying in a vegetative state… kind of. His dead body was rigid and his pale coloring was now dark gray. Holding back a scream every time I checked on him was difficult, but I reminded myself it was Steve—my best friend in the world. It would never matter to me what he looked like on the outside. His insides were beautiful.

"He's the same," I said quietly. "No changes that I can see. He's not trying to communicate as much except for a few words here and there."

"He can hear you?" Heather asked.

"Yes," I told her as the pit in my stomach grew larger. "Can we go after Clarissa yet?"

My stomach was now churning with fury or possibly the combo of cookies and fries.

"When we have an air-tight case," Heather said flatly. "Not a second sooner or we'll lose. She's been around for millions of years. The bitch has something on everyone."

Heather's statement gave me pause. Not the fact that we had to wait. I understood that and agreed. There was no room for error when Steve's afterlife was on the line. Something else entirely set the wheels of my mind racing.

"How old are you?" I asked, still overwhelmed that a secret and ancient world had existed right under my nose my whole life.

"You shouldn't ask questions you don't truly want the answers to," Heather said cryptically.

My friend didn't look a day over thirty-five. However, I was well aware that Immortals could choose their age. Gideon had offered to grow old with me. He wouldn't die, but I would eventually. He'd stolen a piece of my heart when he'd offered that gift. In the end, I'd given him my entire heart. I'd just been stupid and hadn't given him my trust along with it.

Crumpling the empty fry bag and adding it to the mountain of other bags on the counter, I considered what Heather said and decided she was wrong.

"I stand by my question," I insisted, wondering what the hell she was about to tell me. "How old are you?"

"Honestly, I'm not sure," Heather said with a tired laugh. "In the beginning I counted, but after a while, it seemed pointless."

"Ballpark?" I asked, curious how old she could be to have stopped counting.

She looked up at the ceiling for a long moment, and then sighed. "I guess I've been around a couple thousand years."

"Define a couple," I pressed. A couple could mean two or three—even four. There was a huge difference between two thousand and four thousand.

"You're awfully nosey, Daisy," Heather said with a laugh. "But to answer your question, I suppose it's closer to two thousand. Happy?"

"More like gobsmacked," I replied, shaking my head. "How is that possible?"

"The impossible is always possible," she replied. "You just have to suspend your belief in human reality and embrace it."

I mulled that over for a minute and decided the wisest and least complicated plan of action would be to grab the ice cream cake out of the freezer. "Big piece or little one?" I asked Heather as I cut myself a nice large slice.

"Huge," Heather said.

"You got it," I told her as I plopped the rest of the cake in front of her.

"Umm…" Heather looked down at the cake with amused, open-mouthed surprise.

"You said huge," I pointed out with a grin. "I aim to please."

"Well, in that case, thank you," Heather said, grabbing a fork and digging in.

"Welcome," I said as I ate my own piece of cake. "Do you have a favorite time period? One you lived through?"

"I've lived through a whole lot of them. Oh, shit," she said, pinching the bridge of her nose in pain.

"Brain freeze?" I asked.

"Yep. Give me a sec," she said with a pained laugh.

"You gonna live?" I joked.

"Very funny," Heather shot back, raising her brow and middle finger. "As to a favorite time period? Now. My favorite is whatever time period I'm living in. It's a waste to long for something that's gone. If I did that, I wouldn't be able to get up in the morning."

It was almost too much for my mortal brain to take in. I had millions of questions, but they weren't relevant to what we needed to accomplish. If I made it through the next few weeks and lived to tell, I'd ask Heather so many questions her head would spin.

"How long until we're ready to take Clarissa on?" I asked, still unclear of all that needed to be done.

"Daisy, I've learned a lot in my many, many, *many* years on Earth," Heather said as she dug back into the ice cream cake.

"Eat slow," I advised, handing her a napkin.

It didn't matter if I dropped ice cream on my shitty sweats, but Heather's suit was expensive.

"Will do," she said, looking pensive. "Things happen the

way they're supposed to happen—when they're supposed to happen."

"You believe in predestiny?" I asked, surprised.

Heather shrugged. "I believe in free will. I think a plan is laid out for each person. It begins at birth and ends at death."

"Doesn't sound like free will to me," I commented, as I finished off my piece of cake and dug into hers. "If what you just said is accurate, there's no choice in destiny—therefore, no free will."

She pushed the remainder of the cake across the table to me. It was a nice-mean move. Nice because she was sharing. Mean because I was going to polish off the whole damn thing.

"Hang on, I wasn't finished with my thought," she said, leaning over the table and scooping up one last big bite for herself before I demolished it. "Whether or not the person stays on the path that's meant for them is the free will part. There are many ways to get from point A to point B."

"Okay." I swirled the melting ice cream with my fork. "I can follow that. But the dead no longer have free will."

"True," Heather agreed. "And that's where you and I come in."

"And the Grim Reaper and the Angel of Mercy," I added.

Heather nodded. "With most, the afterlife is set by how a person lives their life. No outside assistance is needed."

"Right. I know that," I said. "But… is an afterlife in question truly just in the hands of Clarissa and Gideon?"

"To a certain degree, yes," she said. "But when something goes wrong, a tribunal is called."

That was news to me.

"And how many times has a tribunal happened?" I asked, feeling kind of sick to my stomach.

"Again, don't ask questions you don't want the answers to." Heather leveled me with an emotionless gaze.

"If I ask, I want to know," I said, staring right back at her.

The time for making shitty assumptions was long gone. I'd upended my life by believing I knew truths that turned out to be dead wrong. Been there. Done that. Trying like hell not to do it again.

"Never," Heather whispered.

"Repeat," I said.

"A tribunal has *never* happened," she told me.

"Never ever?" I questioned, not liking the answer at all.

"Never, ever, ever."

"Shit," I muttered. "Are there rules set in place for a tribunal?"

Heather nodded slowly. "There are, but since the rules have never been executed, they're being updated."

"Not following."

"The rules are written in Sumerian," Heather explained.

"What the hell is that?" I asked, getting more tense with each new piece of info.

"Sumerian is the oldest known written language," she said. "Dates back to somewhere around 3500 BC. It was before my time and I don't understand a word of it. So, when I said updated, I meant translated."

"Who's old enough to translate it? *Clarissa*?" I snapped, wondering how much worse everything could get before I just went for it and tried to off her evil ass.

"No," Heather assured me. "Clarence Smith is translating it."

"Her *father?*" I shouted. "I call total bullshit on that."

Heather put her hand up to silence me. "He's not her father."

The hand didn't work.

"Yes, he *is* her father," I insisted, twisting my hair in my fingers in frustration. "What is wrong with you? We all worked at his law firm for years. The only reason she was able to keep her damn job was because he's her father."

I paused as Heather simply stared at me and said nothing. Dammit, I was thinking like a human. I believed the possible and denied the impossible. I had to shift my mindset and I had to shift it fast if I was going to succeed. Failure was not an option. This new way of thinking was going to give me gas, a freaking migraine or a nervous breakdown.

"Okay," I said, getting up to pace my kitchen and throw away all evidence that I'd over-indulged in crappy food. "Clarence Smith is not Clarissa Smith's father."

"Correct," Heather said as she picked up the forks we'd used and washed them.

"I'm going to go out on a limb and say their last name is not Smith," I continued.

"That's a safe limb to go out on," Heather replied.

"Mmmkay," I said, sitting back down at the kitchen table so my knees didn't buckle while I worked out all the new impossible that was indeed possible. "Are they even related?"

"Nope."

"Freaking unreal," I said, grabbing a piece of paper and a pen and jotting down notes. My mind was so full of chaotic thoughts, I knew I'd forget stuff. "Are there more like you and Clarissa and Clarence in our town?"

"While I despise being put in any kind of group with Clarissa, the answer is yes. There are more," she said, scrubbing down my counters with a wipe, and then tossing it in the garbage.

"Make sure you put the child-lock back on or Karen the Chair Eater will eat the garbage," I said, mulling over the bomb Heather had just confirmed.

"Got it." She clicked it shut. "Daisy, this sleepy little town is the strongest portal in existence between Heaven and Hell."

"Gram told me that already," I said. "And I need to be honest with you. I'm still not sure I believe in Heaven and Hell."

Heather was quiet for a long moment. She sat back down at the table. "You've seen the light and you've seen the darkness. Right?"

"I have."

That was true, I just didn't know where they led. To me, it seemed that the light was good because of its beauty. I'd watched several of my dead friends walk into it and disappear after I'd solved their problem. I knew in my heart they were going someplace beautiful.

I'd also witnessed the darkness when it wrongly came for Steve. It was chilling, and I had a difficult time associating it with Gideon. The whole mess of good and evil was so convoluted.

"So, something has to exist beyond what's here," Heather pressed.

I nodded. My nod was a contradiction of my thoughts, but confused was my new middle name.

"You wanted me to send Steve to the light—or for argument's sake, Heaven—when you thought I was the Angel of Mercy. Why?" Heather asked. "Why would you want me to send him somewhere if you didn't believe it existed?"

"I feel like I'm at a distinct disadvantage because you're a lawyer with a few years on me," I told her with a tiny grin. "And yes. You're making me think, if that was your intention."

"Thinking is good, Daisy," she said, giving me a hug. "Keep your mind wide open."

"Is it important for me to believe in Heaven if that's where I want Steve to go?" I asked, feeling like a child asking for confirmation of something that couldn't be explained.

"What's important is justice. What you believe or don't believe isn't relevant," she said, looking around the kitchen. "It's a bit weird here without all the ghosts. I'm so used to the TV being on and silly reality shows playing."

I sighed and realized we were moving on to other subjects. I was grateful. There was only so much *impossible* my brain could hold.

"A ghost was here this morning—after June and Jennifer stopped by," I told her as she gave me an odd look. "It was a woman. I told her I couldn't help her and she finally left after I glued her head back on."

Heather eyed me strangely for about three seconds

longer than was considered socially polite. "After the sentence you just spoke, I find it shocking that you don't believe in the impossible."

"What?" I asked, touching my mouth. "Do I have ice cream on my face?"

"No," she said. "I don't understand why you're still able to see the dead when you quit the job."

"Me neither. I must be a freak of nature." I shrugged and ran my hands through my wild hair that seriously needed to be tamed. "It was difficult not to help her. Killed a little of my soul. I told her she needed to find someone else to help her. I told her the whole story. I was blown away she didn't hightail it out of my house sooner than she did."

"She's probably at the nursing home now," Heather said, standing up to leave.

An icy chill skittered up my spine and my lips flattened into a thin line. "Why would a dead woman go to the nursing home?"

"You don't know?" Heather asked, sitting back down slowly.

"Know what?" I asked, feeling dread rise up from my toes and settle in my overly full stomach.

"They've gone back to Gram," Heather said. "When you quit, the job reverted back to her."

"Bullshit," I snapped. "I've talked to Gram every day, and she's said nothing about having dead squatters in her room."

"She knows about Gideon leaving, and she knows about Steve," Heather said quietly.

Hopping to my feet so I didn't try to use the self-defense skills I'd learned from the YMCA on my kitchen table, I paced the room like a caged tiger. "She's ninety years old," I hissed. "She can't handle that. She doesn't even have the mail fraud box. I do. This is freaking horrible! She's not well enough to deal with a bunch of dead people. Their heads fall off, for the love of everything unappetizing. Gram doesn't eat enough as it is now."

Heather said nothing.

"This is not working for me, Heather," I shouted as I jogged in place, devising some kind of half-cocked plan in my head. Nothing was coming. My brain raced as erratically as my heart. No decision I made lately was a good one. I was harming all the people I loved. "What am I supposed to do? If I call the dead back to me, the darkness will take Steve. If I don't call them back, it will kill Gram. This is an incredibly shitty position to be in. I can't take any more shitty than I already have. Do you feel me?"

"The darkness can't take Steve now that a tribunal has been called," Heather said.

"The freaking rules of the tribunal were written in a dead language," I reminded her in my outdoor voice. "How can I trust anything right now?"

"Can you trust me?" she asked.

I stopped jogging and stared at her. Right now, I barely trusted myself. Trusting someone else was risky. However, not trusting someone I loved was what got me into all of this in the first place. Heather loved me. I loved Heather. More importantly, Heather loved Steve too. She also loved Gram.

"I trust you," I whispered.

"Thank you," she said, walking me out to the living room

and seating me on the couch. "Do you remember who I am? What I do?"

"You're the Arbitrator between Heaven and Hell."

"Yes. I am." She sat down next to me. "And I've decreed that no one can take Steve until a ruling has been made. What I decree stands."

"Where is Clarissa right now?" I asked, worried that she would come here and try to finish what she'd started no matter how much I trusted Heather.

"She has retreated into the light until she is called back to this plane."

"You're sure?" I asked.

"Positive," Heather promised. "She was banished by Charlie. No one crosses Charlie."

"Umm… who the heck is Charlie?" I asked, lost by the reference.

Heather chuckled. "You know Charlie."

I had to think about it. Did I know someone named Charlie? I'd be hard-pressed to remember my own name right now.

"Oh my God," I gasped out. "*June's* Charlie? June's Charlie is Immortal?"

"That he is," Heather said with a smile.

"Is June Immortal too?" I asked.

Heather shook her head. "She's not, and she knows nothing about the secret world that exists alongside the one she lives in. Charlie fell in love with June on sight. He's simply aged along with her. Eventually, he'll have to fake his own death and move away for a while until his children and grandchildren pass on."

"That's so sad," I said as tears filled my eyes.

"And that's where you're wrong, Daisy," Heather said. "When you live forever, much ceases to have meaning. Finding love—no matter how brief in the scheme of an Immortal's lifespan—is something to be cherished. I would trade with Charlie in a heartbeat. He'll have wonderful, loving memories of June for the rest of time. *That*, my friend, is beautiful."

That certainly shut me up. My heart still hurt, but I understood as much as someone who had only lived forty years could. Love was indeed a rare and precious gift.

"What is Charlie?" I asked. "I mean, does he have a title like you?"

"He does," she told me. "Charlie is the Enforcer. He represents science. Charlie is revered by every Immortal, Angel and Demon who exist."

"So, science and religion do go hand in hand," I said, shaking my head at the irony.

"Always have and always will," Heather confirmed.

"Well, hell," I said with a weak grin. "That would certainly blow the minds of a bunch of pea-brained, born-again mother humpers in our town."

"You got that right, girlfriend," Heather agreed with a laugh.

"And Clarence? What is he?"

"The question is, *who* is he?" Heather said.

"Umm… okay. I'll bite. Who is he?"

"How familiar are you with the Bible?" she inquired.

"Not at all," I admitted. "Is that going to be a problem?"

"Nope. Not a problem. Possibly an advantage," Heather replied. "Do you know of the Archangel Michael?"

"You mean, like the one John Travolta played in the movie *Michael*?"

Heather's laugh was real and echoed through the quiet farmhouse. "Close enough," she said, still chuckling. "Clarence is Michael."

"Our old boss is an Archangel?" I asked, squinting at Heather.

"Why should that surprise you? You were dating the Grim Reaper," she said and waited for my reaction.

"Low blow." I narrowed my eyes at my friend. "I don't want to talk about that."

"Grow thicker skin, Daisy," Heather advised.

"Why?"

"Because you never know who you might bump into in the near future," she said, then put her hand up so I wouldn't question her more.

"That hand thing is kind of annoying," I pointed out.

"It scares the living daylights out of most Immortals," she said, surprised.

"Human here," I reminded her. "Until recently, you were just one of my best friends who I enjoyed giving shit to. You can't expect me to toe the line, dude."

Heather's grin grew wide and she laughed again. "And that is exactly why you will win."

"I sure as hell hope so," I muttered. "Need to get something straight though. I'm no longer going by what I think people mean."

"What's that?"

"Are you saying that since Clarissa is in the light and was banished by Charlie, that I can go back to being the Death Counselor?" I asked. "And that the darkness won't take Steve if I do?"

"That's correct," Heather said. "My decree that Steve stays where he is until the completion of the tribunal stands. It cannot be altered by anyone."

"Heather, can I ask a favor?"

"Shoot," she said.

"Can you stay at the farmhouse with Steve for a few hours while I take a way overdue shower and go see Gram?" I asked as I sprinted over to the stairs and took them two at a time.

"I'd be happy to," Heather said as she made herself comfortable on the couch with my puppies. "Do you have Netflix?"

"Yep. Knock yourself out," I yelled over my shoulder.

I had no clue what was going to happen next. However, I knew it felt right to have my dead squatters come home. Plus, I was worried about Gram. Her mind was all there, but her body was fading fast. She didn't need that kind of stress.

One thing at a time.

I'd relieve Gram of her duties.

I'd make sure she was okay.

And then… I'd tackle whatever the hell came next.

Impossible, here I come.

CHAPTER FOUR

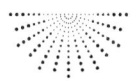

"Okay, I don't want you to say anything," I said as I pulled a sweater over my head. "Which is kind of a redundant statement since you're having a tough time with that right now."

Grabbing my purse and my coat, I sat down on the edge of the bed and made sure the afghan was tucked comfortably around Steve.

"I'm not in a funk anymore and I'm not stuffing my face with junk food," I lied with a smile that I hoped looked genuine. "I'm not sad. I'm not wallowing, and I took a shower. I'd also like to point out that I'm not wearing sweatpants and a crappy t-shirt."

"Dausseeeeee," Steve whispered in the lovingly stern tone I recognized so well.

"What?" I asked, not making eye contact. It sucked being a bad liar.

"Dausseeeeee," Steve whispered again.

"Fine. Fine. You're right," I conceded, running my hands through my wet hair and smiling for real. "That was a lie. Well, most of it. However, I'm wearing nice jeans and a sweater."

Steve grunted and tried to smile back. He was in such bad shape that it was difficult to tell, but I knew him better than anyone. I felt it. I could tell he didn't approve of the sweater, but it was comfortable and I was going to the nursing home to get my squatters back. It would be all wrong to get dressed up for an activity like that.

"Teeeerraaaba swaaater," he said.

"It is not," I shot back.

"Baaaaaagah," Steve said. "Liisssen toooo gaaauh mawn. Ahh nooowah."

"I know it's baggy. And I think it's rude but accurate to imply that a gay man has better taste than I do," I told him with a laugh. "I'm not trying to impress. I'm going to see Gram."

"Giiiddon."

"Is gone," I said, biting down on my bottom lip.

"Naawwwooo."

"Yes. I messed up… umm… bad," I said, hoping he didn't notice the tremor in my voice. "But I'm fine, and I don't want to talk about it. But get this, you're never going to believe it," I said, carefully touching his face and changing the subject abruptly. Gideon was out of sight. Gideon needed to be out of mind. That was my new motto. It wasn't working, but I was trying. "Charlie, June's husband, is

Immortal—some kind of enforcer guy. Could have knocked me over with a feather on that one. And Clarence Smith is not Clarissa's father. He's John Travolta."

Steve made a sound and gazed up at me with an expression of confusion.

"Wait." I laughed and rolled my eyes. "Got that wrong. Clarence is *not* John Travolta. He's Michael the Archangel—like John Travolta in that movie except he's the real dude. Crazy, right? Oh, and his last name is not Smith."

Steve said nothing, as expected. I wanted him to see I was okay. He'd had a horrible guilt complex in life and it was ten times worse in death. A little relevant gossip might make him happy.

"Also, here's the deal," I said, opening up the blinds in the bedroom so he could get some sunshine. I had no clue if vitamin D did anything for ghosts, but hopefully, it would cheer him up. "The squatters are coming back. Charlie banished the wicked bitch until we have a court date of sorts and no one can harm you or take you from me… even if I keep helping the other dead."

"Whheeeerree?" Steve grunted out.

Thank God I had a history of shorthand-speak with him.

"The dead went back to Gram," I said. "That's not a good thing. I'm headed over there now to rip her a new butt for not telling me."

"Goooooouud," Steve said. "Ssssoooorrry."

"There is nothing to be sorry for, Steve," I said softly. "Nothing."

"Dausseeeeee ffeeewl?" he asked.

I sighed and debated how truthful I should be. I was a shitty liar. I knew it and Steve knew it. Imagining how it would feel to be trapped inside of myself like Steve was right now was awful. If I thought about it too long, I got physically ill. But I would want the truth. I would want to know what was happening.

It was honesty time. Steve would worry less if I told him how I felt, no matter how unpleasant.

"It's not pretty," I said.

"S'oookaaay."

Breathing in through my nose slowly then out through my mouth even slower, I bought myself a few seconds. "Sometimes my heart doesn't know how to beat because part of it is missing. And yes, that part is you… and… umm… Gideon, but *you* are my concern, not him. Period. My lungs don't know how to breathe if I think too hard and my brain doesn't know how to focus on anything except how much I want this nightmare to be over for you."

Steve made a soft moaning noise.

"However, that being said," I went on, forcing myself not to cry. "I can see a light at the end of a dark, long tunnel. Along with everything else, I'm also consumed with hope. And if I'm being really freaking honest—which I am—I feel a hell of a lot of anger."

Steve was silent—just watching me with curious eyes.

"My lady balls are huge," I said with a small smile tugging at my lips. "And I'm not going to let that go to waste."

"Gooooooouud. Baaawlls."

"That's right, baby," I said as I gently kissed what was left of his forehead. "I have very good lady balls and I'm about to test them out."

⁓

"What the heck is a cop car doing at the nursing home?" I muttered to myself as I made my way across the parking lot, balancing a box of Gram's favorite doughnuts in one hand and my purse and a jug of apple juice in the other.

Gram hadn't been eating as well as she should, according to the nurses. Of course, doughnuts and juice weren't the healthiest choices, but she loved them and I wanted her to eat. I also needed to get the dead people who had camped out in her room back to my house ASAP.

The nursing home was in a nice section of town and was very well-maintained. As far as nursing homes went, it was really good. But as wonderful as the nurses and staff were, it wasn't home in a real sense of the word. If I could've taken care of Gram at my house, I would've done it in a heartbeat. I'd offered the suggestion up so often, I knew I sounded like a broken record. She'd shot me down every time.

"Crap," I said aloud as I picked up my pace and my stomach tightened with anxiety. Were the cops here for Gram? Had she been busted for mail fraud?

If she had, it was going to be seriously hard to explain why she'd been writing letters and cards to the families of the dead *from the dead*. I suppose we could say she had dementia, but I didn't want to use that as an excuse in case I made it come true somehow.

"Shit, it's freaking Chief Doody's cruiser," I hissed as I started to run toward the entrance of the home.

Dip Doody was the chief of police in our tiny town. His name was a travesty, but we lived in the South. The list of unfortunate names was lengthy. Dip's brother was Deke and his sister was Daffy. They were all cops. I had no clue if those were nicknames or if their mother had been wasted when she'd named them. Right now, that was irrelevant. Dip Doody didn't screw around even though he was a nice guy. However, if he was here to arrest Gram, I was about to show him my lady balls… or beg for mercy.

At this point, I was above very little.

"Son of a butthole," I muttered as I saw the chief standing right outside of Gram's door.

Strangely, Jennifer was with him. What the hell? Was he arresting Jennifer? The only thing my buddy was guilty of was too much Botox.

Dip Doody had to be around sixty. He stood six feet tall and towered over my tiny friend. Jennifer was giggling and flirting up a storm.

Something was not right. Chief Doody had pulled Jennifer over for driving with an expired plate a few weeks back and she'd taken to calling him Big Dick Dookie the Dunghole. Honestly, it wasn't much worse than his actual name, but whatever.

Had Jennifer gotten another ticket and decided flirting her way out of it was the way to go? Maybe the Botox had penetrated her skull and gone to her brain.

"Umm… hi," I said as I approached, unsure if one of my dearest friends was in trouble with the law.

I needed to get to Gram, but if Jennifer was headed to the pokey, possibly for calling the chief of police the awful nickname she'd given him, I'd deal with that first.

"You okay?" I asked.

"Great," Jennifer said as she smacked Dip Doody's ass.

I was shocked, but Jennifer was good like that. I was fairly sure slapping a cop's backside wasn't exactly legal. Was she freaking asking to spend the night in a jail cell?

"You have something you want to tell me?" I asked. I didn't know whether to laugh or drag her away from Chief Doody.

Dip didn't seem to mind being groped by my buddy, but the man was very polite.

"Dick and I were just visiting Gram," she said with what I thought was a wink.

It was hard to tell. It looked more like she had some kind of weird eye tic.

The man grinned and blew out an amused sigh. "It's Dip. Not Dick."

"Whoops, my bad," Jennifer said with a cackle.

He was a good-looking man right around Jennifer's age. His wife had passed a few years ago and all the older gals in town had made a play for the chief of police. He'd paid them no mind and had just gone about his business. Seemed like Jennifer might have cracked that hard shell.

"Dip, let's do our thing for Daisy."

Chief Doody laughed, put his beefy arm around Jennifer and shook his head. "Darlin', haven't we done that enough for one day?" he asked, clearly delighted by my little over-Botoxed fire-cracker of a buddy.

"One more time," she pleaded, giving him a smile that was so damn adorable it was no wonder she'd been married so many times. "Daisy needs it. She's having a bad week."

If that wasn't the understatement of the century...

Jennifer slapped Dip on the ass again, and he laughed like a besotted fool. She'd clearly entranced Big Dick Dookie the Dunghole.

"One more time," he agreed with a wide smile on his handsome face.

Jennifer bounced on her toes and skipped all the way down the hall away from her new *friend*.

"Okay, when I walk by, you say it and I'll answer," she called out, pretending to look down at a watch she wasn't wearing.

"Will do," he replied, pretending to be busy adjusting his badge and gun.

Not knowing what the heck I was about to witness, I felt a little bit like I was in The Twilight Zone. At least the hallway wasn't filled with ghosts. The bizarre *thing* going on with Jennifer and the chief would be impossible to focus on if there were dead people in the audience as well.

Jennifer waltzed down the hallway shaking her hips from side to side so hard, I thought she might throw her back out. I was tempted to ask her if she needed some fries with that shake but figured the timing might be a little off. It was like Jazzercise gone very wrong. The temptation to laugh was huge.

"Well, hello, ma'am," Chief Doody said, puffing out his chest and nodding his head to my friend, who looked like she was trying to dislodge a wedgie without physically pulling her panties out of her crack.

"Are you talking to me?" Jennifer asked, doing her best Scarlett O'Hara.

"Why yes, ma'am, I am," he replied, winking at her.

"HOWDY, DOODY," Jennifer squealed, and laughed so hard that Dip Doody had to whack her on the back when she started to choke. "Get it, Daisy? Howdy Doody! Because Dip's last name is Doody and I said *howdy* like that show with that puppet that scared the shit out of me as a kid. Howdy Doody!"

I couldn't help it. I laughed. It was so ridiculous and she was so proud of herself.

"Jenny, I'm gonna have to get back to work," Dip said, looking mighty pleased with himself as well. "You want a ride back to town?"

"You bet your fine ass I do," Jennifer said with a giggle. "Let me just talk to Daisy for a second and I'll meet you at the cruiser."

"Nice to see you, Daisy," Chief Doody said with a nod of his head as he made his exit.

"Mmkay, *Jenny*," I said with a raised brow.

"That man is hotter than a goat's butt in a pepper patch," Jennifer said as she watched him walk down the hall and out the front door.

"That was a really gross analogy," I pointed out.

"But it's true," she said.

"Just tell me you're not getting married again," I said.

"Haven't banged him yet, so I'm not sure," Jennifer replied.

"Are you serious?"

"Yep," she said. "I need to sample the milk before I buy the cow."

"Your way with words never fails to amaze," I told her.

"Thank you. As far as I can tell, the only thing wrong with him is that he likes to hike," she explained in all seriousness.

"Hiking is a deal-breaker?" I asked, squinting at her.

"I'll let you know after I bang him," she replied with a wicked little grin.

"Alrighty then," I said with a shake of my head. "I need to visit with Gram. You want to come?"

"Just spent an hour with her. Dip and I had her laughing like a loon."

"Thank you," I said, meaning it.

I hadn't been to see Gram in a few days. I'd been too afraid to leave my house.

"Welcome," Jennifer said, pilfering one of the doughnuts. "Odd thing though."

"What?" I asked, worried that maybe Gram had spoken about the dead to Jennifer and Chief Doody—not that they'd believe her.

"She was watching *Survivor*. Never known Gram to watch anything but game shows."

Actually, it wasn't odd at all. The squatters adored reality television.

"I'll make sure she's okay," I promised as I leaned over and gave Jennifer a quick kiss on the cheek. "And thank you again for visiting with her. She adores you."

"Feeling's mutual," Jennifer said as she skipped down the

hallway toward the front door to the police cruiser and potential husband number six. "I love Gram like she was my own."

I loved Gram too. I loved her with my entire heart.

And now I was about to go in there and rip her a new one… because I loved her.

CHAPTER FIVE

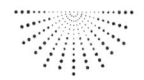

Gram looked tiny and frail in the adjustable bed I'd bought her. The bed had cost me almost three full paychecks and the nursing home had pitched a hissy when I'd moved it in, but I'd prevailed. There was pretty much nothing I wouldn't do for her.

Gram had raised me at a time when her life should have been a whole lot easier. When I was five and my mom died, Gram had stepped up—not one question or doubt in her mind about taking me in and raising me as her own. She loved me something fierce and I loved her right back.

I'd recently learned that my mother's death was no accident. My mother had been a Death Counselor like my gram before her, and now me. She'd taken her own life when a ghost she'd fallen in love with had been sent into the darkness. I hadn't dealt with those emotions yet and wasn't sure I would ever visit that place.

Misplaced anger at my long-dead mother would not be

productive right now. All my anger was reserved for Clarissa at the moment and it burned searing hot inside of me.

"Umm… old lady, you have something you'd like to share?" I asked as I glanced around and took in the scene.

The ghosts were everywhere. Counting them was impossible since they floated in and out of each other. But if I had to guess, I'd say at least thirty had moved into Gram's small quarters. Random body parts were strewn across the floor. Most had congregated around the television and were watching *Survivor* with rapt attention. Only a few noticed I'd arrived.

It was a hot mess, and it was about to end. Thank God Jennifer and Chief Doody had been blind to what was happening under their noses. I suppose I was one of the lucky ones—lucky being a relative word—that I was able to see the secret side. Not to mention, all of the body parts would be tremendously difficult to explain.

"Daisy girl," Gram said with a smile that lit up her eyes. "How are you doin', baby?"

"I could ask you the same question," I said, putting the doughnuts down on her bedside table and the juice next to them.

"Well now, I'm doin' just peachy," Gram lied.

"Really?" I inquired, leveling her with the identical stare she used to give me when she knew I was fibbing as a child.

"Yep," she replied, rearranging her blankets and refusing to meet my gaze.

"Do you really want me to jerk your tail in a knot?" I

asked, picking up a stray arm and handing it to one of the armless ghosts.

I wasn't sure I'd returned it to the correct owner, but I was making a point. Once I got them back to my house, I'd double-check to make sure I glued the right appendage back on the right person.

"Hell's bells on Christmas morning," Gram whispered, paling. "You can still see the dead?"

"Apparently," I sighed as I sat down on the edge of her bed.

"That's not possible," Gram said, confused.

"I'm beginning to believe everything is possible—especially the impossible," I said. "They're coming back home with me."

"No can do," she said, trying to sit up.

It took her so much effort, my heart lodged in my throat. Even the specters were concerned and fluttering around in distress.

Gently helping Gram to a sitting position, I rested my head on top of hers and held back my tears.

"You can't do this," I whispered. "You're too old to have to deal with this anymore. It's killing you."

"Honey, I'm so old I knew the Burger King when he was still a prince," Gram said with a laugh. "We're doin' just fine here. I've sent at least four on their way. Just have to pace myself."

"Are you so old that you knew Mr. Clean when he had hair?" I asked, kissing her wrinkled cheek and breathing her in. She smelled of Ivory soap and dime store perfume. It was the best smell in the world.

"I sure did, baby girl. He was a hottie just like Bob Barker," she said, cupping my cheek and growing serious. "You will not take 'em back. I know what's goin' on."

"From who? Heather?" I asked, realizing I'd forgotten to question my friend when she'd told me Gram knew about Steve and Gideon.

"Nope," she said. "From Tim."

"Tim the nerdy postman?" I asked, shocked and wildly surprised. "The strange little guy who gets possessive about all the packages he delivers? *Tim*, the dude who half the people in town are positive x-rays all the packages at Christmastime and keeps what he likes? I mean, I'm not sure I believe that, but are we talking about the same Tim?"

Note to self, ask Heather for a list of all the Immortals in town.

"Yep," Gram confirmed. "That boy can be as annoyin' as a fart in a fan factory, but he's good at his job."

"Stealing packages?" I asked, confused and wanting to gag at her analogy. Between Gram and Jennifer, I was sorry I'd eaten so much today.

"No, silly girl." Gram laughed and shook her head. "Tim's a Courier."

"Not following," I said, picking up an unattached foot from Gram's bed and holding it up in the air to be claimed.

A large, mostly transparent man missing several appendages and part of his head zipped by, grabbed the foot and mumbled a garbled thank you.

"Some might say Tim can't find his ass with both hands in his back pockets, but he's not that bad," she explained.

"Still not following," I replied, taking a doughnut out of the box and handing it to her.

Gram took a bite and sighed with happiness. "Dee-licious."

"Good. Eat the whole thing while you explain what exactly Tim does."

Gram nodded and took another bite. "He's one of the people in town who never die."

"Immortal," I said and poured her a cup of juice.

"Right. Called him Imodium once and he didn't deliver my mail for a month," she said with a naughty grin.

I laughed. Today, I'd laughed several times. I thought those days were over, but I was realizing time could help you heal… especially if you had no choice.

"How did you know he was Immortal and a Courier?" I asked, swatting at a few of the ghosts who had seated themselves on top of Gram.

"Tim's the one who delivered the mail fraud box to aid the dead when I was in my twenties—told me his secret then. Boy's basically the mailman for the living and dead," she explained.

"He wouldn't have been alive when you were twenty," I pointed out, and then smacked myself in the forehead, much to the delight of the floating specters. "My bad. I'm trying to open myself up to the impossible. Not going great so far."

"The learnin' curve is steep for you, Daisy," Gram said, putting her doughnut back in the box. "I shoulda told you about the gift a long time ago."

"I didn't have the *gift* until recently. I would have

thought you had screws loose if you'd told me," I reminded her, taking the doughnut back out of the box and handing it to her again. "Eat. I stood in line for twenty minutes to get the ones right out of the oven."

Gram took another small bite. It wasn't enough, but it was better than nothing.

"The past is the past," I said. "Dwelling on it is useless. I know what I am now and I accept it."

"But Steve—" she protested.

"Will be fine," I promised. "Charlie sent Clarissa away until the tribunal. Heather decreed that no one can take Steve from me until a decision is made."

"I'm so dang perplexed I don't know whether to check my ass or scratch my watch," she said.

"You're not wearing a watch and I'd rather not see you scratch your butt. So what do you need to know that will help us avoid this un-ladylike conundrum?" I asked, tucking her sparse gray curls behind her ear.

"*Charlie* is Immortal?"

"Yep," I said, surprised she didn't know.

"Well dang," she said, shaking her head. "Tim never told me that. But then again, that boy only has one oar in the water. Are there a bunch of 'em?"

"I'm not sure, but my guess would be yes, since this sleepy little town is the strongest portal between Heaven and Hell," I replied.

Gram was quiet as she mulled over the new information. "Do you believe, Daisy girl?"

It was my turn to be quiet. I didn't want to upset her, but telling half the story wasn't working anymore. The truth might not set someone free, but it was far easier to remember than a lie.

"I don't know," I admitted as I moved around the room collecting body parts and handing them to the ghosts. "A month ago, I would have said no. Today? I hope I'm wrong."

"Faith," Gram said. "You gotta believe without proof."

"Yep," I said. "I'm trying."

Gram took another little nibble off the doughnut. "Daisy, it doesn't matter a lick what you believe. Just follow your heart and do what's right by others. Living it is far better than preaching it."

"What is *it*?" I asked.

"Faith," she replied. "The invisible belief that life will expand until it fills up the Universe."

"That's pretty deep," I said with a laugh.

"I think Bob Barker said it once on *The Price Is Right*," she informed me with a giggle and a wink.

"I think you need to put your hearing aids in more often," I shot back.

"Hate 'em," she griped. "With those little nuggets in my ears, I can hear every damn sound in this here prison I'm in."

My stomach tightened. "Gram, are you unhappy here?"

"Ohhh Daisy," she said and reached out for a hug. "I'm just playin' with you. I like it here. Got plenty of company and I love the gals who take care of me. Don't you be worryin' about that. You have enough goin' on right now."

"While that might be true, you come first," I said, still feeling off as I hugged her. "Always."

"Gimme some sugar," Gram insisted.

I did as told and it felt like home. Being in my gram's arms even as an adult was so right.

"Here's a good thing," I said, adjusting her bed so she was sitting more upright. "You can get back to your boyfriend, Bob Barker, when the dead leave. No more crappy reality shows."

"Fine point," she said with a giggle. "Don't forget about my side dish, Pat Sajak."

"How could I ever forget Pat Sajak?" I replied with a laugh as I grabbed the remote and turned the channel from *Survivor* back to the game show channel.

"How are you gonna get the dead to go with you?"

"Same way I got them to leave," I replied and glanced around the room at the ghosts who hovered in anticipation.

Closing the door to Gram's room so the staff didn't think we were off our rocker, I eyed the ghosts, and then smiled. Of course, we *were* off our rockers, but that wasn't for anyone else to know.

Taking a deep breath, I closed my eyes and centered myself. "I rescind my notice. I no longer deny who I am or what I'm meant to do. I am the Death Counselor. Go home. Now."

The deceased squatters were beside themselves. They flew around so fast, a sharp wind blew the box of doughnuts right off Gram's bedside table.

Diving to save the treats from falling to the floor, I missed the mass exodus.

Gram did not.

"Holy hell in August on a Sunday," Gram gasped out as

she looked around the empty room in shock. "What kind of power do you have, Daisy girl?"

"Can't you do the same?" I asked, getting back to my feet.

"Not even close," she said, shaking her head and pointing to the far corner of the room.

One ghost remained. I knew her. She'd been at my house earlier.

"That one just arrived today," Gram said quietly. "She breaks my heart."

"Mine too," I muttered as I crossed the room and squatted down in front of her.

"Sssiiiiiiinngea boooooooouuns," she said.

"What'd she say?" Gram asked, popping her hearing aids in and leaning forward.

"I don't know," I replied. "I'd have to enter her mind to find out."

"I don't like that one bit, Daisy," Gram said sternly. "Not one little bit."

I didn't reply. I didn't like it either, but sometimes it needed to be done. If the Ouija board didn't work for this poor woman, I would hug her and learn her story. I could already tell it was tragic.

"Gram, does she look familiar to you?"

Gram squinted her eyes and stared at the woman. "Can't say she does. Do you think you know her?"

"No," I said softly as I touched the dead girl's hand. "I feel like I've seen her before though."

"She was pretty in life," Gram said.

"She's still pretty now." I kept my eyes on the girl as she trembled. "Go back to my house. I can help you there."

She continued to tremble and tried to smile. It was macabre but appreciated.

"Sssiiiiiiinngea booooooouuns," she repeated.

"I'll figure out what you mean soon," I promised. "Go now. You'll be safe at my house."

The young woman shimmered for a brief second, and then disappeared.

"You okay?" Gram asked quietly.

I stood up and faced her. "I have no choice, so yes."

"What can I do to make that frown turn upside down?" she asked.

Well," I said as an idea came to mind that made me smile. "You can eat an entire doughnut. That would make me happy."

"Deal," Gram said, taking a nice big bite. "Can you get me a glass of milk, baby? I have a carton in the fridge over there."

"That I can do," I said, feeling a small bit of relief she was eating. Granted, it took a little bribe, but that was fine by me.

Bending down to get the milk out of her small refrigerator, I grabbed the container—and then dropped the carton to the floor as if I'd been burned. Milk splattered everywhere and Gram gasped.

"Daisy, what's wrong?"

Slowly picking up the paper carton, my eyes blurred with tears as I looked at the face of the missing woman on the container. She was lovely. Her smile was bright and her eyes twinkled even in the black-and-white photo. She'd been missing for a year. Clearly, the search was still on.

"It's her," I whispered.

"It's who?" Gram demanded, trying to get out of her bed.

Quickly crossing the room so she would stay put, I held out the container with the picture on it.

The reason I recognized the ghost was because I had indeed seen her before… on a milk carton.

"Her name is Lindsay Macon. Only twenty-five years old," Gram said, with her hand on her heart. "Poor child. You have to let the family know somehow."

Nodding because talking might make me cry, I hugged Gram.

"I can help you," she said, holding me as tight as her weakening arms could.

"I've got this. Sorry about the milk," I said. "I'll let the staff know I spilled it."

"No worries, Daisy girl. Tell 'em I got doughnuts in here and they'll come runnin'."

"Will do. You have to eat at least two, please," I said, kissing the top of her head before grabbing my coat and purse.

"You have my word," Gram promised. "Keep me up to date, please. I worry about you."

"Back at you, old lady," I said with a watery smile. "I love you."

"Love you more," she shot back.

"Not possible."

"Everything's possible," Gram said with a wink. "Especially the impossible."

Truer words had never been said.

CHAPTER SIX

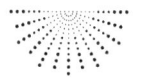

"Hey," I called out as I walked into Missy's bookshop. "Anyone home?"

My BFF since childhood owned and ran a fabulous kitschy bookstore in town. It was loaded with bestsellers along with books on magic and all sorts of other new-agey stuff that I used to roll my eyes about.

Not anymore. I was living magic and new-agey stuff. My eyes were no longer rolling.

"Be out in a sec," Missy called from the back.

I wandered the shop and ran my fingers over the spines of the books. The scent of jasmine filled the air and it felt like the world might be normal for a moment. It was a fleeting wish. The moment passed as quickly as the feeling. My new normal would never be *normal* again.

Part of me was fine with it. Part of me was terrified. Hence, I was going to arm myself with knowledge… or at least try to.

I wondered if Missy would have what I was searching for. She'd probably have to order it. That is, if it even existed. The internet would be helpful if necessary, but I loved books. I liked the way they smelled and the feel of them in my hands. I'd considered the library, but this particular book I wanted to own.

"Shot of iced espresso with an obnoxiously large squirt of chocolate syrup and a buttload of milk for your pleasure," Missy announced as she came out of the back room of the shop and handed me my favorite drink.

"I think I love you," I replied, taking a big sip.

The sweet caffeine slid down my throat and felt heavenly. Missy made my special drink as perfectly as I did… and as perfectly as Gideon had.

Nope. Not going there. Since there was no time to think about the biggest mistake I'd made in my life so far, I pushed all thoughts of Gideon to the back of my mind. Unfortunately, he didn't seem to want to stay there.

"I know you love me," Missy said with a grin.

She leaned on the counter and waited for me to speak. I was grateful. Plus, the coffee was insanely good. From knowing each other as long as we had, we innately knew what the other needed. I wasn't sure how much I wanted to say or even *what* I wanted to say. Telling her everything wasn't fair. She was human and didn't need to know. I was human, but I had no choice.

"How did you know I was coming?" I asked, taking another sip and pointing at the coffee.

"You stood outside the shop for five minutes talking to yourself," Missy told me.

"Right," I said, closing my eyes and taking a deep breath.

Missy was correct that I'd been standing on the sidewalk outside of her shop. She was incorrect that I'd been talking to myself. I'd run into three ghosts who seemed lost. I'd given them directions to my house and they'd disappeared. The fact that I'd forgotten I was in public didn't bode well for the townsfolk questioning my sanity.

Note to self, ignore dead people in public settings.

"I have a lot on my mind," I said, which was a massive understatement.

"I know," Missy said, giving me a hug. "Can I help?"

My bestie was beautiful, inside and out—tiny with wild curls and perfect mocha-colored skin. Her fashion sense was Boho-chic slash artsy-fartsy slash I'll-wear-whatever's-clean, evidenced by the mini skirt, combat boots and gauzy shirt she was wearing. It was November, but somehow Missy made it work and look fabulous. Her normally dark curly hair was enhanced with bright green braids today.

"I'm looking for a book," I told her, wanting to change the subject. Getting deep was off the table right now. I was about to drown.

"You're in the right place, dude. It's a bookstore," she answered with a smile.

"Obnoxious much?" I asked, putting my coffee down on the counter and smiling back.

"You're an easy target," Missy pointed out. "What kind of book?"

Walking over to the reference section, I bent down to examine the spines. "I'm looking for a book on the Sumerian language."

"You and everyone else," Missy said, shaking her head. "Surprisingly, I had three. However, I sold all of them. That's why I was in the back of the shop. I was about to order more."

My chest tightened. I stood up and leaned on the bookshelf so my knees didn't buckle. Who else wanted to learn Sumerian? Was I about to add to the mental list of those who never died?

"Bizarre," I said, keeping my eyes on my fingernails, which were in desperate need of a manicure.

"Exactly what I thought," Missy agreed, walking over to the children's story corner and flopping down on a tie-dyed couch. "What do you know that I don't?"

The answer to the question was so absurd, I almost laughed.

"I saw a documentary on it recently," I lied, hoping Missy wouldn't notice.

She was very much aware that I was a crappy liar.

She paused for a long moment and waited for more. None came.

"Well, that must be it," she replied.

I was fairly sure she didn't believe me, but she didn't push.

"Who else wanted the book?" I asked, hoping like hell I sounded casual.

"Tim the postman, June's husband Charlie, and Clarence Smith."

Tim and Charlie wanting the book didn't surprise me. They must not have been alive during the Sumerian time period. The fact that Clarence Smith aka John Travolta aka

Archangel Michael needed the book was so alarming, my head started to throb. If he didn't already know the language, how was he supposed to translate the instructions for the freaking tribunal?

Shit. I needed to talk to Heather.

"Dude, you okay?" Missy asked, hopping up and leading me to the couch. "You just turned five shades of pale."

"I'm… kind of okay," I admitted without adding any of the damning facts. "Is anyone else working today?"

"Nope," Missy said, sitting down and wrapping her arms around me. "Just me."

I rested my head on her shoulder and fought back my desire to tell her the truth about the nightmare my life had become.

"Look, I liked him, but he's an asshole," she whispered as she hugged me tighter.

"Who's an asshole?" I asked, so deep in my own thoughts, I had no clue to whom she was referring.

"Gideon," she said, giving me an odd stare. "Gideon's a player. You can do much better than a jerk like him."

While talking about Gideon was like removing my fingernails with pliers, it was safer than the rest of the *impossible* crap that was happening.

And maybe talking it over with my lifelong best friend wasn't such a bad idea.

"It was my fault," I told her. "I told him to leave."

Missy squinted at me. "And he did?"

"Umm… yes."

She raised a brow and snorted in disgust. "Proves my point. No man who's worth it would just up and leave."

"Missy, no means no, and leave means leave," I pointed out, defending Gideon.

"Agreed," she conceded. "But a guy who had it as bad for you as he did wouldn't just leave without fighting for you."

"Maybe he didn't have it that bad," I said with a shrug to hide the fact I wanted to scream or cry. "I'm a big girl. I'll be fine."

"Fine?" Missy pressed.

"Eventually," I said. "It didn't work out. The end."

"You're sure?" Missy asked, searching my eyes for the truth.

I forced a smile. "Yes. I'm sure," I lied. I was getting better at lying. Nothing to be proud of, but right now it was helpful. "Steve's death was devastating. We'd spent a lifetime together. Gideon… he was only in my life for a little while. I'll survive."

Missy stared at me for what felt like an eternity, and then nodded her head. Clearly, she was satisfied with my answer. "I still say he's an asshole for leaving. You're drop-dead gorgeous on the outside and even more beautiful on the inside."

"And you're a bit biased," I pointed out. I almost giggled at the drop-dead part but realized my sense of humor had become far too morbid and swallowed it back.

"Possibly," she agreed with a grin. "But I'm also always right."

"And don't forget humble," I added.

"That too," she said with a giggle.

Her logic was wildly flawed. Missy had no clue that Gideon was the Grim Reaper. Nor was she aware that I saw the dead and helped them solve their problems so they could move on to whatever came next. My best friend had no idea that her former girlfriend, Heather, was around two thousand years old, or that I was probably going to mind dive into a woman whose picture was on a milk carton. She had no clue that my dead husband had come back to let me know he was gay and was now going to trial so he wasn't sent to an afterlife he didn't deserve. By the grace of God or whoever was in charge, Missy was blissfully ignorant.

"I'm forty," I reminded her. "I'm a widow. I'm past childbearing years and I've started collecting dogs. I wouldn't say I'm a great catch."

I left out the part about gluing dead people's parts back on.

"You are *not* past childbearing years, dude," she said. "Women are having babies into their fifties."

"Not my idea of a good time," I said, scrunching my nose. "I can barely take care of my dogs."

"I feel you," she said with an arched brow. "My cats own me. I can't even imagine what a child would be like."

A long time ago, kids were something I'd wanted badly. Life didn't always work out as planned. Right now, I was living in a world I barely recognized. I was thankful I'd never had kids. Especially since they'd be saddled with the very same *gift* I had.

"So, you'll order the book for me?" I asked, abruptly changing the subject.

"Screw Gideon. And yes, I'll order the book for you," Missy promised. "Clarissa came in for the book on Sumerian as well. I escorted the bitch out of my shop and let her know her money and her presence were not welcome here. Told me she was leaving town for a bit and implied she was going to see Gideon. The man is a player and a loser."

I was glad I was seated. The news Missy had just shared was almost more than I could take. The words were so sharp they felt like a bite.

"Had to sage the entire place after she left," Missy said with a shudder. "So, like I said, Gideon is an ass and he deserves a skank like Clarissa."

I couldn't fake it anymore. My heart felt shredded in my chest. It was none of my business if Clarissa went to Gideon, wherever he was. It was none of my concern if they took up where they'd left off hundreds of years ago. I'd told him it was over and that I never wanted to see him again.

Nothing he did was my business ever again.

My reasoning had been fatally flawed. I'd assumed that he'd been the one who had made the decision to send Steve into the darkness. He was the Grim Reaper, for the love of everything unholy. That's what Grim Reapers do.

Except it's not.

It's not even close.

"Oh my God, Daisy," Missy said, grabbing me as my body crumpled forward and the tears I'd been holding back flowed freely. "I am so sorry. So damn sorry."

It could have been ten minutes. It could have been ten hours. My mind raced and my heart thumped so loudly in my chest I could feel it through my whole body. Missy held me and let me lose my shit. Maybe if I hadn't had this conversation, I wouldn't have known Clarissa was making another play for Gideon. However, it was better to know than to be surprised if I ever saw them together.

My need to destroy the Angel of Mercy grew irrationally larger. While I had no right to be hurt if Gideon chose to be with her, I was human. I couldn't help it. I was still in love with him.

"Daisy," Missy whispered as she rocked me back and forth like a child. "It will be okay. I am so sorry."

"Not your fault," I said weakly and gave her a watery, lopsided smile. "My fault."

"I don't know why you ended it and I won't ask," she said, smoothing my wild dark curls away from my tear-stained face. "But things have a way of working out the way they're supposed to. Miracles are possible when you believe."

"Believe what?" I asked, glancing over at my best friend.

"In the impossible."

I was sure my mouth hung open. I was so tempted to ask Missy if she was Immortal, but something stopped me. Heather would have told me if Missy was like her. I was sure of it. Although, so much of what I'd been sure of had turned out to be wrong.

I'd simply ask Heather. If Missy was human, as I suspected, I didn't need her worrying that I'd truly become unhinged.

"Do you believe in the impossible?" I whispered.

"All the time, my friend," Missy said. "After the way I grew up, there's no reason for me to be a semi-functioning adult. Yet, here I am."

"You're a miracle," I told her, cupping her cheek in my hand.

"And you are too," she replied, placing her hand over mine. "Do not forget that."

I smiled. It was real. Missy was one of my miracles. She and I had been through so much together over the years. While I might not ever be able to tell her everything, she was still my rock and I would always be hers.

Missy was a miracle I could believe in.

∽

"THAT'S NOT YOUR ARM," I SAID FOR THE FOURTH TIME TO the squatter who floated in front of me holding an appendage that clearly didn't belong to her. "I understand that you want an arm, but stealing someone else's isn't going to work."

"Miiiiiiiuuune," she insisted.

"Nope," I said with an eye roll. "That arm belongs to a man about twice your size. I will not glue that onto your body."

"Yausssss. Miiiiiiiuuune," she repeated.

"No. Not yours. This is not my first day of dead squatter surgery," I informed her, using my outdoor voice in case she was hard of hearing. "And I'm not blind. So, do not be a dick about it. Manners go a long way at my house—not that it's nice to call you a dick. Sorry I called you a dick. That was rude. It's been a long week, but that's no excuse to be mean."

My polite Southern DNA was so ingrained it was ridiculous.

The ghost hissed before she zipped away, and I was pretty sure she flipped me off. Fair enough. I had called her a dick. It was difficult to tell if she'd given me the bird since she was missing a few fingers. She was definitely not Southern.

"They're like little kids," Heather commented as she watched the gluing party with open-mouth awe.

"Profane little kids," I added with a tired smile. "Most are sweet, but that gal was spicy."

"And the superglue holds them together?" she asked.

"For a while," I replied, quickly and efficiently reattaching a hand to a decomposing man who had patiently and politely waited his turn. "When they get too wild, heads fly. Literally."

Heather's laugh made me laugh too. The impossible absurdity of what was happening didn't escape me. Although, I had to admit squatter surgery was far more satisfying with someone to witness my newfound skill.

Steve had been my observer for a while, but now that wasn't possible. At least he was resting safely upstairs with my two dogs. Heather had watched television in our bedroom with him while I was gone. She was sure he enjoyed her company. I was sure of it too. Steve and Heather had been dear friends when he was alive.

"I've never seen anything like this." She tilted her head to the side and took in the peculiar process.

"Welcome to my world," I replied as I glued a foot back onto a large man who was missing an arm as well. "Find the spicy gal. Pretty sure she has your arm. She'll probably flip you off, but I think she highjacked your body part."

"Thaauanuak yooouah," he said as he disappeared, looking determined to find the gal with the active middle finger.

"So, let me get this straight, Missy is not Immortal—or *Imodium*, as Gram likes to say?" I asked, opening another tube of glue and continuing my rounds.

"*Imodium*? Seriously?" Heather questioned with a grunt of laughter.

"She called Tim an Imodium back in the day and he didn't deliver her mail for a month," I replied.

"Priceless," she said. "And no, Missy is not *Imodium*. Missy has a gift though. Her intuitiveness is unusual for a human."

"She's psychic?" I asked. I'd always thought Missy could see things.

"I suppose you could put it that way. She definitely has a sixth sense," Heather said, reading the instructions on a tube of glue. "Can I help you glue on body parts?"

"No clue," I said. "No one's ever offered."

"Can't really see you getting many offers, dude," she said with a chuckle, walking over to a specter and putting out her hand.

An older gentleman gave Heather his leg and it went right through her hand. She tried twice to pick it up off the ground and the same thing happened.

"Guess that answers the question," she said, trying once more. "How odd. The ghosts seem almost corporeal but they're not."

"To me they are," I told her, marveling at the bizarre fact.

"I mean, I can see through parts of them, but when I touch them, they're very real."

"Daisy, you are a rarity," Heather said. "An abnormal phenomenon."

"Was that a compliment?" I asked with narrowed eyes and a half-smirk.

"Absolutely," she replied. "Should have used the word miracle instead of phenomenon."

"Then thank you… I guess," I said. The word miracle had been thrown around like confetti on New Year's Eve lately. However, a compliment was a compliment no matter the semantics. Again, my Southern gene required me to say thanks.

"Can I ask you something?" Heather inquired, sitting back down on the overstuffed couch and wrapping one of the afghans Gram had made around herself.

Heather fit in perfectly at my bed and breakfast for the dead—well, not breakfast, thank God. I'd be bankrupt in a week if the ghosts ate food.

My old farmhouse was lovely and warm—just like Heather. I'd done all the painting and some of the other manual labor things, but Steve had been the one with the great decorating skill. All of the furniture was overstuffed and in soothing patterns and faded florals. The floors were a lightly stained, pitted cherry and the walls were repossessed barn wood we'd bought at an estate sale years ago. It had always been my safe haven and was even more so now.

"Can I ask you something first?" I countered.

"Shoot."

"Well, I have a couple of questions," I said.

"And I have a lot of time," Heather pointed out.

"As in an eternity?" I asked with a raised brow and a giggle.

"Your comedic skills are seriously lacking," she said with a grin. "However, the attempt was appreciated. And yes, I have an *eternity* of time on my hands."

"My comedic skills are *not* lacking," I shot back and pointed to all of the laughing squatters. "They think I'm hilarious."

Heather glanced around with amusement and sighed. "I'm outnumbered. You win. Ask away."

"Why does Clarence Smith need a book on the Sumerian language if he's John Travolta?"

Heather shook her head. "You do realize you're going to call him John Travolta by accident if you keep that up."

"Fine point. Well made," I said, realizing she was correct. Clarence Smith had always been kind to me when I'd worked for his firm as a paralegal. He had a medium-rare sense of humor. He might laugh if I called him John Travolta. Then again, he might not. Whatever. I was going to get my jollies wherever I could at this point. "So why does John Travolta need a book on the language if he was alive during that time period?"

Heather laughed and let her head fall back on the couch. "John Travolta probably needs to brush up on Sumerian since it's a dead language. I'd hazard a guess he hasn't spoken it in several thousand years. And the particular book Missy stocked is very unusual."

"That's why you say she's intuitive?"

"Yes," Heather said. "It's a good example. Anyhow, that's

why I think John Travolta wanted the book."

Heather's answer was logical.

"Why would Tim and Charlie need the book?"

"Tim is nosey," Heather explained. "He's been nosey for the thousand years I've known him. Charlie is just one of those thorough kind of people. He came into being right after the Sumerians were gone. I would think he could understand some of it possibly."

"Tim is a thousand years old?" I asked, still trying to wrap my mind around the impossible.

"Not sure," Heather said. "I've known him for around a thousand years. He could have been around much longer than that."

"You think he's been stealing mail for thousands of years?" I inquired with a naughty grin.

"I'd guarantee it," Heather replied with a groan. "They don't come any nosier than Tim. However, as nosey as he is, don't discount him. The bizarre little man has been everywhere."

"Do you realize how strange this conversation is?" I asked.

"No stranger than watching you glue body parts onto the dead," Heather pointed out.

"True," I agreed. "Clarissa wanted to buy the book as well."

"Did Missy sell her one?" Heather asked in a tone that wasn't light anymore.

"No, she only had three. She's ordering one for me," I said, growing uncomfortable.

Heather nodded and relaxed.

"Why is that a big deal?"

"The tribunal directions are in the book," Heather said, sounding old and tired. "We were aware that Missy had the book. No one was to touch it unless the need arose."

"Wait," I said, sitting down and ignoring the ghosts who were still missing appendages. "The directions were in Missy's shop? How?"

Heather shrugged. "When I told you that Missy was special, I wasn't exaggerating."

"Do you think she knows what's in the book?"

"No. I don't. But I think she was guided by her sixth sense to have stocked it. Why in the hell would anyone have a book on the Sumerian language in a tiny bookshop in the outskirts of Atlanta?"

Again. Logical.

Also, impossible…

Believe the impossible.

"The impossible is real," I whispered.

"It always has been and always will be," Heather said. "You just have to believe."

I hoped to heck and back that I wouldn't find believing—truly believing—impossible.

"One more question," I said, mulling over all the new information.

Heather sat silently and waited.

"Is my family the only line of Death Counselors?"

Heather stayed silent. Her lack of reply made me wonder if I'd asked the question aloud. Was I losing it that much that I couldn't remember if I'd spoken?

Heather leaned forward, placed her elbows on her knees

and rested her chin in her hands. It made me antsy.

"As far as I know, yes," she said. "I've known a lot of people you're related to over time."

"My mother?"

She nodded and didn't say anything.

"I see." I wanted to question her but refrained. Information could be upsetting. There was enough going on without adding to the load. At some point I would ask, but not today. "How far back do you know my family?"

"At least a thousand years," she admitted, sounding weary. "And by the way, you come from good people."

"And we were all Death Counselors?"

"Only the women," she replied.

"What the heck? Seems kind of unfair for the gals to get stuck with it," I said, speaking the first thought that came to my mind. "I mean, women in general get screwed. We have periods then menopause. In many cases, even today, we're second-class citizens. Not to mention, the pain of childbirth—not that I would know about that one. As far as pain goes, all men have to worry about is getting kneed in the nuts."

Heather's laugh rang out in the quiet house and I joined her. The reference to a man's junk getting smashed lightened what had been getting very dark. True, but dark. I was thankful I was still able to laugh. It was saving me.

But wait…

"Umm… I don't have children," I said, piecing together a rather large and potential problem.

Heather stopped laughing, turned her head and gazed out of the window. That didn't bode well.

"Am I the last of the line?" I asked a question I wasn't

sure I wanted her to answer. I mean, maybe I had distant relatives I didn't know about who were gluing on body parts too. That was logical. That made sense.

Heather nodded slowly and watched for my reaction. I had no clue what she expected. I was pretty sure I wanted to throw up. Not sure she wanted to witness that.

"So, umm… it ends with me?" I muttered, unsure how I felt about that. Would the dead just roam the earth without help to move on? "I don't have a daughter, and I don't think Donna the Destroyer and Karen the Chair Eater count, even though they're girls."

Heather listened to me point out the obvious then looked down at the floor. "It's been discussed."

"By who?" I asked, narrowing my eyes.

"All of us," she said.

"Want to be more specific?"

"I can't," she replied. "Not yet."

"You're freaking me out here." My tone was a little sharper than intended. "What do you know that I don't?"

"Actually nothing," Heather said. "No one does. That's why there's nothing to say."

A horrid thought crossed my mind. "Was Gideon a setup? Was everyone hoping I would have a baby with him? Was he put up to it by the others, whoever the hell they are?"

"No," Heather insisted firmly. "Absolutely not. In fact, there were those who were concerned about your relationship tremendously. The chances of Gideon procreating—or any of us who have been in existence for as long as we have—are very slim."

"So, the Immortals were pleased that we didn't work out?" I demanded, as my emotions bounced from rage to despair like a thousand Ping-Pong balls dropped off the roof of a skyscraper.

"Some," she admitted.

"You?" I asked.

"Yes and no," Heather said, rubbing her temples and sighing. "Sometimes I get attached to people. I'm attached to you. For centuries I didn't let myself experience affection for humans. It was devastating when they died. I became guarded and emotionless—a dangerous and empty way to live."

Her words made my heart hurt, but I wasn't about to be swayed towards compassion yet.

"And?" I pressed.

"And about a hundred years ago, I let myself feel emotions for others. The pain of losing them eventually was worth the time I got to spend with them. If my lot is to live forever, I decided to actually live—in each moment."

"Not following," I said.

"Eventually you'll die, Daisy," Heather said in a whisper. "Someone will have to take the job. So, while I was thrilled for your happiness at falling in love with Gideon, I suppose I was hoping you would meet a human man and fall in love… and have a daughter who I could become attached to like I am to you."

It was my turn to be silent. There was nothing to say.

"I think you should go," I told Heather as I stood up.

"Are you upset with me?" she asked.

"Honestly, I don't know. I can see it your way if I divorce

myself and my feelings from the situation," I replied, running my hands through my hair and wanting to go to sleep for about a month. "I just need some time alone to be with Steve."

"I can give that to you," Heather said sadly. "I'm sorry, Daisy."

"For what?" I asked.

"For the truth. It's not always pretty."

"The truth isn't always the truth either," I said. "Free will mixed with the winds of change can skew results."

"How so?"

"The impossible is real, Heather," I said. "You told me so yourself. If that's the case, then what one knows as the truth could cease to have meaning. The term can be relative depending on the user."

"Holy shit," Heather muttered with a surprised laugh. "You've grown up one hell of a lot since you turned forty."

"When you have no choice, you do what you have to do," I stated.

"There's always a choice, Daisy. Remember that."

Heather left without giving me a hug. That was fine. As much as I loved my friend, hugging her felt wrong right now.

If there were indeed choices to be made, I would make them one day at a time.

One choice at a time.

Otherwise, I'd crack.

"Okay," I called out to the dead who had been listening the entire time. "Who needs some repairs? The squatter surgery center is back open."

CHAPTER SEVEN

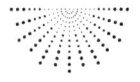

It was 6:00 PM and most of the ghosts had disappeared. This was normal. I had no idea where they'd gone, but I'd become accustomed to the late-day break and was pleased it still existed.

They'd be back. I hadn't solved one single issue other than reattaching a missing body part or two… or three in a few cases. The little birdie finger woman had not wanted to give up the arm she'd claimed as hers, but after a long chat where I was fairly sure she called me a hooker several times, she gave the arm back to its rightful owner. Sadly, we didn't find her arm. I suppose she could have died without it—might be why she was so keen on stealing one.

Honestly, I was looking forward to using the Ouija board with Birdie—as I'd secretly nicknamed her. I was sure it would be a memorable and profane experience.

"What a mother humper of a day," I muttered as I sat down on a kitchen chair with a thud and continued to talk to myself as I made a list. Lists calmed me. Actually, calm was a place I couldn't find lately, but it was worth a shot. "Steve is fine—fine being a relative word, but he's not getting worse. That's good. I'm not mad at Heather. Actually, I'm grateful she didn't lie to me. Heather is my friend. I love her. This is very good. John Travolta is going to figure out the tribunal. Also, good. Gram's health? Iffy and not good. The number of dead squatters I need to help? Not sure… I think about thirty. I hope they like it here because with everything going on, they might be guests for a while. Thoughts of Gideon? Still far too frequent to be healthy. My sanity? Teetering on the edge of an abyss—to be expected."

The tranquility I usually felt in my home was missing. Everything resembled a warzone to me right now. The farmhouse had been a dream of Steve's and mine. We'd bought it ten years ago and had spent the last decade fixing it up. It sat in the middle of twenty acres surrounded by lush forest. Steve had been a far better decorator than me, but I was a pro with a hammer and a gallon of paint. The hours spent improving our dream house were some of the best memories I had of my husband.

I'd also had dreams of filling our home with our children and dogs from shelters. I had the dogs now. The children? No. Steve was gay, which explained a whole lot. However, the bomb that Heather had dropped made me wonder if I should do something wildly stupid, like getting artificially inseminated.

For all I knew, that's what my mother had done. I knew nothing about my father and neither did Gram. All she'd ever told me was that my mother was secretly seeing someone and ended up pregnant. It had been the talk of our small Georgia town for a while, but then some other juicy piece of gossip must have replaced it.

Whatever. I didn't exactly have the time to get knocked up on my own, nor did I want to. Taking care of dogs and Steve were about all I could handle.

Speaking of…

"Donna. Karen, come on downstairs. It's peepee-poopoo time," I called out as I stood up and stretched. I really needed to run, but that would have to wait. "And if either one of you furry buttholes took a dump upstairs, you're going to eat it. Well, not really. That would make your breath smell even worse than it already does."

Hearing what sounded like a snicker of amusement, I whipped around. My eyes landed on Lindsay. She was obviously unaware that this was my alone hour. I didn't mind. She'd stayed close to me the entire time I'd done surgery on the others. It almost felt like I had an assistant of sorts. Not that she could help… more of a moral support ghost. I liked it.

Her body shook. I was pretty sure it was laughter, not fear. Her face was so badly damaged and decomposed, it was hard to tell if she was smiling, but I was going to go with a yes.

"You think that's funny?" I asked, putting my hands on my hips and giving her a look.

"Yausssss," Lindsay said, reaching out in excitement as Donna and Karen bounded into the kitchen.

Karen, my goofy black lab, had no clue that the house was filled with dead squatters. Karen had belonged to John, one of my dead guests who had moved on into the light. One of his most fervent wishes was that I would adopt Karen from the pound and give her a home. That was a no-brainer for me. I adored animals and even though Karen was in a battle to the death with all of my shrubs, I couldn't imagine my life without her.

The biggest gift for John, besides knowing Karen had a loving home, was that his murderous wife was locked away in a prison awaiting a trial she couldn't win. Sarina Dunn wouldn't see the light of day for the rest of her miserable life. John's murder had been avenged.

On the other hand, Donna, my fuzzy, red furball of a puppy, absolutely did know we had squatters from beyond the grave. She had been a gift from my friends for my fortieth birthday last month so I wouldn't be lonely. Turned out she was a Hell Hound who saw the dead as well as I did. It had given me a brief moment of pause when I'd learned the news, but I was already completely in love with her.

Donna the Destroyer was also instrumental in helping me return to reality when I went mind diving into the dead. The two times I'd done it thus far, I'd followed the sound of her bark to come back.

"Well, Lindsay," I said, using her name because I knew it from the milk carton and because having a name made a person feel like they mattered. "If I find a chocolate stinky laying around, I'll be sure to have you do the honors of cleaning it up. Cool?"

"Naawwwooo," she said, shaking again with laughter.

Donna went right over to her, sat down and wagged her tail. Lindsay covered what was left of her mouth in surprise.

"Daaaaaggguh. Sssssseeeeeee."

"Yep," I said, shooing Karen away from the trash. She was a bigtime garbage eater. "Donna can see you. Karen can't."

"Hoooowah?" she asked.

"Donna's special."

"Sssspeeusaul," Lindsay said, pointing at Donna.

"Yep. We're all special," I told her. "You're special."

"Sssiiiiiiinngea booooooouuns."

I sighed and let my chin fall to my chest. "Lindsay, I can't understand what you're trying to tell me, but I promise I'll figure it out."

She nodded her head and I was happy it stayed attached. Heads were tricky. Using two tubes of superglue earlier had been a good move.

"Okay doggies, outside," I instructed, opening the door and following them out. Turning back, I saw Lindsay hovering with uncertainty. It made my heart clench with sadness. "You want to come? You might enjoy watching Karen dig a massive hole. It's one of her not-so-hidden talents."

"Yausssss," Lindsay said and zipped right past me out the door.

The Ouija board would be a bad choice for Lindsay. I knew it in my bones. Her demise was going to be complicated. The state she was in now told me her death had not been a peaceful one. Mind diving was my plan for the young woman.

"Do not encourage the dogs," I yelled with a smile as I watched Lindsay fly around the yard with Donna as she did her zoomies while a crazed Karen dug a hole like she'd ingested a vat of sugar.

I was sure Lindsay's story wasn't a good one. Therefore, I would make sure her stay with me was.

∽

THE COLD. THE COLD WENT ALL THE WAY TO MY BONES AND TORE through my body like sharp, frozen daggers made of ice. Trying to catch my breath, I gasped for air but stayed calm.

My head pounded violently and every single cell in my body screamed for oxygen. I knew it was momentary, but it still sucked.

My mind went numb and I couldn't feel my limbs.

Knowing what was happening made it slightly less terrifying, but not by much.

"Lindsay," I choked out, closing my eyes as I had been taught by my dead friend Sam when I was inside his head. "Can you hear me?"

"I can," a soft and sweet female voice answered, sounding wildly surprised. "Daisy?"

"That's my name. Don't wear it out," I said, and then groaned internally. I was turning into one of those out-of-touch older folks who made embarrassingly shitty jokes.

Lindsay laughed. I was fully aware she was being polite, but it made the mortification easier to swallow.

"You can understand me?" Lindsay asked.

"I can," I told her, keeping my eyes squeezed shut.

Never go to the light. Never go to the dark.

Those were the two rules I was told to follow by both of the lovely men who I'd visited in their minds. Sam and John held very special places in my heart. Helping them had been a joy—a semi-illegal joy that could have landed me in the pokey, but a joy nonetheless.

"Thank you," Lindsay whispered. "What am I supposed to do?"

It was a good question. The others had seemed to know, but Lindsay was so much younger than either Sam or John. Her life had ended far too early.

"We can talk," I said. "You can also show me your memories."

Lindsay was quiet.

"It's okay, Lindsay," I assured her. "I won't judge and I might need to know what happened to help you."

"I... I don't want you to see," she said, brokenly.

"That's fine," I assured her. "Tell me what you've been trying to say, please."

"Singing bones," Lindsay whispered.

I was still lost. "Is that a band?" I asked, feeling wildly out of touch with pop culture.

While I wasn't old enough to be Lindsay's mother, I definitely felt maternal towards her. God, I wondered if her mother was still searching for her.

"No. Not a band."

Each time I'd gone mind diving, I'd controlled how long I'd stayed. The first time had been devastating on my body and I'd slept for sixteen hours. The second time, I'd recovered quickly. Maybe third time would be a charm and I'd have no recovery time.

However, the longer I stayed, the riskier it was for me.

"Explain," I urged her. "I can't stay in your mind too long without side effects."

"Daisy, go," Lindsay said, sounding frantic. "I'm not worth it. Really."

"Lindsay, you are worth it. Really," I said firmly. "I want to be here. We just can't beat around the bush. Tell me about the singing bones. Please."

"It's a fairy tale," she explained in a shaky voice.

"Tell me."

"My mom read it to me as a little girl. It's about two brothers who set out to kill an evil boar. The prize is that whoever eliminates the dangerous monster will get the princess's hand in marriage."

"I've heard this," I said, remembering. "The younger brother kills the monster and his elder brother finds out, and then kills him and takes the credit."

"Right," Lindsay said. "The older brother buries his younger brother's body beneath the bridge where he killed him."

"Until one day, a shepherd comes along and finds a bone that he uses to make a mouthpiece for his horn," I continued.

"Exactly," Lindsay said, getting excited. "And when the shepherd blows his horn, the dead brother's story comes out in the song. So, the shepherd goes to the king and plays the song."

"And the king finds the rest of the bones under the bridge and the evil older brother is punished by death for his deception," I finished as a pit formed in my stomach. "Will your bones sing, Lindsay?"

"They will," she said softly.

"Are you from around here?" I asked, wondering about the logistics of helping her. There was no way I could take a trip anywhere right now.

"I'm not, but I died near here."

"Where are you from?"

"Atlanta," she said. "I grew up there."

I nodded and realized she couldn't see me. "And your parents?"

"My mother died when I was a teenager. My stepfather raised me like I was his own daughter. And I have a stepbrother," she said flatly. "My stepfather was very ill when I... umm, died."

Okay, that was interesting. From the tone of her voice I took it as an important piece of information.

"Who is searching for you?" I asked.

"No one if my father died," she told me, still emotionless. "Possibly the executor of my father's will."

"Father or stepfather?" I asked for clarification. It would be difficult to communicate once I left her mind.

"Step, but he was my father for all intents and purposes," she explained as her voice began to grow weaker.

"Do you know where your bones are?"

She made a sound that ripped my soul open. I wanted to wrap my arms around her to comfort her, but we were in a place that defied reality and touching wasn't possible.

"Kind of," she choked out. "Off a trail by a waterfall."

There was only one waterfall in the area, so I had a decent idea of where she was describing. It was along one of the paths where I ran. Dense woods surrounded the area so finding her bones could be difficult. And what the heck would I do with her bones if or when I found them?

Shit.

"Is that where you died?" I asked, not wanting to upset her, but needing to know as much info as she felt comfortable telling me.

"It is."

"And your bones will tell the story?" I pressed, not wanting to screw this up.

"Yes," she whispered as her voice began to completely fade away.

"Lindsay, I know you don't want me to see what happened, but I can't hear you anymore," I said, keeping my voice even and calm. "I need you to remember. I'll be able to follow that."

She made a sound that reminded me of a wounded animal then went silent.

Pictures raced across my vision so quickly, I couldn't make them out. It was like an old, static-filled black-and-white TV screen was inside my head. It had been the same with Sam and John. Catching glimpses of a smiling little girl with her mother at a lavish child's birthday party, I forced myself to relax. I was fully aware the ending would not be happy, but I wanted to see who Lindsay was.

Scene after scene flashed by of an adorable young Lindsay—on a cruise, at a formal dance, cheerleading at a high school football game. Her laugh was pure and clear. Her smile was beautiful.

Lindsay had come from a very wealthy family. If the man I was seeing was her stepfather, he seemed to dote on her. Quick starts and stops of family outings flitted by so fast it was hard to make them out.

"Lindsay, slow down. Let me see," I told her.

The screen went to static, and then the ugly parts began to play out.

"He's not your father," a boy of about fourteen hissed at a ten-year-old Lindsay.

"Yes, he is," she insisted with tears in her eyes.

"He's mine, not yours. Your mother is a stupid whore," he snarled as he shoved the small girl to the ground.

"You're a stupid whore," Lindsay yelled back, clearly unaware of what the word meant.

The screen went static again. My stomach began to roil. My imagination went wild with scenarios and I pretty much figured out where we were going. My instinct was to save the little girl, but that was not going to happen. Lindsay was dead. There was nothing I could do to change that.

What I could do was bring her closure. Hopefully.

"She's dead," a young man of twenty said with a wide smile. "You're going to get thrown out on the street."

"Daddy wouldn't do that to me," a teenaged Lindsay snapped.

"He's not your daddy," the young man spat. "Your whore of a mother was a gold digger just like you. You won't get a penny of my money."

"I don't want your money, asshole," Lindsay shouted.

The screen jumped and went to black for a brief moment. I held my breath and waited. Some of the perks of being a Death Counselor were not great. Seeing someone die in order to help them was the most horrifying one.

"No," a bruised, battered, and older Lindsay screamed. "Stop. Please stop."

"I told you to disappear and you didn't listen," the man roared, coming unhinged. "I told you that you would never get a penny of my money and I meant it."

"I don't want your money," she choked out as blood poured from her mouth and nose. "You can have the money."

"Not how it works, bitch," he hissed as he hit her in the head with some kind of metal rod.

Picking up a barely conscious Lindsay, he tossed her limp body into the trunk of a very expensive car.

I took the entire ride with Lindsay in her mind. I gasped as I realized this mind dive was vastly different from the others. Involuntarily—or possibly not—I began to take on Lindsay's pain. The more I took, the more relaxed she got.

For a brief second I wondered what I was doing to myself, but an instinct I couldn't control took over.

At first the pain burned like a fire, and then it faded to an iciness that I felt in my bones. Dark gray clouds filled the edges of my vision until all I could hear were the gasps of breath coming from my mouth as I tried to take oxygen into my crushed lungs.

Shit, was I going to die? I couldn't die. Steve's afterlife was on the line and I had Gram to think about. Lindsay was already dead. It had happened. It was fact. I could not undo what had been done by taking on her pain.

And if I died, I couldn't give her closure.

With effort that took everything I had, I pulled back and became an observer again. Lindsay convulsed and threw up blood as she was tossed around in the trunk of the car.

The man who did this would pay. If it was the last thing I ever did, I would make the bastard pay.

The screen filled with static as Lindsay was pulled from the trunk and beaten to death with a rock as she fought for her life. She scratched at his face and tried to deflect the blows, but she was no match for someone so huge, lethal and filled with greedy rage.

She did not win.

Lindsay was left lying in a puddle of her own blood as the son of a bitch drove away. There was a flash of something shiny in her hand, but before I could make out what it was the screen went back to black.

"Oh my God," I said. "Lindsay, I am so sorry."

"It's okay," she said, barely above a whisper. "Can you find my bones so they can sing?"

The truth was that I wasn't sure. If she had been dead for a year in the forest, there was a chance we wouldn't find much. However, I'd cross that bridge with her if I ever came to it.

"Yes," I said. "I can. I need to think about a few logistics, and I'll need your help, but yes."

"Thank you, Daisy."

"You're welcome, Lindsay."

CHAPTER EIGHT

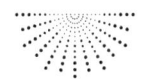

The aftermath of the mind dive was brutal. I'd curled up at the bottom of the bed where Steve was and slept from nine in the evening until noon the next day. Every bone in my body ached and my head felt like it was going to explode.

Taking on a dead person's physical pain was now on my *What Not To Do* list. No matter how much I wanted to help them, it was debilitating. The outcome would remain the same. My suffering would only keep me from what I had to do for the dead.

I'd let the dogs out before I'd gone to bed and had forgotten to let them back in. Thankfully, it wasn't too cold out and they were curled up on the porch swing when I went looking for them this morning. The upside to the dog-mom blunder was the lack of poo and pee surprises to greet me when I woke up.

I hadn't told Steve about the Lindsay mind dive. He'd

worry. He didn't need any extra stress right now. I could have used someone to lean on, but that was just too damned bad. I'd had someone and I'd sent him away.

"Lindsay," I said as I made my coffee drink with an obnoxious amount of chocolate syrup. "I have an idea about how to find your bones that will kill a lot of birds with one stone."

Donna barked and gave me a little growl.

I smacked myself in the forehead and wanted to go back to bed. I was being incredibly politically incorrect with my squatters.

"My bad," I said, shaking my head. "Shouldn't have said kill. Should have said… umm… Should have said nothing."

"S'oookaaay," Lindsay said, patting my head awkwardly.

She'd been hovering worriedly above me when I awoke and hadn't left my side. She'd missed the rule that no ghosts were allowed in my bedroom except Steve. However, to be fair, I hadn't really laid out the rules to the new group. I'd have to gently tell her the bathroom was off- limits. I did not need her floating around while I took a shower.

"Hoooooooookaaah," the little birdie woman hissed as she whipped around the kitchen like a mini dead tornado.

"Did you just call me a hooker?" I asked, pressing my temples, unable to believe the conversation I was having.

"Hoooooooookaaah," she repeated with a cackle that sounded somewhat similar to a cat coughing up a furball.

"That's extremely rude," I chastised her. "If you want my help, you'd better clean up that nasty mouth. You feel me?"

"Beeeeeeooootch," Birdie announced before she disappeared in a huff.

"Lovely," I muttered as I sat down at the kitchen table and peeled a banana. It was lunchtime, but I'd missed breakfast. "Lindsay, if you went for a run with me, do you think you could find your bones?"

"Yausssss," she said, seating herself in the chair across from me.

My gag reflex had disappeared. When the ghosts had first shown up, I couldn't eat when they were hanging out. The partial jaws and missing appendages deadened my appetite—pun intended. However, my compassion for my squatters had overcome my gag reflex. It was a seriously good thing that the ghosts had no odor. Not sure I would have been able to overcome that.

"My plan is a little screwy, but I think it could work," I said, grabbing a butter knife and slathering some peanut butter on my banana. "However, it's not illegal, which is an improvement for me."

Lindsay giggled. It was slightly off as far as giggles went since she was dead, but it warmed my heart.

It was the little things that counted most right now.

∼

"YOU DO WHAT?" HEATHER ASKED, LOOKING AT ME LIKE I'D lost my mind.

She wasn't too far off on loss-of-mind assumption, but I found her shock a little much.

"I mind dive," I replied, tying my tennis shoes and yanking a fleece hoodie over my head.

"How?" she demanded, crossing her arms over her chest and squinting at me.

I looked at her and grinned. She did not grin back. "A hug."

"You hug the dead and dive into their heads?" Heather questioned as she paced my bedroom in agitation.

"Yep."

"Does it happen every time you touch them?"

"Nope. Just when I hug with intent," I explained. It would suck if it happened every time I touched a ghost. With the amount of squatter surgery I did, it would be a problem.

"Daisy, that can't be a smart thing to do."

"Not sure I know the meaning of the word anymore," I said, stretching my hamstrings and wincing.

I hadn't run for real in a week. I wasn't exactly going on a run right now, but the stretching felt good in a painful way.

"How do you get out of their heads?" Heather asked, sitting down on the bed next to Steve and observing him carefully.

"Donna."

"What the hell? Donna mind dives too?" Heather asked, clearly shocked as hell.

I laughed and shook my head. "God, no. She barks and I follow the sound back."

Heather sat silently and contemplated what I'd just revealed. She was disturbed, but her curiosity was piqued. "I've never heard of this before. Did Gram mind dive?"

"Nope," I said. "She wasn't too happy about the prospect

either, but she's come to accept that I do it my way with my squatters."

"How did you figure it out?"

"Dumb luck," I replied, wanting the conversation to be over. It was what it was. I was fine—tired, but fine. "With some, the Ouija board won't work. Lindsay was one of those cases."

"I just…" Heather began.

"You just what?" I asked.

She was thoughtful for a long moment. "I just don't know."

"Join the club," I said with a smile, trying to lighten the mood, which was getting too weird for me. "Anything new on the tribunal?"

"No, but from what I understand, John Travolta is getting close."

"You do realize you're going to call him that by mistake," I said with a smile as I repeated her warning to me.

"Already did," Heather replied, shaking her head and groaning.

"And?" I asked.

"Thankfully, he had no clue what I meant."

Putting my phone into the pocket of my fleece, I winked at Heather. "I'd be delighted to send him a copy of the movie."

"While the thought is amusing, the reality might not be," she replied, tossing me a hat that Gram had knitted for me.

"Thanks." I put it on and glanced down at a very quiet Steve. "You're good to stay with Steve while I'm gone?"

"Always," she replied.

"Love you," I told her.

"Back at you," Heather said with the first real smile she'd given me since her arrival. "Be careful."

"Careful is my middle name," I replied.

"No, it's Leigh," Heather reminded me with an eye roll.

"New times, new name." I waved as I left the room. Although, *careful* wasn't accurate. *Hellbent on self-destruction* might be a better fit, but I was going to do my damnedest to avoid that one.

~

"For the love of Jesus in a jockstrap, you had work done, Daisy," Jennifer insisted as she huffed and puffed her way up a tiny hill on the trail.

"I did not have any work done," I told her for the third time.

"You look ten years younger than you did the other day," she said, wiping the sweat from her Botoxicated brow. "I just want to know who did your work. It's fabulous."

"No work done," I repeated.

"You're using a new cream?" she asked.

Jennifer wasn't going to leave it alone until I gave an answer that satisfied her. I'd barely looked in the mirror in a week. I was exhausted and on the verge of tears at all times. I had no clue what she was seeing. I was a hot mess.

"I use the drugstore brand of moisturizer," I told her. "And I wash my face with regular soap."

"Are you shitting me?" she shouted as Donna barked and ran up ahead. "Dip, did you hear that shit? Daisy uses soap on her face! I might have just wasted two hundred dollars on the fancy crap from the department store in Atlanta."

"Heard it," Dip said as he brought up the tail end of our little hiking party. "Don't see a problem with it. I use soap too."

Jennifer giggled like a loon and slapped her knee. "Dip is a real comedian."

I didn't exactly agree, but I wasn't about to speak my thought aloud. Dip was a good man and a nice guy. If Jennifer thought he was funny, then good on both of them.

Dip grinned from ear to ear at Jennifer's delight. It was cute and bizarre at the same time. However, if Jennifer was happy. I was happy. Apparently, Jennifer had sampled the cow and enjoyed the milk. When I asked if she and Chief Doody wanted to come on a hike with me, she was all for it.

I guess the hiking wasn't a deal-breaker.

So far, my plan was on track. Lindsay floated about three feet ahead, and I ignored her completely. She was aware of the scheme and on board with her part. Hiking with the chief of police and finding the bones was the best strategy I could come up with without incriminating myself in any way.

"So, Chief Doody, what kind of soap do you use?" I asked.

"Whatever's on sale," he said with a grin as Jennifer hooted and hollered like a dumb-dumb. "And Daisy, you can call me Dip."

"Okay, Dip," I said with a laugh. "You're my kind of guy. I get whatever's on sale too."

Jennifer rolled her eyes and shook her head. "Fine, I'll

start using soap," she muttered. "And I'd like to point out that I'm colder than a penguin's balls."

"That was colorful," I said, watching Lindsay out of the corner of my eye.

"Dip, tell Daisy some of the fun facts," Jennifer begged. "That'll make up for me being colder than a witch's tit in a brass bra."

"Well, now, I can certainly do that," Dip said, wrapping an arm around Jennifer to keep her warm as we hiked. "Did you know if you keep your eyes open when you sneeze, you could pop an eyeball out?"

"Seriously?" I asked, wrinkling my nose. It occurred to me that I hadn't glued any eyeballs back into a squatter's head yet. Thankfully, I caught myself before I shared that news with my hiking buddies. That probably wouldn't have gone over too well.

"Yep," Dip confirmed. "And if you ever need to escape from the grip of a crocodile's jaws, just shove your thumbs into his eyeballs and that sum-bitch will let you go instantly."

"Have you tested that theory?" I asked with a wince. Dip's useless trivia knowledge was even grosser than Jennifer's.

"Nope," Dip said. "And hopin' I never have to."

"I've got one," Jennifer volunteered.

"Is it gross?" I asked, hoping it was less graphic than her boyfriend's.

"You bet it is," she answered with a laugh as Dip joined her.

They were a perfect match.

"Tell us, sweet thing," Dip said to Jennifer as he kissed the top of her head.

"A banana slug's penis grows out of his head," she announced with great pride.

I snuck a peek at Dip to see if he was appalled. He wasn't. Jennifer had definitely found her new man.

"I believe I can beat that, sweetheart," Dip told Jennifer with a grin.

"Try it, big boy," she challenged.

"Alrighty," he said with a grin that made me kind of regret our hike. "King Tut was mummified with his Johnson erect."

My forward motion stopped and I gaped at the chief of police. "How is that possible? I mean, is it possible?"

"Probably rigor mortis," Dip offered as I gagged a little. "Dead bodies are a fascinating subject."

His statement was so bizarrely appropriate for what I had planned, I almost laughed.

I didn't, but Lindsay did.

It took all I had not to glance over at her. I was happy her sense of humor was intact considering what she'd been through and the fact that we were about to find her dead body—even if her humor was a bit morbid for my taste.

"I've got one," I said as I watched Lindsay begin to shudder and point to the right of the path. "Every time you lick a stamp, you consume one-tenth of a calorie."

"Get out of town," Jennifer yelled. "I'm buying the self-stick ones from now on. Gotta watch my sexy figure."

"You're perfect just the way you are, Jenny," Dip said as Jennifer literally swooned.

"You just want to get into my pants," she informed him with a delighted laugh.

"TMI," I said as I felt a tingle of dread whip through my body. It was incredibly difficult to sound normal when all I wanted to do was freak out.

"Your point?" Jennifer asked, nudging me with her elbow.

"No point," I said, trying to keep my focus on the human conversation. "Just an observation."

"We might be in our sixties, but we've still got it going on in the boudoir," she announced as Dip blushed and stammered a bit.

I would have laughed except I was too busy wondering if the banana and peanut butter I'd eaten earlier was going to stay in my stomach.

Donna keyed in on Lindsay and darted off the trail.

"Donna," I yelled. "Come back here."

Donna barked like the forest was on fire. My little Hell Hound was brilliant.

"Oh shit," I muttered as I started off the trail and into the woods.

"Step back, Daisy," Dip Doody instructed, turning from the guy who knew about King Tut's pecker back into the chief of police. "I'll get Donna. There might be a wild animal."

I said nothing. We didn't have many wild animals around here other than deer, opossum, foxes and a few coyotes, but Dip taking the lead was perfect for the outcome I desired.

"That man is as fine as a frog hair split four ways,"

Jennifer gushed with a happy sigh as he disappeared into the dense woods.

"You're going to marry him, aren't you?" I asked with a shake of my head.

"He does like my junk in the trunk, and I like the junk in his jeans," she said with a giggle. "But you know what I really like?"

"Umm… his butt?" I asked, terrified of her answer.

"Well, of course. You could bounce a quarter off that fine ass," she overshared. "I love that he gets me and likes me anyway."

Jennifer rendered me silent. She did that often, but mostly because she'd grossed me out. This time it was because her statement moved me. It was beautiful.

"So, he's going to be husband number six?" I asked.

"Hell to the no," Jennifer said, throwing her little hands in the air. "We're gonna get permanently engaged."

"Mmmkay," I said. "Not following."

"I have shit luck with marriage. I love that man too much to marry him. Every time I've chained myself to a man, it ends in divorce. Not gonna happen with my Dip Doody."

"That might be the smartest thing you've ever said," I told her.

"Nah," she said with a wicked little grin. "Smartest thing I've said is that a whale's penis is called a dork."

"You made that up," I said, trying not to laugh since my body felt like a live wire knowing what was about to happen.

I failed. Jennifer was good like that. I really did love my friends.

"I most certainly did not make that up," she replied, crossing her heart.

"Jenny," Dip called out. "Need you to call the station. I need backup."

"Are you okay?" she asked, getting frantic.

"I'm fine," he said.

"Then why don't you call?" she asked, confused.

"You have my phone, darlin'. I have a little issue down here."

"Is Donna okay?" I yelled, walking into the woods.

"She's fine," Dip said. "Y'all might not want to come down here."

"Why?" Jennifer demanded, marching right past me as she called the station house.

No one told Jennifer what to do, not even the chief of police.

The scene wasn't bloody. It was oddly quiet and calm. Considering the way Lindsay had died, I'd expected it to be horrifying. Not that it wasn't horrifying to see human bones, but it wasn't what I'd thought it would be. My heartbeat accelerated, and my chest tightened, but I also felt so much relief I wanted to drop to my knees and weep with joy.

Instead, I simply stared. I forced myself to separate Lindsay my friend from her bones on the ground.

The bones were scattered from the elements, and I suppose the wildlife. I quickly pushed the macabre thought away. The visual was too much. In the short time I'd known Lindsay, I already loved her. I'd lived through her death with her. I didn't want to imagine what had come next.

Lindsay floated over her bones and pointed to something shiny on the ground. I gave her a tiny nod and approached what used to be my new friend.

"Oh my God," Jennifer gasped out and slapped her hand over her mouth in horror. "Is it a woman or a man?"

Dip sounded weary and sad as he looked down at the bones and sighed. "Looks like a female skeleton. You can tell by the pelvis," he said, squatting down and examining the bones. "That part of a female is adapted for gestation. It's not as high as a male's and it's wider."

My eyes filled with tears. They were happy tears, not that Dip or Jennifer would know. The expression on Lindsay's decomposing face was so peaceful, she appeared angelic.

Lindsay's bones were about to sing.

"What's that?" I asked, pointing to the shiny object on the ground tangled in the bones that had once formed Lindsay's hand.

"Looks like a medical bracelet," Dip said, moving over to the object and taking a look. "Apparently someone by the name of Scott Macon is deathly allergic to bees."

"You think that's Scott?" Jennifer asked, sitting down on the ground in her distress.

"No, Jenny girl," Dip said, glancing over at her. "The victim is a woman."

"You think she was murdered?" I asked, wanting to make sure we were going in the correct direction.

Dip nodded and blew out a long, slow breath. "I do. Look at the poor girl's skull. It was bashed in. I'd guess these bones to be about a year old, give or take a few months.

Probably no DNA evidence on the killer would be left due to the elements, but you better believe I'm gonna find out who this little gal was."

Dip was a very smart man.

"Scott Macon did it," Jennifer shouted, pointing at the bracelet on the ground. "I could be a cop!"

"Maybe," Dip said, shaking his head. "If it is Scott Macon, it'll be the easiest dang case I've ever solved."

I had no intention of telling him, but it was indeed going to be the easiest dang case he'd ever solved.

I just hoped that Scott Macon was arrogant enough to have stayed in Atlanta. If he did inherit his father's fortune, my guess was that he was living it up in style.

The backup arrived, and Jennifer and I made our way back to the trail.

"I'm never going hiking again," Jennifer griped as we waited for Dip.

"I'm kind of with you on that," I said, glancing around for Lindsay.

If she went into the light without me, I would be heartbroken. Yet, at the same time, I would be happy. Lindsay deserved peace. I was humbled that I got to be a small part of it.

After about an hour, Dip joined us with Donna on his heels. "The boys will take care of it now," he said. "You gals okay?"

I nodded. Showing my excitement would be bizarre and wrong. Mostly, I was thankful the plan had worked.

"Do you think Scott Macon is the murderer?" Jennifer asked as we walked back to where we'd parked our cars.

"I made a call after talking with my men. Turns out Scott Macon's sister went missing about a year ago—right before their rich daddy passed," Dip said darkly. "Young gal named Lindsay Macon."

Lindsay's name on his lips sent chills skittering up my spine. I knew Lindsay was dead. This was no surprise. However, when the chief of police said her name, everything became cold and factual. Lindsay simply became a statistic. She was so much more than that to me.

"Holy shitballs," Jennifer said, going pale. "Her brother murdered her for the inheritance."

"Can't be jumpin' to conclusions, but it doesn't look real good for Scott Macon right now," Dip said.

"Will you have a case?" I asked.

"I'm not a lawyer," Dip said. "We're gonna gather up all the evidence carefully then the DA will take over."

Again, I nodded. Heather knew everyone in the law world of Georgia. I'd make triple sure that the DA who took the case enjoyed bringing people to justice.

CHAPTER NINE

"You did good, Daisy," Heather said, handing me a plate of homemade peanut butter cookies.

"You baked?" I asked, surprised as I bit into a delicious cookie.

Heather was a fabulous lawyer, a dear friend and an all-around kickass person, but she was a disaster at baking. She made a mean pot sticker, but I'd never met a cookie or pie that she hadn't destroyed or burned beyond recognition.

"Heck no," she said, sitting down at the kitchen table and nibbling on a cookie. "June and Charlie stopped by. June baked the cookies."

"They were here?" I asked. "At my house?"

"Umm… yes," she said. "I did not bake these cookies, which we should both be thrilled about, and I haven't left the house."

"Why were they here?"

Heather sighed and ate the rest of her cookie while I waited. "June wanted to bring you cookies."

"And?" I pressed.

"And Charlie had some information."

"How did that work?" I asked, squinting at her as I dragged the plate of cookies over so they were sitting in front of me. Sugar was a necessity if I was going to make it through the rest of the day.

"He slipped me a letter," Heather said.

"Are you going to tell me what it said?" I covered the cookies with my body, keeping them hostage until she gave up the goods.

"I am." She sighed. "But first tell me about Lindsay."

Her hesitation to share the news was worrisome. However, I would play along. It had been a rough afternoon and I needed a short break before I took in anything else.

"I think she went into the light. Breaks my heart because I'll miss her, but I'm happy about it," I told Heather, letting her have a cookie.

"Nope," Heather said. "She's upstairs watching over Steve. She got back long before you did. She hasn't left his side."

"Why?" I asked aloud. It was more a question directed at myself since I was aware Heather couldn't understand the ghosts like I did.

"Not sure," Heather admitted. "But Steve seems calmer in her presence."

That was a mystery to be unraveled later. I had another puzzle to put together first.

"Interesting," I said, wondering how well the dead could

communicate with each other and if Lindsay and Steve were talking. I'd never asked my dead guests that particular question. I needed to remedy that.

"Lindsay's bones sang just like she said they would," I told Heather as we both ate cookies like we were starving and hadn't eaten in a week. "Her brother's medical bracelet was wrapped around the bones from her hand, implicating him. Dip called his name in and connected them as sister and brother."

"Excellent. What was the medical bracelet for?" Heather asked.

"Apparently, the greedy, murdering asshole is deathly allergic to bees."

"How inconvenient for him," Heather muttered with disgust.

"He lives in Atlanta. Do you know the DA in Atlanta?"

Heather nodded. "I do. I'll be making a call."

"Thank you," I said, glancing down at the empty cookie plate. "Are there more?"

"Is June the sweetest, cutest woman in the Universe?" Heather inquired with a lopsided grin.

"Yes. The answer is yes," I said without hesitation. It was the truth.

"Correct." She grabbed a bright orange plastic container from the counter and plopped it in front of me. "June bakes for an army. Always."

"Thank God for that," I replied, digging in.

"Amen, sister," Heather agreed as she joined me. "Amen."

"That's not really news," I said, watching Karen examine the outdoor trashcan with great interest. So far, she hadn't been able to get it open, but she clearly had nefarious plans.

"Yes and no," Heather agreed, picking up a stick and tossing it for Donna. "We'll meet tomorrow. More will be revealed."

"Oh my God," I said with a strained grunt of laughter. "That sounded like a line from a bad B movie discussing a secret society."

Heather shrugged and tossed another stick since Karen had stolen the first one from Donna. "If the shoe fits…"

"Who will be there?" I asked.

"Clarence, Charlie, Tim, you, me and possibly a few others," she told me.

My body grew tense and my voice tight. "A few others?"

"Not Clarissa," Heather assured me. "She's not welcome back to this plane until the tribunal."

I heaved a sigh of relief, but then felt light-headed and off-balance. "Gideon?" I whispered.

Heather was silent as she accepted the stick from Donna and tossed it again. "No. And that is an issue."

"Why?"

"Because he needs to be here and no one knows how to reach him," she replied.

I digested that for a few minutes. My heart still felt raw and torn apart where Gideon was concerned, but I had no one to thank for that except myself. I'd destroyed any chance I had at real love, and now it seemed like I might have destroyed the chance for a tribunal to help Steve as well. My track record was abysmal and possibly catastrophic.

"No one?" I whispered.

"That's what we're going to figure out tomorrow."

"How?" I pressed, wanting information she didn't have.

"Remains to be seen, Daisy. I've asked June to come by tomorrow and sit with the dogs while we're out."

"Didn't she think that was odd?" I questioned. She didn't know Steve was here, and the point of someone being here was to protect him.

"Karen ate part of the couch," Heather informed me. "I told June the dogs couldn't be trusted and it would take a load off your mind if she stayed with them."

"She bought that?" I asked, doubting the merits of having June here while I was out. I had a mail fraud box and so much superglue it could raise questions. However, June was not nosey at all. I couldn't imagine her snooping in a million years. I was fully aware Karen had eaten part of the couch. I'd covered it with one of Gram's afghans but obviously hadn't hidden the destruction well enough.

"Bought it hook, line and sinker. Even said she might be able to repair the sofa. I also told her if Clarissa stopped by to call the police and me."

"Clarissa is in the light. You told me she couldn't get to Steve," I said, my voice rising in alarm. "What don't I know?"

Heather took my hand and pulled me over to the porch swing. "Clarissa *is* in the light. She isn't allowed to do anything to Steve or take him anywhere. However, she's tricky."

"Explain," I snapped, feeling a massive headache coming on.

"Clarissa is a rule follower to a certain point," Heather said, slowly. "She would never touch Steve right now because she would have to forfeit all of her powers and her title if she broke the rules."

"Okay," I said. Relief washed over me. "Then what gives?"

"If she slips back through the veil, she could go after you."

My fury spiked and my body tingled with rage. Needing an outlet for my ire, I walked out into my yard and straight to the largest oak tree. It was probably two hundred years old. I was aware I was about to break one or both of my hands, but I needed some physical pain to remove the need to peel my skin from my body. Running forever might help, but that was out of the question. Punching a tree was not. Plus, the tree would be fine.

Me? I didn't care.

My eyes rested on the pattern of the bark. It was cracked and chaotic like the thoughts racing through my head. The crisp, brown late-fall leaves underneath my tennis shoes were as lifeless as the ghosts who suddenly surrounded me. I circled the tree. The leaves crunched under my feet. The sound was strangely satisfying.

The gnarled limbs of my favorite tree were twisted and naked. The enormous size represented power to me—power that was elusive. Power I would never have.

Making a fist and keeping my thumb on the outside like

I'd learned in my self-defense class at the Y, I reared back and laid into the tree.

"Daisy," Heather yelled. "What the hell are you doing?"

"Letting out a little steam," I shouted back and punched the tree again.

My knuckles were bleeding and I felt the impact of the punches all the way up to my shoulders. It was tremendous and liberating. I wanted more.

"Daisy, stop," Heather insisted, sprinting over to my side and grabbing my arms. "This will result in nothing except a trip to the hospital."

"That's where you're wrong," I said, breaking out of her strong grip with surprising ease. "It's solving a lot. Trust me."

Heather shook her head and stepped back to watch me break both of my hands.

Boxing with a tree was wildly gratifying.

Until it wasn't.

"Oh shit!" Heather screamed as she grabbed me and yanked me back.

We landed on our rear ends in a tangled pile and watched in utter shock as the massive tree swayed and groaned. The thick, skeletal branches twisted and snapped like tiny twigs. The tree seemed to lift its arms to the sky begging for mercy.

"What the fu…" I cried out.

With one last mighty and furious groan, the massive two-hundred-year-old oak swayed and split. It crashed to the ground with an enormous thud, taking out my mailbox and missing my car by inches.

Heather and I sat in freaked-out silence for at least twenty minutes. Even Donna and Karen were subdued and sat quietly beside us.

"I didn't do that," I choked out on a whisper.

"I think you did," Heather said, glancing over at me with concern.

"Not possible."

"You mean impossible?" she questioned.

"Yes. That's what I mean," I said, taking in the carnage.

"Everything is possible—even the impossible," she said. "You just have to believe."

"What's happening to me?" I whispered, looking down at my bloody hands as if they belonged to someone else.

Heather leveled me with a worried stare. "I'm not sure. Maybe we can get some answers tomorrow. In the meantime, I'd suggest you refrain from punching things."

"Is that a joke?" I asked, closing my eyes and letting my body fall back into the grass. "Because if it is, it sucks."

"Not a joke," Heather replied. "I'm deadly serious."

"Roger that." I kept my eyes shut. If I opened them, I'd have to see the damage I'd done—the *impossible* damage I'd done.

"You want more cookies?" Heather asked.

I laughed. The request was absurd, considering that I'd just knocked a two-hundred-year-old tree over by punching it. However, it was also perfect.

"I do," I replied, sitting up. "At least I didn't crush my car."

"There is that," Heather said, helping me to my feet.

"Although, not sure how Tim is going to feel about you demolishing your mailbox. That might be a federal offense."

"I'm into the illegal stuff." I gave her a weak grin. "A little federal offense is not a problem. You want to be my lawyer if I get thrown in the pokey?"

"You're a hot mess, and yes. I will always represent you, Daisy. Let's go bandage up your hands and eat cookies."

Right now, it was the little things that definitely mattered most.

Cookies were at the top of that list.

CHAPTER TEN

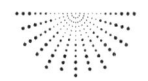

"Listen up everyone," I shouted above the early morning din of the squatters. "First of all, you're not supposed to be in my bedroom."

"Hooooooooookaaah," Birdie screeched as she dove into a basket of clean clothes.

"I've had about enough of you," I snapped, dumping her out of my freshly washed sweats, t-shirts and panties. "You're a freaking menace."

"Hooooooooookaaah," Birdie snapped as she faded away with her middle finger lifted.

"For the love of everything annoying," I huffed as I put the clean clothes back in the basket. "I've been remiss about telling you guys the rules. So, let's fix that now."

"Yausssss," said the large ghost who was the victim of Birdie's arm-stealing adventure.

He sat down at my desk and tried to pick up a pen to write down the rules. He was my kind of dude. Walking over to him, I patted him on the back when he got upset about his inability to hold a pen.

"It's okay. No worries," I said. "I love your organization skills."

"Yausssss," he replied, trying to give me a salute and losing his hand in the process.

He started to cry. Well, as much as a semitransparent specter could. His distress pulled at my heartstrings.

Retrieving his hand from the floor and giving it back to him, I then picked up the pen and grabbed a sheet of paper. My hands were still bandaged, swollen and sore. Heather and I were both shocked I hadn't broken them. There was no logical explanation for yesterday so I decided to block out the fact that I'd knocked over a two-hundred-year-old tree with my fists.

It wasn't working.

"How about I write down the rules and you can be the Mayor of Squatter Town and remind everyone to follow them?" I asked, focusing on the matter at hand.

"Yausssss. Thaauanuak yooouah," he said and nodded his large head so vigorously, I was concerned he might lose that as well.

"Mmmkay," I said as the crowd hovered around me. "The bathroom is a hard no. No one is to set a ghostly foot in there. You feel me?"

There was a chorus of murmured assents.

"Good," I said as I finished writing it down for the mayor. "Normally, you're not allowed in the bedroom, but today I'm making an exception."

The excited applause from my squatters created a sharp

wind that blew everything around willy-nilly except the furniture.

"And that right there is one of the reasons why," I said, hopping up to make sure Steve was okay.

He was. Lindsay sat right next to him and gave me a smile.

"Heeeve fauuiiine," she told me.

"I can see that Steve's fine. Thank you, Lindsay." I sat down next to her. "Honey, if you want to, you can leave and move on. Your brother is going down. I promise you."

Lindsay nodded and smiled again. It was beautifully horrible.

"Sssiiiiiiinngea booooooouuns. Thaauanuak yooouah, Dausseeeeee."

"You're most welcome, Lindsay," I told her, gently touching her caved-in cheek. "So, no pressure, but when you're ready to leave it's fine."

Truthfully, I didn't want her to go anywhere. My instinct was to keep her close and protect her.

"Liiiiinsay staaaawauy," she said, patting my head with one hand and Steve's with the other. "Taaaawk caaaure oowt Heeeve aawnd Dausseeeeee."

Clearly, Lindsay had a protective instinct too. The fact that she wanted to take care of Steve and me made me want to cry. The dead were thrilled with the development and zipped around the room cheering like they were at a championship high school football game and their team was kicking some major ass.

"Oh baby," I said, leaning in to hug her and being careful not to pull off a body part by accident. "That's probably the sweetest thing anyone has said to me in a very long time."

"Yausssss," Steve added, looking at me, and then at Lindsay. "Gooodah guirrul."

"She is a good girl," I said, giving Steve a kiss on the top of his head.

"Hoooooooookaaah," Birdie yelled as she appeared from out of nowhere and scared the bejesus out of me. "Meeeeah heealup toooah."

"You want to help me?" I asked, narrowing my eyes at the fouled-mouthed little hot mess of a ghost.

"Yausssss, hooooooooookaaah," she announced with a cackle.

Shaking my head, I laughed. "Well, I suppose I should take help where I can get it," I muttered as I stood up to get Steve's approval on my outfit.

When Steve died, I'd stopped caring about myself. I did shower and brush my teeth, but that was about it. When he came back, he was appalled at the way I'd been dressing—had a fit. I hated to admit it, but he'd been correct. Since my fashion flair was iffy and I had something important to do, I ran my outfit past my gay dead husband slash best friend.

"Is this okay?" I asked, making sure I was in his sightline.

I was about to attend a meeting with people who had been alive for thousands of years. They'd been through so many fashion eras it had to be difficult to keep up. After trying on far too many outfits that had gone out of style ten years ago, I settled on a pair of slim black pants, a golden yellow silk shirt that matched my eyes, and black pumps. I felt pretty good about my choice. Of course, the hand bandages weren't all that attractive, but they were necessary.

"Buuuummmmbalah beeeeeee," Steve announced, much to the amusement of my dead guests.

"Shit," I muttered, glancing in the mirror. He was right. Black and yellow wasn't the best color combo. Getting dressed up sucked all kinds of butt. "What the hell should I wear? It's a business meeting of sorts."

Birdie flew into my closet and started to shriek. I wasn't sure if my clothes terrified her or she was trying to lend a hand. Either way, it was slightly unnerving.

"What?" I walked into the closet and found her trying to put on a long-sleeved, black silk, square-neck blouse that still had the tag on it.

"Yausssss, hooooooooookaaah," she hissed.

Rolling my eyes, I took the shirt, removed the price tag and changed into it. "Better?"

Birdie flipped me off and disappeared. Such a delightful woman.

Checking my watch, my stomach tightened. I needed to leave in twenty minutes. June would be here in five. I didn't have time for a freaking fashion show.

As I caught a glance of myself in the mirror, I had to admit Birdie—as unpleasant as she was—was correct. I looked put-together and professional. The mayor grunted and pointed to my jewelry box. It was open and waiting. Clearly, the Mayor of Squatter Town had an opinion.

"Okay," I said with a raised brow. "Which earrings and which necklace?"

Using his detached hand as a pointer, he touched the

diamond studs and the teardrop diamond necklace that had been gifts from Steve. I quickly put them all on. The mayor nodded his approval.

"Am I good?" I asked Steve as I got back into his sightline. "I don't have time to try on much more."

"Gooooodah," he said with approval. "Haaaaur doooowun."

"But I think it looks more professional up," I told him.

"Naawwwooo," he disagreed as the dead chimed in with a loud chorus of agreement.

"This is ridiculous," I griped, taking the pins out of my bun and letting my dark, long, wild hair fall free.

Again, my posse of squatters applauded wildly.

"I'm done," I said, taking a bow. "My friend June will be here while I'm gone. She can't see you guys, so no funny business. You all feel me?"

Quickly turning on *Survivor* in the bedroom to occupy my squatters, I gave Steve another quick kiss on his head.

"I'm gonna get this solved for you, baby," I told him. "I promise."

"Looooovah yooooah," he whispered.

"Love you too."

∼

"Daisy, you look gorgeous," June said, wrapping me in a warm hug.

I would have killed to have had someone like June for a mother but having her as a dear friend was almost as good.

"Thank you," I said, not wanting to let go. I completely

understood Charlie's adoration of June. Everyone loved her. She was all kinds of wonderful, and then some. Not to mention, she baked an amazing cookie.

"You look so lovely you should grab Missy and get some lunch today. Have a good time," she suggested. "My goodness, what happened to your hands?"

"Umm… wiped out running," I lied and forced a laugh I hoped didn't sound as fake as it felt. "No biggie, and thanks, but no lunch date, not today." I grabbed my dress coat and a purse with a strap that wasn't frayed. "I have no clue how long this meeting is going to last."

"Not to worry," June said, pulling out an upholstery kit from her massive tote. "Charlie has a work meeting today too, and the kids are all out of town. I need a little project and, from what Heather told me, I do believe your couch might be it."

"It's pretty bad." I laughed as Donna and Karen bounded into the room and attacked June with wet doggie kisses.

"Which one of you little furballs is the culprit who did this?" she inquired with a giggle, pointing to the chewed-up section of my sofa.

"While I didn't see the criminal in action, I'm going to have to go with this one," I told her, scratching Karen behind her ears and hitting her tickle spot.

Karen's furry foot slapped the floor as I nailed her favorite spot and Donna did zoomies to impress June. Her laugh rang out in my quiet house, and I noticed a few ghosts float in and gravitate to her. Even the dead adored June.

"Daisy, I'm serious about you having a little fun today. If you want to take a run when you get home, I can stay for that too," she said, having no clue that she was being worshiped by my dead squatters.

Even Birdie was taken with her. As far as I could tell, Birdie had yet to flip off my dear friend.

"Oh my God," June said, reaching into her bag and pulling out a huge cookie tin. "Jennifer told me about the hike and finding the body of that poor girl. Must have been awful."

"Mostly sad," I said.

"So sad," June agreed with a sigh then put the tin on the coffee table.

"Are those cookies for me?"

"Well, they're not for Charlie or me," she said with a grin. "Our waistlines are a little out of control. We're starting a diet this week. All my baking has to leave the house. My Charlie has such a sweet tooth. If there's a sugary treat in the house, he'll find it."

"I will happily accept anything you have to offer," I told her, wondering if Charlie could control his weight like he could control his age. I wouldn't be the least bit surprised if he gained pounds on purpose so June never felt bad. "Is Jennifer still upset about seeing the body?"

"No," June said, pilfering one of her own cookies and taking a bite. "She wants to become a cop now because she said she solved the crime. Can you believe that? I think that Botox fried her brain."

I laughed and grabbed a big handful of cookies. Maybe I'd give Charlie one…

"Anyhoo," June went on, stacking her upholstery tools

on the table. "Justice was served pretty dang fast on that one."

"What do you mean?" I asked, startled.

"The killer—who confessed, by the way—got stung by a hive of bees," she said, shaking her head. "Cops in Atlanta found a big bee's nest under the mansion that the horrible man lived in. They came up through the heating system and stung him to death—not that I wish death on anyone, but the way he killed his sister was dreadful."

"How do you know this?" I asked.

We'd only found the bones yesterday. Did karma work that fast?

"I'm not supposed to know," June whispered so no one would overhear.

"June, we're alone," I told her, quickly checking to make sure Lindsay wasn't within earshot. I would tell Lindsay myself.

She giggled and smacked herself in the forehead. "Whoops! Jennifer told me. She wasn't supposed to, but she can't keep her trap shut… and apparently I can't either."

"No worries," I told her. "And not that I'm happy to hear about anyone dying… but that guy? Seems like he had it coming."

"Agree. He was a very bad man," June said, checking her watch. "What time do you have to be there? And where are you going anyway? Heather just said it was a meeting. Is it for the firm?"

We all worked as paralegals at Heather's newly opened law office—June, Jennifer and me.

"Umm... no," I said, leaning down, wrapping the cookies in a napkin and tucking them into my purse so June wouldn't see my face. Being a crappy liar wasn't in my favor at the moment. "It's a meeting about the settlement from Steve's death."

Actually, it was only a partial lie... or a lie of omission. The meeting was indeed about Steve's death in a roundabout way.

"Oh sweetie." June hugged me again. "I'm so sorry. Will Heather be with you?"

I nodded, afraid if I said any more the lie would grow, and possibly my nose, as well. After knocking the tree over with my bare hands yesterday, I had no clue what my body was capable of doing. Becoming Pinocchio would suck hard.

"I have to go," I said. "Thank you so much for making sure the dogs don't eat the house."

"We'll have a grand old time," she assured me. "Oh, and sorry about your oak. It was such a lovely old tree."

Again, I nodded and raced out the front door. Hopefully, one day, there would be nothing in my life that June would have to feel bad about or worry over. I had no clue when that time would come, but I sure as heck hoped it was soon.

CHAPTER ELEVEN

"I'm nervous—like high school marching band on speed in my stomach nervous," I told Heather, noticing a small tear on my purse and flipping it so the good side was showing.

If I had to keep meeting with people who were older than dirt, I was going to have to invest in a new purse. For the love of everything Southern, a forty-year-old woman should own at least one decent bag that wasn't falling apart. I mentally noted that I needed to up my game or I was going to have to turn in my Southern Gal Card.

Our heels clicked on the highly polished hardwood floor as we made our way down the hallway of the law firm where we both used to be employed.

"Nerves are good," Heather said. "Keeps you on your toes. Going in casual would be dangerous."

"Well shit," I muttered, grabbing her arm and halting her. "I have a few questions."

"Make them quick," Heather said, checking her watch.

"Do I look okay?"

Heather clinically examined me from head to toe. With a curt nod, she gave me a thumbs up. "You look like a gorgeous princess from the depths of Hell. All you're missing are the red eyes, but your gold eyes are a nice angelic touch."

"Umm… not exactly the look I was going for," I said as my stomach roiled. A bumblebee might have been a better choice than a demon princess.

"Trust me, a princess all in black who talks to the dead and can take out a tree with a punch is a very good thing right now."

"Okay," I said, trying to calm my racing heart. "Am I supposed to speak during the meeting?"

"If you have something to say, then yes. Any more questions?"

"Yes, but I can't think of any right now."

Heather gave me a quick hug. "This is not the tribunal, Daisy. Steve's afterlife is not on the line today. It's more of an informational meeting."

I nodded and took a deep breath.

"Wait," I said as Heather began to walk again.

"One more question, Daisy," she said. "Being late isn't smart."

"Got it," I replied, feeling woozy about the words on the tip of my tongue. "Scott Macon was killed by bees. Did you know that?"

Heather's pause was approximately seven seconds too long. "I did. Karma worked pretty fast on that one."

My mouth hung open. I wanted to ask another question, but I didn't want the answer. Scott Macon's death, no matter how it happened, didn't affect Steve's afterlife or my job as the Death Counselor. Therefore, it should be none of my business. The evil man deserved to die after his vicious murder of Lindsay, in my opinion, but that was all it was—an opinion. I would never act on it. I felt ill that maybe Heather had. It made going into the meeting all the more terrifying.

I dealt with the dead. I helped them. I cared about them. I wasn't the reason for their deaths.

"Oh," Heather said, breezing right past Scott Macon's demise without concern. "Candy Vargo will be in attendance."

"Freaking Candy Vargo is Immortal? Candy Vargo? Candy Vargo, who has hammertoe and an ear wax issue? Candy Vargo, who works as a cashier at the Piggly Wiggly?" I asked, shocked to the core.

"Yep," Heather said with a chuckle. "That Candy Vargo. Thank God there's only one. My advice is not to piss her off. She has a short fuse. You ready?"

"Hell no. Let's do this."

"That's my girl," Heather said with a wide grin.

∼

I'D BEEN IN CLARENCE SMITH'S OFFICE BEFORE. THIS TIME was vastly different.

The office was very masculine—dark wood and leather furniture. The walls were painted a hunter green and a very expensive Persian rug covered a large portion of the shiny wood floor. My eyes were immediately drawn to the ornate wooden table in the center of the room. The Immortals were already seated and waiting for Heather and me.

I would have liked to have been anywhere else in the world. I could literally feel the power in the room crawling along my skin.

Heather was correct. Candy Vargo was here and sitting at the head of the table. Charlie, Tim and Clarence Smith, aka John Travolta, gave her a wide berth and appeared to be slightly uncomfortable with her presence. I wondered if she'd monologued about her bone spurs. Once Candy Vargo got going about her feet, it was tremendously difficult to make her stop.

Charlie—short, round and adorable—gave me a covert wink, which relaxed me some. Tim, on the other hand, stared at me as if I were some kind of unpleasant science experiment. Tim was slightly unfortunate-looking. His eyes were a little too close together, and his thinning hair was parted unstylishly in the middle. He wore his postal uniform. Did he own any other clothes?

Candy Vargo simply picked her teeth and looked bored. She was a disaster—untucked, unbathed and rude.

"Thank you for coming, Daisy," Clarence Smith said kindly as he put his hand out to indicate we should be seated. He was a handsome man, with thick white hair and golden-colored eyes, in his early seventies—or at least it was the version of himself he chose to show—and, funny enough, didn't look a thing like John Travolta.

"I didn't think there was much of a choice," I said,

making a joke that made no one laugh. "Umm… I'm kidding. I'm… umm… honored and you know… kind of, somewhat pleased to be here. So, thank you for having me."

If I could have melted like the Wicked Witch of the West, I would have gladly done it. My lack of sophistication was showing and I was fairly sure it wasn't going to be in my favor.

"Yes, well, let's get right to it," Charlie said, giving me a smile that warmed me all over.

He was as lovely and kind as June. Having him and Heather here was a gift and an incredible relief.

"Shall we start with introductions?" Clarence Smith suggested.

"I already know all of you," I pointed out, confused.

"Yep, as far as you know, you do," Candy Vargo said, tossing her toothpick to the floor and sitting back in her chair.

"Got it," I said, wanted to gag at her manners. "My bad."

"I go by Clarence Smith. My real identity is Michael the Archangel. It's self-explanatory."

I nodded because I was terrified that I was going to call him John Travolta.

"I go by Charlie Calvert. My real name is not easy to pronounce, so I stick with Charlie," Charlie said with a chuckle. "I'm the Enforcer of the Immortals."

"Tim. Just Tim. I can't remember the name I was given," Tim said with a shrug. "I'm the Courier. The almighty mailman of the Immortal Universe."

I noted a slight eye roll from the others but Tim was oblivious. I was tempted to ask him if he stole mail from

Heaven and Hell, but thought one shitty joke had been enough for this meeting.

"My name is Heather George. I've had a variety of names over the years. Occasionally, I can't remember who I am this century—comes with living forever, I suppose. I'm the Arbitrator between Heaven and Hell."

The group chuckled. I forced myself to join them. Immortal humor was a bit above my scope of understanding and pay grade, but if I was anything, I was polite. Only Candy's alias remained. I couldn't even imagine what her Immortal job was. Her manners were heinous.

"I go by Candy Vargo." She pulled a fresh toothpick out of her pocket and had another go at her teeth. "My real name is Karma. My job is my name. Figure it out."

Karma grinned from ear to ear as my entire body chilled to the core. She then made a noise that sounded distinctly like a buzzing bee. I immediately regretted all the cookies I'd eaten. Heather wasn't joking when she'd advised it would be unwise to be on Candy's bad side.

My stomach churned and I stole a quick glance at Heather. She wouldn't look at me. I had my answer about Scott Macon. I was too taken aback to know how I felt about it. Part of me wanted to thank Candy on behalf of Lindsay. The other part of me was appalled. I decided to feel nothing, or at least show as little on my face as possible. I didn't want Candy to start *helping* me with my job. Blood on my hands, even if it was the blood of a murderer, was something I wanted no part of at all.

Taking a deep breath and remembering why I was here steadied my confidence. Steve was the only person who mattered, and I was his representative. "I'm Daisy Leigh Amara-Jones," I said, using both my maiden and married surnames. "I'm the Death Counselor."

"Names are such a telling thing," Candy Vargo said darkly.

I was half tempted to shout *no joke*, but I bit it back. The fact that a sloppy, tooth-picking, hammer-toed Immortal was in charge of Karma was very dark indeed.

I really wanted to get out of here. The chances of me offending *Karma* with my new and constantly growing lady balls was high. There was no room for more trouble on my plate.

"Have the instructions for the tribunal been deciphered?" I asked, getting back to the reason we'd gathered so we could finish and I could get the hell out. I was seriously thinking about taking June up on her offer to stay at the house while I took a run. Running was about the only activity that made my mind go blank.

"We're close," Tim said, still watching me with a sour expression on his face.

I wondered if he'd heard I'd crushed my mailbox with a tree and was pissed. He was such a strange little man.

"However, there are some issues," Clarence added, staring at me too.

They were all staring at me. Did I have food on my face? Shit. Heather would have told me if I was sporting cookie crumbs. Maybe there was lipstick on my teeth. I hadn't asked for a teeth check.

Lady balls. Use my lady balls. If I had lipstick on my teeth, I would own it and pretend I meant to put it there.

"Issues such as?" I asked, leveling Clarence with a stare that meant business. "What was done to Steve was wrong. I will not abide by the decision."

"You will have no choice other than to abide by the result of the tribunal," Clarence shot back with a raised brow and an expression I couldn't quite decipher.

"I'll win," I said flatly.

My confidence might be lacking for myself, but when it came to the people I loved, I had it in spades.

"Ballsy," Karma commented.

"Correct," I replied. "What is the issue?"

I knew the issue. The issue was Gideon. I wanted to hear the solution.

"The Grim Reaper must be in attendance in order for the tribunal to be legal—so to speak," Charlie said with a concerned expression aimed at me.

"Fine. I have no problem with Gideon being here," I said with a shrug.

"You sent him away," Tim pointed out.

"And you know this, how?" I asked, narrowing my eyes at the bizarre man.

"Word gets around," he replied easily. "He… *or she* who caused the problem must solve it."

"What does that mean?" Heather demanded tightly. "Explain yourself, Courier."

Tim sat silently and stared right back at Heather.

Great. Was I about to witness an Immortal smackdown? If so, my money was on Heather.

"It means that since Daisy sent the Grim Reaper away,

Daisy must bring him back," Charlie chimed in, avoiding eye contact.

"Impossible," Heather snapped, jumping to her feet and eyeing the group with disgust. "That's a death wish."

"Out of order, Arbitrator," Candy Vargo said with a laugh. "You should know better. Getting attached does have its pitfalls."

Candy Vargo was a walking cliché. *Karma was a bitch.* She was mean, disgusting and deadly.

"Nothing is impossible," I said, putting my hand on Heather's arm to calm her. "You just have to believe."

Heather closed her eyes and slowly sat back down. Steve's afterlife was on the line. I would make the impossible happen. There was no choice in the matter. I just had no idea how to do it.

"Wise words for one so young," Clarence said with admiration in his eyes.

For a while, I'd secretly pretended Clarence Smith was my father since I had no clue who my sperm donor was. He'd always been kind and fair to me all the years I'd worked for him. Of course, the distasteful fact that his daughter was Clarissa ruined the fantasy. Ironically, now I knew they weren't related. It made sense. Clarissa was the essence of evil and Clarence was not.

"I'd say thank you, but I think it's a little premature," I replied cryptically. "What do I have to do?"

No one said a word. That did not bode well, and I was grateful to be seated. I'd accepted a whole lot of impossible recently. I wasn't sure how much more my brain could hold.

"You knocked down a massive tree with your bare hands?" Karma inquired casually.

"With my fists," I corrected her. "And what does that have to do with anything?"

"Nothing," she replied with a rude grin. "Just curious."

"I see," I said, getting irritated with the games. I didn't like the rules. It was time to play by mine. "What else are you curious about while you have me here as a captive audience?"

The exchanged glances of surprise felt empowering. Hoping like heck I wasn't reading them wrong, I crossed my arms over my chest and waited. My bandages were on full display. I thought it was a nice touch—a bit arrogant, but a nice touch.

"You go into the minds of the dead?" Charlie asked, confused and concerned.

"I do," I confirmed.

"How?" Clarence asked, sounding truly curious.

Should I tell them? Was it safe? Would I endanger my squatters by sharing my methods? Shit.

"It's okay, Daisy," Heather promised. "No one here has your power. No one in this room can harm the dead."

Slowly letting my gaze hit every person in the room, including Heather, I nodded. "Fine. However, I want some kind of proof that what I say stays in the room."

"Again, I say ballsy," Karma said with a cackle and went back to digging in her teeth. "Who does this little chit think she is? I could eat her for dinner."

"Dude, *gross*," I snapped, rolling my eyes. Candy Vargo was an asshole. "Can you wait until the freaking meeting is done before you pick your teeth? I'm going to lose my cookies. And I do mean cookies," I said, reaching into my purse and whipping out the napkin full of June's masterpieces. "How about this? If you can contain your rank habit until I leave the room, you can have a cookie. If you can't, no cookie for you. And just for your information, *Karma*, June made these cookies."

The room went deathly silent. I would have laughed at the expressions on all of the faces if I hadn't just stepped so far over the line and probably signed my own death warrant.

To say Candy Vargo was shocked would have been an understatement. I just hoped she would wait to kill me until after the tribunal.

"Can I have two?" Candy inquired with a wide grin as everyone let out a collective sigh of relief, including me.

"You going to put that toothpick away?" I asked.

"Yep." She snapped her fingers and burnt it to ash.

"Well, that was certainly unnervingly impressive," I said, handing her three cookies to be on the safe side.

"I'm good like that," Candy replied, biting into a cookie. "Balls are good, little girlie."

"My name is Daisy, and thank you," I said, passing the cookies around the table. "I want proof that what I say doesn't leave the room."

All eyes landed on Charlie.

"Your secret is safe," Charlie promised.

"That's it?" I asked, surprised. "No blood oath or weird ritual?"

Charlie laughed and put his hand on his heart. "Trust me," he said. "My word is law. *No one* goes against it."

Karma shuddered and Tim looked terrified. I was satisfied. Apparently, sweet Charlie was quite the badass.

"I hug the dead who have needs more complicated than others. Most of the issues can be resolved by using a Ouija board, and then…"

I paused. I remembered Gram telling me that Tim had delivered the mail fraud box to her. However, the man was so strange, I didn't want him to get his panties in a wad. Plus, I didn't have any more cookies in my bag to calm him down if he threw a fit.

"And then?" Clarence asked.

"Tim?" I questioned.

"What?" he asked.

"Would you like to explain what I do then since you're the one who provided the materials?" I asked.

"No."

I shook my head and sighed. "Alrighty then, I forge letters and cards to the dead's loved ones. I postdate them. It's their final wish so they can move on. It's illegal and I enjoy it. I've also committed a misdemeanor, and my lying skills have vastly improved."

I was pretty sure I heard Heather snort.

"Is that all?" Clarence asked, looking a little dazed.

"Umm… no. I do squatter surgery regularly," I explained to confused stares from all but Heather. "I glue appendages back onto my ghosts."

"With what?" Charlie asked, trying not to laugh.

I smiled at him. "Superglue. I should take out stock. I

go through a lot of it. The dead are a hot mess and incredibly clumsy. A detached head requires two tubes of glue. I'd also like to add they adore reality shows and I don't."

I was greeted with amused silence. It was a relief to speak about what I did and not be locked up in an institution for it.

"Now that I've spilled my secrets, someone needs to tell me what I have to do to find Gideon."

The room went from light to dark in the time it took to take a breath. The answer to my question was not going to be pretty.

"You must go to him and convince him to come back," Clarence said.

"Got that much. Where is he?"

"In the mist," Charlie said softly.

"Can you be a little more specific?" I asked.

"Gideon is in the darkness," Heather ground out, unhappy with the fact. "Apparently, they want you to enter the darkness and convince him to come back."

"And if I don't?" I asked, feeling disengaged from my body.

"Then the Angel of Mercy's edict stands. Your dead husband will never go into the light," Karma informed me, sounding bored by all of it.

Refusing to go was a very bad option.

"Is there any other way?" I asked.

No one said a word. My answer was in the silence.

"Fine. I'll do it," I said, feeling shaky. "How do I find the darkness? Is there a map?"

"You find the darkness in the minds of the dead," Clarence explained with no emotion in his voice.

"Shit," I muttered as I struggled not to scream. I'd been told never to go into the light and never to go into the *darkness*. Never is a very long time. I supposed my never was very close on the horizon.

"You may choose one of us for guidance on how to navigate the darkness," Charlie told me. "Choose carefully. Once the decision is made it cannot be retracted."

"The rules are archaic," I said, holding back an eye roll with effort. I'd pushed my luck far enough.

"We *are* older than dirt," Heather pointed out.

"Speak for yourself," Karma said.

"I am," Heather replied. "And for all of us in the room."

Glancing at each person seated at the table, I had no idea who to pick. None of them were familiar with what I did and how I did it. None of them had gone into the darkness.

Wait.

One of them might have…

"I choose Tim," I said, staring right at the persnickety man.

Two conversations rang in my mind as I watched Tim preen for a moment and Karma get pissed. Gram had told me that Tim was the mailman for the living and the dead. And Heather had said not to discount him and that the bizarre little man had been everywhere.

I was betting my life—literally—that Tim had been to the dark side. Tim was the most logical choice.

Both Heather and Charlie blew out audible sighs of

relief and made me feel more confident of my choice. Karma was back to picking her teeth.

The odd reaction was from Clarence Smith. If I wasn't mistaken, the man looked proud.

Whatever. I didn't need John Travolta to be proud of me. I needed him to declare Clarissa wrong so that Steve could go into the light where he belonged.

"When would you like to travel?" Tim inquired.

"Umm… tomorrow morning?" I said, mentally cataloging what I needed to do just in case I didn't make it back to this plane. Number one on the list was a visit to Gram. She needed to know how much I loved her if I didn't come back. "Is there anything I should do to prepare?"

"Yes," Tim replied.

I waited.

And I waited.

God, he was an asshole.

"What do I need to do?" I ground out as politely as I could, which wasn't very polite.

"Choose someone," he said.

"I already did," I snapped. "I chose you."

"Quit being a dick," Heather hissed to Tim. "Out with it. Now."

"I quite agree with Heather," Charlie said, sounding so ominous I blanched.

Tim practically peed his postal pants.

"Yes. Yes, of course," he stammered. "You must choose one of the dead. You will go into their mind and enter the darkness that way."

"And you'll teach me how to come back out?" I pressed, wanting to get it all out on the table with everyone present.

He nodded. "It will not be easy… at all."

Well, that sucked. However, nothing worth doing was ever easy.

I was scared. I was scared to walk willingly into the darkness. I was scared of never coming back. I was scared to face Gideon after all the things I'd said to him.

But I was terrified of what would happen if I couldn't convince him to come back.

Standing up and grabbing my purse and coat, I nodded to the group. "I'd say it's been a pleasure, but it hasn't." I realized that for the first time, my Southern manners didn't own me. I owned me. "Tim, I'll expect you around ten in the morning. Does that work for you?"

"It does," he replied. "Get some sleep. You're going to need it."

"Noted," I said as I turned and walked out of the office.

I didn't look back. I didn't say thank you. From now on, I was going to move unapologetically forward. It was the only way to survive.

CHAPTER TWELVE

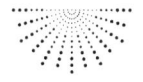

Gram's mouth was wide open. I could see her molars.

"Shut the front door! Candy Vargo is *Karma*?" Gram asked for the third time. "Always thought that woman was slower than a herd of turtles. Little concernin' that someone who wears leggings as formalwear and digs for gold up her nose in public is in charge of fate."

I closed my eyes and tried to remember if I'd ever shaken hands with Candy the nose digger. "Please tell me that was an exaggeration."

"Nope. Bless her heart. That woman is a hot mess of nasty," Gram announced with a grimace.

"Gross," I said with a shudder, as I unwrapped the burgers and fries I'd picked up for us to eat. Thankfully, thus far in life I'd missed Candy Vargo having a go at her nose. If I ever saw her hands getting close to her sniffer in the future, I'd be sure to look the other way.

June had been delighted when I'd called to let her know I

was going to bring Gram some lunch and sit with her for a bit. She insisted that I take my time and enjoy the day. She needed a few more hours with my couch. I adored my friend.

"Well, butter my butt and call me a biscuit," Gram said as she squirted mustard all over her fries. "Can't get over that Candy Vargo is gonna live forever. Next you're gonna tell me that the cross-eyed gal at the bank is a dragon."

Mustard on fries was one of Gram's stranger habits, but if it made her eat, I didn't care what she slathered on her food. I'd tried mustard on my fries once and hated it. I was a catsup and extra salt girl all the way.

"Nope, not as far as I know," I said, unwrapping the extra hamburger I'd gotten for myself. A gal couldn't live on cookies alone. "However, very little would surprise me at this point."

"How is it that you eat all that crap and never gain a pound?" Gram asked as she tore open a few more mustard packets.

"My guess is early menopause," I said with a mouthful of hamburger.

"Don't know where you're getting your information, Daisy girl, but that ain't the way it works."

I shrugged. It wasn't the best idea to tell her I took out a tree in the yard with my fist. Her health was declining and that would worry her to no end.

Heck, it worried *me*.

"Call me lucky," I said with a laugh. "It won't last, so I'm taking advantage of it."

"Should have named you Lucky," she said with a sigh. "Might have counterbalanced the rest of the name."

"Not following," I said, wiping a little mustard from the corner of her mouth with a napkin.

"Amara," Gram said, checking her hamburger for extra pickles. "Means Immortal being—one who is blessed without end or death. Dang it, only one pickle."

The bite of hamburger felt like sandpaper going down my throat. "Here." I handed her the extra burger. "I just lost my appetite."

"Baby girl," Gram said with concern, putting her food down and taking my hands in hers. "Did I say something wrong? My mind seems to be goin' and I just talk nonsense all the time."

"Our name. Our last name," I said. "Do you think it's an omen?"

"Hells bells, Daisy," Gram said with a laugh. "You mean like that little adopted devil boy who's slicker than goose shit and kills his whole family, and then smiles at their funeral like he just had a good BM?"

"Umm… no," I said, shaking my head and pressing the bridge of my nose. "You missed your calling, old lady. You should have reviewed movies for a living."

"I would have been right good at that," she said, pointing a fry at me. "Could've called it Siskel, Ebert, and Gram. Betcha I could've gotten into Bob Barker's britches if I'd been a famous movie reviewer."

"If I hadn't already lost my appetite, that would have done it," I told her, shoving all my food her way. "June and Charlie are going on a diet. I'll tell them to stop by every day around dinnertime and you can help them out with a Banging Bob story or two."

"Least I'm still good for something," Gram said with a giggle.

"You're good for everything," I told her firmly. "What I meant was, is our last name an omen about us?"

"Gonna have to go with a no on that, sweetie," Gram said, checking her new burger for extra pickles. "I'm about ready to be one with the earthworms. Immortality—or *Imodium*, as I like to call it—ain't in the picture for us. Always just kind of figured we got saddled with the name Amara because we help the dead."

"Enough pickles?" I asked.

"Yep, has four."

"Good. Eat it." I gave her a look that meant business.

As far as our name went? It was a strange coincidence… I hoped. For right now, I'd stick with Gram's explanation. At the very least, it was semi-logical.

The changes in me were not logical. I'd forgotten to ask about it at the meeting. However, I hadn't come here for Gram to help me figure out why I was turning into a freak of nature with superpowers. I'd come to let her know how much I loved her. The name game was irrelevant.

"Gram?"

"Yes, baby girl?" she answered, taking a bite of her lunch.

"I need to tell you something you're not going to want to hear."

"Well then, spit it out. Bad news is easier when you tell it quick—like rippin' a Band-Aid off a hairy leg. Speaking of… what in tarnation happened to your hands?"

"Are you saying my hands are hairy?" I asked, trying to veer her towards another subject.

"Don't you be smart with me, Daisy girl," Gram chastised. "You might be forty, but I'm still your Gram."

Shit.

Truth or dare… or lie. Lies really weren't kind or fair. Gram would read right through a lie. Even the ugly truth was sometimes less painful than trying to protect someone with deception. I knew she'd worry, but she'd worry more if I wasn't honest.

"I… umm… punched a tree and it fell over."

She was silent for a long moment. "In a dream?"

"No."

"A little tree?" she asked, still searching for the joke.

"No."

"Mmmkay," Gram said, pulling one of the pickles off the burger, dipping it in mustard and popping it into her mouth. "What kind of tree are we talkin' about here?"

"You know the oak in my front yard?" I asked.

Her eyes widened in surprise. "The huge one?"

I nodded.

Gram slowly chewed her mustard-covered pickle and swallowed it. I could see her mind working and absorbing what I'd just told her. Her expression went from disbelief to shock to confusion and finished with a resigned acceptance.

"Did it hit the house?" she inquired.

Of all the questions I thought she'd ask, that was not one of them.

"Nope. Demolished the mailbox, but missed my car by inches," I told her.

"You break your hands?" she asked, eyeing the bandages.

"Shockingly, no," I admitted. "Heather couldn't believe it."

"Might be because it's impossible," Gram pointed out.

"Nothing is impossible. You just have to believe."

We both stared at my hands for a while. Gram ate a few more fries as I tried to think of a solid reason as to why I was able to take out a tree with a few punches.

There wasn't one.

"Daisy girl," she said, gently touching my bandaged hands. "You've always been different—since the day you were born."

"Good different or bad different?"

"Remains to be seen, but I say good different. The gift came late to you," she pointed out correctly. "Maybe that's because your gift is greater than that of any other Death Counselor in our family tree."

I was so tempted to make a joke about punching our family tree but refrained. The timing was way off.

"What if I don't want that *big* of a gift?" I wondered aloud.

"Not sure you have a choice, darlin'," she said, sounding worried.

"I suppose I could get a job with a tree-clearing company," I muttered with a laugh.

She who laughs first has the last laugh, or something like that...

Gram's giggle delighted me and calmed my chaotic mind.

Our acceptance of the impossible was mind-boggling.

But then again, talking with the dead should be impossible. Solving their issues so they could move on was not exactly normal either.

"Alrighty then, now that we've discovered you're the new female Hulk—albeit not green and ugly, thank Dolly Parton's plastic surgeon—let's get to the rippin'-off-the-Band-Aid part of the talk," she said, still staring at my hands.

"I'm going to mind dive and go into the darkness. I have to bring Gideon back to save Steve."

The last thing I expected in reaction to the news was a hamburger with extra pickles being lobbed at my head. Had to hand it to Gram. She was creative when she was pissed.

"Absolutely not," she snapped as her frail body began to shake.

I immediately regretted my decision to tell her, but if I didn't come back, I needed her to know why. Wrapping my arms around the most precious woman in my world, I held her close and rocked her trembling body.

"There's no other way," I whispered. "Tim is going to teach me how to do it."

"Tim, the scrawny little Imodium bastard who steals mail?" she demanded.

I laughed. "Yes. The scrawny little Imodium bastard who steals mail. You said yourself that he's the mailman for the living and the dead."

"Lord have mercy on a Thursday," she said, giving me a little shake. "Don't listen to what I say. I'm a crazy old woman with the hots for game show hosts. I'm not right in the head."

"You *are* a little nutty," I agreed, cupping her pale cheek in my hand. "But you're also the most amazing woman alive. I love you more than anything in this world even though your taste in men is a bit off."

"Bob Barker is a looker," she said with a small smile. "You're really gonna do this?"

"I am," I told her. "The Angel of Mercy can't do what she did to Steve and get away with it. She did it to hurt me. If Clarissa wants to come at me, fine. But there's no way in Heaven or Hell she's going to do it by destroying Steve's afterlife with a vicious lie."

"That gal is an abomination," Gram said. "Never actually had to deal with her during my time on the job."

"There were never any questions about a ghost's afterlife?" I asked, surprised.

"Not a one," Gram said. "How a life was lived usually determined the path for what came next. But then again, I never saw the dead go into the light like you do. Also never took a dive into their minds."

"Do you think that's why I'm changing?" I asked.

"Wish I had an answer, lovey," she replied, sounding tired. "Life ain't as simple as *The Price is Right*."

Cleaning up the remains of our lunch, I thought about what she'd just said. Gram was correct. Life was not a game show.

"You want to see Gideon again," Gram stated as I sat back down on the edge of her bed and tucked her covers around her frail body.

She was right and she was wrong. I wanted to apologize. I wanted to beg his forgiveness for being blind. But I needed him to save Steve. My apology might be misconstrued as selfishness for myself. I was unsure if he would believe I was truly sorry. Truthfully, I didn't know if he would even care.

I wanted to see him again. However, I would have liked our reunion not to have included massive strings attached.

"Yes," I admitted. "Not too excited about seeing him in Hell, though."

"So, you believe now?" she asked, trying to salvage the burger she'd attacked me with.

"In the biblical definition? No. That some form of Heaven and Hell exists? Yes."

Gram's eyes began to flutter closed. My visit had exhausted her.

"I want you to know I love you more than anything," I said, kissing her wrinkled cheek.

"Right back at you, sweetheart," she replied with a smile. "You're my world, little girl. I need you to promise to be careful. Whose mind you gonna dive into?"

It was an excellent question, and one I didn't have an answer for yet.

"Not sure, maybe Steve's," I said, thinking that was probably not a good plan.

He was in terrible shape and it could be a traumatic event for him.

"I suppose I could go into the Mayor of Squatter Town's mind, or Birdie, the foul-mouthed little mess who keeps flipping me off," I told her, drawing her shade down so the sun wouldn't disturb her nap.

"Or Lindsay's," Gram suggested.

"She's been through enough," I said, grabbing my coat and crappy purse.

"Hell's bells. Get your rear end into my closet right now and take a few handbags," Gram said, eyeing my torn purse with horror. "That bag looks like it fell out of a tree and hit every branch on the way down."

I laughed. Of all the things discussed in the last hour, she was most appalled by the unfortunate state of my purse. Knocking the Southern out of a Southerner was one thing that was *not* possible.

"Thank you," I said, still laughing as I opened her closet door and took a pretty black leather bag and a sharp-looking brown one. "I'll bring them back."

"Heck to the no you won't. Those are yours now. I don't need them anymore," she informed me with a shake of her head. "I'll sleep much better knowing you're not walking around in public with a crappy bag. That's not acceptable in Georgia. Might even be against the law."

"I'll keep that in mind. Wouldn't want to end up in the pokey for breaking the Ugly Purse law."

"Speaking of not ending up in the pokey, did you hear about little Lindsay's murderin' brother dying from bees?"

I nodded and raised a brow. "Karma worked quickly on that one."

Gram paled and put her hand to her mouth. "You sayin' what I think you're sayin'?"

I nodded my head. "Yep. And the weirdest part is, I'm not sure I'm angry about it. Appalled? Yes. Freaked out? Absolutely. Angry? No clue. I'll tell you this though, I don't want to ever be on Candy Vargo's shit list."

"Boysireee," Gram said. "Karma is a bitch."

"Cliché intended?" I asked.

"One hundred percent."

"I love you, Gram," I said, trying to hold back the tears that begged to flow.

I was fully aware that this might be the last time I saw my beloved Gram.

"Love you more, child. Loved you something awful since the day you were born. Gimme some sugar, and then skedaddle before we both start blubberin'," she said, staring at me as if she were memorizing my face. "I expect to see you tomorrow night… safe and sound. And you best be carryin' one of those new purses."

"Deal." I prayed I was telling the truth. Coming back for Gram and Steve was on my agenda. I had no plans to fail either one of them.

But only time would tell.

CHAPTER THIRTEEN

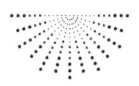

"Have you always been a dick?" I inquired, glaring at a smug Tim as he marched around my front yard and examined the tree I'd punched and knocked down.

The beautiful, broken oak would probably be in the yard for a while. Calling the tree removal company was low on my priority list at the moment.

"Yes. I've always been a dick."

He'd arrived a half hour late. My stomach was in knots. I'd run ten miles on the treadmill at six in the morning to stop my mind from racing with horrifying possibilities. I hadn't broken a sweat. I decided not to dissect the reason why. I figured if I had to run through the darkness, my Energizer Bunny ability might come in handy.

Heather had stopped by at eight with bagels, fruit and the book on Sumerian that Missy had ordered. I was grateful she was alone. There was no way I could have behaved *normal* in front of Missy. She knew me far too well for me to hide one of the biggest freak-outs I'd ever had.

"How's that dick attitude working out for you?" I questioned.

Tim stared at my mailbox with horror. I knew he'd hone in on that.

"Working out just fine," he said.

I rolled my eyes. He hadn't taught me anything yet. "Awesome."

I was going to do my part. He was going to have to do his.

After hours of internal mental debate with myself last night, I'd narrowed my choices down to Steve or Lindsay as my host for the mind dive into the darkness. As sweet as the Mayor of Squatter Town was, he cried an awful lot, and I was concerned it would be too much for him. Birdie was crossed off the list when I found her head in the refrigerator. She thought her joke was hilarious. I did not.

I was going to need therapy after Birdie finally moved on.

In the end, I'd chosen Lindsay, who was thrilled to help me. Heather's information earlier was the deciding factor. She'd learned more about the tribunal after I'd left the meeting yesterday. Part of the process would be to prove Steve's death was an accident. The only way to do that was to relive his death in his mind.

It was not good news. The thought of watching him die was so abhorrent to me, I almost got sick when she relayed the news. The tricky part was that a witness was needed. One way to accomplish that would be to bring someone into Steve's mind with me. I had no clue if that was possible or who was insane enough to agree. The only person who I could imagine coming with me was Gram, and the Immortals might think she was too biased to be neutral. Not to mention, she wasn't well. The aftermath of a mind dive could destroy her.

I would cross that bridge when I got to it. I had to live through today first.

The thought of something happening to Lindsay after what she'd been through was upsetting. There was a chance the host could be harmed. Steve wasn't strong enough to withstand it. Lindsay knew the risks and had insisted she was the one to protect me.

Lindsay won. I threw up a quick prayer to a God I wasn't sure I believed in to watch over her. I requested nothing for myself. Just in case He or She was listening, I didn't want to overwhelm.

"Are you going to tell me how to get in and out of the darkness?" I asked, squinting at the strange little man in the cold morning sunshine.

"You walk," he said, picking up the pieces of my smashed mailbox and examining them carefully.

I was ready to shake him until his brains fell out. Choosing Tim might have been a huge mistake.

Lindsay zipped around the yard and followed Tim's every move. Several times he swatted her away, but the rest of the time he ignored her. His rudeness knew no bounds. However, Donna and Karen seemed to adore the man, and the feeling was mutual. Maybe my dogs knew more than I did. It was possible, but doubtful. Tim was an ass.

"Loooounlahy," Lindsay said, pointing to Tim, who was still gently touching the pieces of my splintered mailbox.

"Of course he's lonely," I muttered. "He's a dick."

Lindsay floated over and we watched Tim meticulously stack the pieces of my mailbox into a neat pile.

"Naawwwooo fraaaaunds," she whispered. "Saawd. Loooounlahy."

"He's a wanker," I whispered back. "It's not a mystery why he has no friends."

"Yausssss," she agreed. "Dausseeeeee fraaaaund Tiiauum."

"Are you serious?" I asked. Becoming Tim's friend wasn't on my to-do list.

"Yausssss. Sssooooo saawd."

With a sigh of resignation, I walked across the yard and began to help Tim pick up the shattered wood and metal of what used to hold my mail.

"Be gentle with the flag," Tim instructed sternly.

"Will do," I said without an ounce of sarcasm in my voice.

"If it can be saved, we will save it."

Carefully picking up the bent red piece of metal, I handed it to him. "This might be a goner."

Tim took the flag in his hand and stroked it lovingly. Under other circumstances, I would have laughed, but he was so serious and committed, I felt sorry for him. He tried twice to unbend the flag. Twice, he failed.

"Give that to me," I said, reaching for the twisted metal. If I could knock down a tree, surely, I could straighten a piece of metal.

"Do *not* hurt it," he warned, grudgingly handing it over.

"Wouldn't think of it," I replied as I carefully unbent the red flag. I was cautious since I was a little unclear of how much strength I had. "Success."

I glanced up at Tim—and saw he was crying.

"Umm… are you okay?" I asked, concerned for his sanity.

"That was beautiful," he said, reaching out for the fixed flag. "You're ready."

"For what?" I asked, confused.

"To join the postal department for Heaven and Hell," he replied with the first real smile he'd ever given me.

"Is that the key?" I asked, hoping he hadn't lost his debatably sane mind.

He nodded and tucked the flag into the pocket of his postal uniform coat. "It's the key to the Universe," he told me. "Well, the key to traveling the Universe. Are you willing to take the oath and abide by the rules?"

I had no clue what I was agreeing to, but my gut said to go for it. "I am."

"Are you willing to wear the uniform with pride?"

Shit. "Is that a deal-breaker?" I asked with a wince.

Tim shrugged. "Your choice, but the uniform has pockets."

"Pockets are important?"

"Very."

"Are you screwing with me?" I asked.

"About the pockets? No."

"About the uniform?" I asked with a small grin pulling at my lips.

Tim looked down at the ground and tried to hide his

own grin. He failed. "Yes. I'm screwing with you about the uniform," he admitted with an uncharacteristic chuckle. "But I would be proud if you wore one."

Counting to ten inside my head so I didn't scream the word no, I resigned myself to the awful fact that I was going to wear a heinous postal uniform to Hell to make my new friend—using the term very loosely—proud.

"I will wear the uniform," I promised, and then wanted to take it back as a mortifying reality hit me hard.

Tim's whoop of joy stopped me. He did a little jig and was joined by Donna, Karen and Lindsay. His smile was wide and his spirits were high. I refused to take that away from the lonely man... even if it meant that at my reunion with Gideon, I would be sporting a hideous postal uniform.

I suppose I could carry my crappy purse to finish off the look.

Or not.

⁓

MY POSTAL UNIFORM WAS NOT GOOD. BOXY AND unflattering would be outstanding words to describe it. Tim was so excited, I didn't have the heart to tell him how much I hated it. It was also two sizes too big. The pants were too long and the top could work as a muumuu. Whatever. It did have nice pockets.

"People think you x-ray their packages and steal the stuff you like," I told Tim as I served him a sandwich and a soda. "That might be one of the reasons why everyone is a little... umm... wary of you."

"Great sandwich," Tim said. "I love turkey."

"Are you ignoring what I just told you?" I asked, sitting down across from him at the kitchen table and taking a bite out of my sandwich.

"Yes."

I almost choked on my turkey due to the laugh that came up from my gut. "Oh my God," I said, swallowing the bite so I didn't need to have my new *friend* perform the Heimlich maneuver on me. That would be a little too personal at this point in the relationship. "You *do* steal mail."

"I do *not* steal mail," Tim snapped. "I rehome some of it."

"Rehome?" I repeated.

"Yes. Some people do not deserve the glorious items within," he told me with a huff.

"Dude, they ordered it and paid for it," I pointed out, putting my sandwich down and gaping at him. Since I had no clue what he would say next, I couldn't risk choking to death on my lunch. "Or it's a gift from a friend or family member."

"You think *married* women should have *vibrators*?" he asked indignantly.

"Yes!" I practically shouted. "You rehome vibrators?"

"A few," he admitted, blushing. "I believe we live in an oversexed society, and I feel that the Universe would be a more productive place if the human population was focused on spiritual rather than carnal endeavors."

"Dude," I said, shaking my head. "You need to get laid."

"Inappropriate," Tim huffed.

"True," I shot back. "Have you ever had a relationship?"

"Define," he said.

"Umm… like a physical relationship with another person who you care about and who cares for you."

"Define care," he said, growing uncomfortable.

I rolled my eyes. "For the love of everything normal, you need to make some major life changes."

Tim mulled over what I said as he continued to eat his sandwich. "Do you have chips?" he inquired.

"I do. Did you hear what I just said?" I asked as I stood up and grabbed a bag of chips from the cabinet.

I completely ignored the unappetizing fact that Birdie had put her leg and half of her ass next to the chips. The less attention I gave her for the atrocious behavior, the better. She would also have to wait for me to glue it back on. If she was intent on tearing off body parts to freak me out, she was going to have to get by without those body parts for a while. At the rate she was going, she was going to be scattered all over the house soon.

"Do you happen to have any books on this life-changing process?" Tim asked.

I had to think about that one. I did have a whole lot of self-help books, but most were on the grieving process. I'd amassed a large quantity after Steve died.

"How about we start slow?" I suggested. "You stop x-raying packages and stop rehoming people's stuff."

"How about I stop rehoming first," Tim countered. "If I cold turkey everything it's a recipe for failure."

I nodded and tried not to laugh. "Reasonable."

"Can we hang out?" he asked, concentrating on the chips as if his unending life depended on it. "I mean, occasionally. Not all the time."

"Yes," I said as his head jerked up in surprise. "However, you will not be a dick. I'll call you out on that and train you until I feel you're ready for a group situation."

"Why would you do that for me?" he asked, confused.

"I don't know," I replied honestly. "As unpleasant as you are, I kind of like you. I think there might be someone fun underneath the mail-stealing guy who is anti-vibrator."

Tim threw his head back and laughed. The dogs barked and joined in while Lindsay zipped around the kitchen giggling. Several of the other squatters came in to see what was happening. Even Birdie… who was missing her head, a leg and part of her ass. However, she still had a hand and proudly flipped me off. The saving grace was that since I'd left her head in the fridge, she couldn't call me a hooker with company present.

"Oh my," Tim said, pointing at Birdie. "What happened there?"

"It's a long story. We'll save it for our first hang out evening," I told him. "Right now, I need you to help me understand what I have to do to navigate the darkness."

Tim sighed and looked very old for a moment—far older than the age he presented himself.

"You've chosen the one to host?" he asked, picking up his plate and taking it to the sink.

"I have. Lindsay," I told him. "She's willing and wants to do it."

"She's aware that you might be stuck in her mind for eternity and that she will never progress to an afterlife if something goes awry?" he asked, glancing over at Lindsay.

"Shit." I closed my eyes and let my head fall to the table with a thud. "I didn't know that was a possibility."

"Probably won't happen. It's the worst-case scenario," Tim assured me. "But both of you need to be aware of the ramifications if something goes wrong."

"Yausssss," Lindsay said, floating to the ground, standing next to me and putting her hand on my shoulder. "Yausssss."

Tim tilted his head to the left and stared at me. "You are like no one else. Never have I seen a Death Counselor so in tune with the dead."

"I've heard that before," I said, worried about Lindsay. "Lindsay's been hurt enough in life. Is there any other way to travel to the darkness? There has to be. How do *you* do it?"

Surely, he didn't go through the minds of the dead to deliver mail to Hell.

Tim pressed his lips together and looked up at the ceiling. "I come from the darkness," he said with no emotion. "All I have to do is wish myself there."

"Okay," I said, wondering if Tim was a Demon of sorts. "Then how are you allowed in Heaven to deliver mail?"

"I am from the light as well," he replied.

"Want to explain?"

He sighed, and then placed his hands over his eyes. "When I open my eyes, stare straight into them."

"Umm… okay, is this going to hurt?" I asked, wanting to be prepared.

"No."

As he pulled his hands from his eyes, I gasped. The

ghosts whipped around the kitchen and screeched with shock and delight.

The iris of Tim's right eye sparkled a bright red, just like Gideon's had. The left one was a brilliant gold, very similar to John Travolta's eyes.

Tim blinked and it was gone.

"So, your mom was a Demon and your dad an Angel?" I asked, putting out the only logical explanation I could come up with.

"The other way around," he said with a shrug. "That's how I'm able to travel. You, on the other hand, would only be able to wish yourself to the light."

"I'm sorry. What?" I asked, positive I'd heard him wrong.

Snapping his fingers, he produced a mirror. The magic stuff freaked me out a little, but I was more freaked out by what I thought he'd just said.

"Look at your eyes," Tim instructed.

Picking up the mirror, I stared at my image. My eyes were indeed a golden color, but they were not like Tim's or John Travolta's.

"They're not the same," I said, handing him the mirror. "I'm not an Angel. I'm a ridiculously strong, forty-year-old human female widow with shitty purses who talks to the dead."

Tim shrugged and put the mirror into one of his many pockets.

"What?" I demanded. "Do you know something I don't?"

"I only know what I see, Daisy," he said.

"And what do you see?" I asked, feeling way off center.

"I see an Angel hybrid who doesn't believe."

"Tim," I said, leveling him with a hard stare that he met without flinching. "I think you need to get out more. Maybe you're correct in your assumption and maybe you're not. It would certainly explain a few things. However, unless your conjecture about me will help me get in and out of the darkness without dying, I'd like to table the discussion for another time. You feel me?"

Tim grinned. "Karma was right. Ballsy."

"Karma is disgusting," I said, without thinking. "I mean..."

"Disgusting," Tim agreed. "I tried to hang out with her a few centuries back and it didn't go well. Due to you extending your hand in friendship, I shall give humans a shot."

I had nothing to add to that. The visual in my head of Tim and Candy hanging out had to be less offensive than the actual story. I'd leave that one alone forever.

"Tell me what I need to know," I said.

"As you wish," he replied. "Time doesn't run the same on the other planes."

"Faster? Slower? Explain what you mean, please."

"Meaning, you may feel like you've been gone a few minutes, but a year will have passed on the human plane," Tim explained.

"Can I control that?" I asked. I couldn't leave Gram and Steve for a year... or my dogs.

"I can't, so I doubt you can," Tim said, and then paused. "However, you are unique, Daisy. I will be interested to hear your experience when you return."

I heaved a sigh of relief. "You believe I'll return?"

"Well, I have great *hope* you will," he amended. "It's quite new having a friend and I'd like to explore it."

"Right," I muttered, sorry I'd asked. "So, I'll go into Lindsay's mind, and then walk toward the darkness?"

He nodded.

"And then what?"

"And then you'll look for Gideon," he replied, as if I should have already known that.

"Yep, I'm aware of why I'm going, but I want to know what I should expect."

Tim rolled his eyes and grunted. "Okay. Fine. Don't touch the walls. They have teeth. If there is a turn in the path, always go to the left. If you were going into the light, you would always take a right, but that's irrelevant in this conversation."

"Okay, then when I return, do I retrace my steps back the way I came and take rights instead of lefts?" I asked, wondering if I could bring a cheat sheet. However, since it wasn't my physical body going on the trip, I was fairly sure props wouldn't work.

"No. Always to the left in the darkness. Just like time runs differently there, directions do as well."

"Shit," I muttered and ran my hands through my hair. To the left, to the left. Thank God for Beyoncé.

"I'd suggest Lindsay recite something the entire time you're in the mist so you can find your way back. If Gideon agrees to come back, you'll have an easier time returning. If he doesn't…"

"If he doesn't, then what?" I pressed. I was going to do

my best, but it was not a done deal by any means. I had no clue if I could convince Gideon to return with me.

"If he doesn't, I'd suggest that Lindsay speak very, *very* loudly."

"Sssiiiiiiinngea. Sssiiiiiiinngea looouwd," Lindsay said. "Yausssss, Dausseeeeee."

"Hear me out," I said, giving Lindsay a quick hug. "I walk into the darkness while Lindsay sings. I won't touch the walls. Turn left always, and then wing it. Get a lift from Gideon if he agrees to come back. If not, hope like heck Lindsay can sing loud enough for me to hear."

"Yes," Tim said with a curt nod of approval. "Oh, and Gideon will not be as you knew him."

"Will I recognize him?" I asked, ready to scream. The hidden curve balls just kept coming.

"Did you love him?" he asked.

It was a little personal, but I was about to walk right into Hell… "I *still* love him."

"Then you will know him no matter what form he has chosen," Tim told me. "Are you ready?"

"Umm… two things," I said, knowing I was probably going to regret number one. "Will you stay here and watch over my dead squatters and my dogs while I'm gone?"

"You trust me to stay at your home?" Tim asked, shocked.

"Actually no, now that you mention it. However, if we're going to try this friendship thing out and you want to be my friend *for real*, you will not mess with my stuff."

"Reasonable."

"You will not steal anything."

"Again, reasonable."

"You can eat anything you want but you will not hide, throw away or destroy my vibrators."

"How many do you have?" Tim inquired, clearly appalled.

"None of your business."

"I can make that work," he said. "And the second request?"

"I need about fifteen minutes," I told him as I stood up. "I have to say goodbye to Steve."

Tim nodded respectfully. "The window to the dark side is easiest to traverse this time of day. Fifteen minutes will not affect the outcome. I will be waiting for you when you are ready… friend."

"Thank you, my friend," I replied without hesitation.

He was an odd one, but then again, so was I.

∼

STEVE DID NOT NEED TO SAY A WORD. THE APPALLED LOOK OF shock on his decaying face said it all.

"Yep," I said, glancing down at myself in despair. "I know it's awful. But the story is too long to explain why I have to wear it."

"Awwwwwufahul," Steve grunted with what sounded like a laugh.

"Maybe if I belt it and roll up the pant legs?" I suggested with a grin.

"Naawwwooo."

"Hoop earrings? My black stiletto heels?"

"Naawwwooo," he said as his normally still body shook with the little laughter. "Gaaaayah maaaaaauns niiiii-itamaarah."

"You did *not* just call me a gay man's nightmare," I said, laughing.

"Yausssss."

"You are correct as usual," I said, sitting down next to him. "I'd have to go out on a limb and say gay or straight, I'm definitely a nightmare in this sexy outfit. However, I have to roll up the legs or I'll trip in the darkness."

"Caaaaarahfuuuwl," Steve said.

I nodded. "I promise I'll be careful. I'll be inside Lindsay's mind and my new friend Tim the Immortal postman, who does indeed x-ray and steal mail, has given me a few tips."

"Naawwwooo," Steve said with a smile so scary it warmed my heart.

"Yep, and get this… he pilfers and rehomes vibrators," I said, and watched with delight as Steve's body trembled with laughter.

My friends were so wrong about me not being hilarious. Dead people thought I was a riot.

"So anyhoo, I'm not sure how long I'll be gone since time runs differently on the other planes, but I plan on getting in and getting out. And just so you know, I chatted with Heather this morning. If for some absurd, ridiculous, unheard-of reason I can't get back, Heather will go to Clarence Smith and demand mercy for you. She said Charlie will back her, and everyone is terrified of Charlie.

And I added an extra surprise for John Travolta if he plays hardball."

"Waaahat?" Steve asked, trying to reach for my hand.

I saved him the effort and took his hand in mine.

"It's not exactly ethical. Or at least not very nice," I said with a wince. "As you know, I've gotten a taste of living on the edge, so I made a deal with the ghosts. If John Travolta gives Heather a hard time, the ghosts have pledged to make his life unbearable for the rest of time. Birdie was thrilled with the prospect and the other thirty in residence agreed. The man won't have a moment of peace for eternity."

Steve gave the tiniest shake of his head and smiled. "Naawwwooo, Dausseeeeee," he said. "Dausseeeeee stuuuucuk innnn daaaaaaurk. Meeeeeee coooum daaaaaaurk wiiiiuth youuuuah."

"Oh my God," I choked out as tears filled my eyes. "I'm making a choice here. Yours was stolen from you by a vindictive bitch. You've been wrongly accused because Clarissa is jealous. You belong in the light, babe. I need you to be in the light. Promise me you won't follow me into the dark. Promise."

Steve was quiet, but he smiled.

I was going to take that as a yes. If I had the time, I'd make him say it. I didn't have the time. I also had no intention of getting trapped in the darkness. So, the entire conversation was moot. Hopefully.

"I love you, Steve," I said, gently kissing his forehead and tucking in the blankets around him. "I'll see you soon."

CHAPTER FOURTEEN

THE COLD. THE COLD WENT ALL THE WAY TO MY BONES AND TORE through my body like sharp, frozen daggers made of ice. Trying to catch my breath, I gasped for air but stayed calm.

My head pounded violently and every single cell in my body screamed for oxygen. I knew it was momentary, but it still sucked.

My mind went numb and my body felt weightless.

I knew where I was. I'd chosen to come. Pride, terror and determination consumed me. It was my decision to be here. There were no alternatives and it was the right thing to do.

This time was different. My emotions were in a freefall. The thought of seeing Gideon—no matter the circumstances—was intoxicating and chilling. Holding my breath for a moment, and then exhaling slowly, I touched my arm with my bandaged hand. I'd never thought to find out if my body felt corporal when I was mind diving.

It did.

The shock of being in a solid form was bizarre.

A wildly uncomfortable sensation of feeling a knife to my throat, daring my heart to keep beating, was unsettling.

Stop. I couldn't let my mind send me into the starring role of a bad B horror movie. That would be counterproductive and stupid. Been there, done that. I'd already been stupid enough for one lifetime, especially where Gideon was concerned. I didn't need to add any more stupid to my resume.

Forward not backward was my motto. Beyoncé was my guide. To the left. To the left.

"Lindsay," I called out softly. "Can you hear me?"

"I can," she said. "Open your eyes, Daisy."

"Can't." I kept my eyes squeezed shut. "I was told never to open my eyes when I was inside someone's mind."

"Do you plan on walking into the darkness with your eyes closed?" she asked with a giggle.

"Was that a loaded metaphor on top of a question?" I inquired with a laugh as I cautiously opened my eyes.

In the past, I'd gotten glimpses of the nothingness. I hadn't been able to see a thing. It was pitch black.

Not today.

There was no floor. No walls to speak of—more of a vast landscape of nothing. Lindsay and I floated in a silvery mist. It wasn't necessarily frightening, but it was devoid of any kind of joy.

"Did you do something?" I asked.

Lindsay stood in front of me looking like she had before she was murdered. She was lovely.

"Tim explained that I could light your way when you were talking to Steve. I'm relieved to see it's a golden glow."

"Is that important?" I asked.

"It means that when it's time for me to move on, I'll be going into the light," she said as the golden light shimmered, making her appear celestial.

"No brainer," I said. "I could have told you that."

"I hoped I'd be going to Heaven, but it's nice to get confirmation," she told me with a wide smile, and then winced. "Oh. Wow. I'm so sorry."

My stomach tightened. My heartbeat sped up and thumped like a jackhammer in my chest. "For what?" I asked, dreading she'd changed her mind.

"That outfit." She scrunched her nose. "It's really some serious bad."

"Oh shit," I moaned, glancing down. "I was hoping since I'm not technically physically here that the shitshow I was wearing wouldn't have made it through."

"No such luck," Lindsay said. "You're still beautiful, Daisy."

"Thank you," I replied. "However, I do believe you're a little biased."

"Possibly," she agreed. "But you are truly beautiful—inside and out—even in that eyesore of an outfit."

There was nothing to say. I didn't agree, but I was thankful she believed it. My outsides were hereditary, thanks to my mom. Pretty shells could hide a multitude of sins within. I was aware that I was a good person—or at least I tried to be. However, beautiful on the inside? No. I was immensely and tragically flawed.

"You ready to sing?" I asked as a tingle of anticipation and dread danced through my body.

"Yep. You have any requests?" Lindsay inquired.

"Umm... do you know Journey?"

"Not really," she said, shaking her head. "A little before my time."

"Right," I replied. "What do you know the words to?"

"I know Beyoncé's entire catalog."

I was stunned to silence. It was an omen, and not like the omen Gram had so eloquently grossed me out with recently about the devil child smiling like he'd had an excellent BM. Nope. This was a good omen.

Feeling light-headed and more hopeful than I had in days, I grinned.

"Do you know 'Irreplaceable'?"

"Like the back of my hand," she replied. "To the left. To the left."

"Do you mind singing that one over and over again?"

Lindsay raised a delicate brow and giggled. "How long will you be gone?"

"A few minutes... a week... a year?" I estimated with a shudder, hoping my first guess was correct.

"Seeing as I'm dead and have nothing on my social calendar right now, I think I can manage that."

The absurdity, the irony, the danger and black humor of the situation, did not escape my attention. If someone had told me two months ago that I was going to stroll into Hell in search of the man I'd loved and lost to save my dead gay husband's afterlife while listening to a sweet ghost who was murdered by her brother sing Beyoncé songs, I would have laughed until I passed out.

I wasn't laughing now.

"Lindsay, I can't find the words to say thank you appropriately," I said, reaching out and touching her soft cheek. "If it looks like it's going to Hell—unfortunate pun intended—I'll turn around and come back. I don't want to harm you."

"Silly Daisy," Lindsay said, placing her hand over mine. "You made it possible for my bones to sing. You've already saved me. While going into the light sounds cool, I am happy where I am. If this is my destiny, so be it. I'm more worried about your destiny."

I was a little worried about it too, but at this point there was no turning back. Life had been a lot less complicated not so long ago. The past was just that. The past.

"I'll be fine," I said with far more confidence than I felt. "I punched out a tree and won."

"Would you like to know why?" Lindsay inquired, looking very serious for such a young soul.

Her question was unexpected, and I was so tempted to let her explain.

"Will it help me survive the darkness or freak the shit out of me?" I asked, only able to focus on one thing at a time.

"I'd have to go with freak."

"Then hold that thought and start singing."

"You've got it," she said with a thumbs up.

Turning away from the hauntingly lovely sound of Lindsay's voice singing the song that would remind me to turn left, I took my first step into the darkness.

∽

IT WAS SURPRISINGLY SIMPLE. AS SOON AS I TOOK THE THIRD step, Lindsay's voice became a soft, distant echo. The silver-gray mist thickened, but I could still make out the path.

The emptiness was devastatingly depressing.

"To the left," I muttered as I came to the first turn in the path.

As I continued to put one foot carefully in front of the other, a bone-chilling breeze blew and clung to my body. It pressed against me and tugged at my soul. Trying to counteract the sadness and despair flashing through my mind, I hummed an off-tune version of 'You Are My Sunshine'. The song was the only good memory I had of my mother. The rest of my memories had faded with anger over time. I wasn't her sunshine. If I was, she never would have left me for a dead man.

"Hello, anyone home?" I called out, and then laughed at the ridiculousness of my words.

No one answered. I didn't think anyone would. This wasn't going to be easy—not that I'd expected it to be. However, it was nothing like what I'd imagined.

I'd expected so much more than the eerily silent void. Maybe clanking chains, blood-curdling screams, fire, howling, grinding, hissing, moaning…

Nope. Nothing. Absolutely nothing. It was enough to make a person go insane.

"Bingo," I whispered as I tried to figure out if I'd made any progress. Everything looked the same. There were no points of reference to hold on to. "Slowly going insane is definitely a form of hell."

Since I had no clue where I was going or where Gideon might be in the expansive oblivion, I simply kept walking.

"How much time has passed?" I wondered aloud as I studiously avoided the wall along the path. I saw no teeth, but decided not to test Tim's theory that the walls could bite. My hands were already a mess from my altercation with the tree. Bandages were fine. Amputation? Not so much.

From the mist came a noise that chilled me to the bone and made me want to run. It was a sound no living being could make. An explosion of screams, crashing waves and pure agony—like thousands of sharp metal nails on a chalkboard made of glass—reverberated through Hell.

"What the…?" I choked out as I crouched down and waited to die.

I'd made a wrong turn. At least I hoped I had.

"Mother humper," I gasped out as I stood up and ran headfirst into a wall that I couldn't see. "What now?"

Tim had neglected to inform me that Hell was filled with paths that led to dead-end walls with monsters behind them. Fine. Slight change of plans. I'd simply turn around and keep going to the left like Beyoncé wanted me to.

Except the path had disappeared. Beyoncé and Tim hadn't prepared me for this part.

"Time to wing it," I whispered, gingerly touching the wall with my bandaged hands, hoping it didn't sink its teeth into me.

I'd punched a tree and knocked it down. Could I break a teeth-sporting wall in Hell?

Only one way to find out.

"Okay, God," I said with an internal eye roll. I figured covering all bases at this point wasn't a bad plan. "I'm still not completely on board, but just in case, I'd like a little help here. Not for me… I want it for Lindsay, Steve and Gideon. That's all and… umm… thank you for your time."

I thought the thank you was a nice touch on the off chance that someone was actually listening.

"Nothing is impossible. You just have to believe," I said in full voice as I cocked my arm back and punched the wall with everything I had.

The shock of the contact threw me back about ten feet. I landed on my ass with a thud and was grateful for the thick back pockets in my postal pants and all the extra material in my muumuu top. It cushioned what could have easily resulted in a broken tailbone.

The floors in Hell were seriously hard.

I stayed low. If the monster came at me, I'd have to fight. While I was thankful for my self-defense classes from the Y, we hadn't covered sparring with Demons.

The wall creaked ominously—and then turned to dust, creating a sandstorm that rivaled anything I'd ever seen in the movies. It came down with a blinding crash and I closed my eyes against the onslaught.

I hoped there were no more walls to punch. I could feel the blood seeping through the bandages. A burning pain shot from both hands all the way up to my shoulders. I hadn't broken them on the tree, but I was fairly sure they were broken now.

As the dust settled, I opened my eyes and gasped.

My gaze was drawn to the most beautiful monster I'd ever seen.

He was shirtless and furious. As his ire mounted, he began to growl and speak in a language I'd never heard. My damaged hands went to my mouth involuntarily as shimmering black ebony wings erupted from the monster's back and a golden glow surrounded him. The span of his wings had to be six feet and the glowing light made them sparkle.

The juxtaposition of the light around him in the darkness didn't surprise me. The monster was dark, but he was also good.

Sadly, I'd figured that out too late.

His eyes were a glittery blood-red and they narrowed to slits when they landed on me. His beauty as a human was only amplified in this form, and I longed to touch him. Gideon was the absurd kind of gorgeous—messy blond hair, ridiculously muscular body, full lips and eyelashes that most women would kill for.

Right now, he was also a beautiful, deadly winged beast. The Grim Reaper was a sight to behold.

"What are you wearing?" he demanded, eyeing me curiously.

"My uniform," I whispered, horrified that it was the first thing he noticed.

"And how exactly did you get here," he questioned coldly, crossing his arms over his chest as a ring of red fire exploded around him and framed him in a deadly glow.

"I walked," I replied, getting clumsily to my feet, trying to save a tiny shred of my dignity.

"Preposterous," he snapped. "State your name and your business and be gone."

His gaze held no recognition. Nothing. It was far more devastating than his anger or hurt, which I deserved. But this…

"I repeat," the Grim Reaper ground out. "State your name and your business and be gone. You do not want me to have to say it again, Messenger."

My eyes filled with tears and my body felt as if it had turned to ice underneath my ugly uniform. I'd considered many different ways this reunion could go. This was not one of them.

"You don't recognize me?" I asked in a voice that sounded annoyingly small and pathetic to my own ears. My lady balls needed to show up. I was about to drown.

"I don't," Gideon replied in a cool tone. "Should I?"

"Umm… no," I said, taking a deep breath. I wasn't here to get back together with the man I'd sent away. I was here to bring the Grim Reaper back to the human plane so a tribunal could be held to condemn the Angel of Mercy.

I was not here for me. That ship had sailed and if I needed proof, it was in the eyes of the man I still loved.

"Why do you bleed?" he demanded, pointing to my hands.

"The door was locked so I punched the wall down," I replied.

His laugh warmed me all over. I'd craved his laughter. Even now, when it was clear he'd forgotten me, his laughter was still something I longed for.

"A violent Messenger," he said with sarcasm dripping from his voice. "How cliché. Who sent you and what do you want?"

I want you to recognize me, I screamed inside my head. *I want you to still love me. I want your anger and your hurt. I want to be able to apologize.*

Instead, I said, "John Travolta has requested you come back to the earthly plane."

"I'm sorry," Gideon said, looking at me like I had screws loose. "Who?"

"Shit," I muttered and closed my eyes. Heather had warned me that I'd call Clarence Smith by the wrong name at an inopportune moment. I didn't think it would be this inopportune, though. However, I suppose I could change my motto to *go big or go home*. I'd definitely gone big. I just couldn't go home quite yet. "I meant, Clarence Smith, the Archangel Michael."

"I know his title," Gideon said, appearing to grow bored. "What does the man want and why on earth did he send you? Someone like *you* should not be here."

His assholeyness was rude. However, I needed him and pointing out he was a jerk surely wouldn't help my case.

"Well, someone like *me* is here," I said, trying my damnedest to sound polite and reasonable. Being Southern was saving my ass right now. "There's going to be a tribunal. Your presence is required."

This piqued his interest. "How fascinating. Who is being accused? If it's me, I can assure you, I shall not be returning."

"Have you done something that would require a tribunal?" I asked before I could stop the words from leaving my lips.

The explosion was enormous and I regretted my curiosity immediately.

"If I had," he snarled, "do you really think I would tell you? Trust is earned."

I winced at the trust comment. "Umm… nope. My bad."

"Say that again," he demanded.

"Say what?" I asked, wondering if he was playing some kind of sick game where if I repeated something enough, he could legally fry me where I stood.

"Say, *my bad*," he requested, staring at me with a strange expression.

"My bad," I repeated and waited to be incinerated to ash. "Better?"

"Indifferent," he replied. "I will need more information from you in order to decide if I will abide by John Travolta's wishes, Messenger."

"You mean the Archangel Michael," I corrected him.

"Right. *My bad*," he replied, and then waited for the information he'd requested.

I took a deep breath and bit back all the things I truly wanted to say. They were unnecessary. They would never be necessary. I took a little solace in that he was still a funny man. He might not recall our time together, but if his sense of humor was intact, he could still be happy.

"The tribunal is against the Angel of Mercy. She wrongly damned someone to the darkness. It was done out of spite and jealousy. The decision must be reversed."

"Is this personal for you, Messenger?" he inquired, studying me with interest.

I nodded. "It is."

"I see. So, you walked willingly into the darkness for the accused?"

"I did."

"Any other reason?" he asked emotionlessly.

I stared at the man I had loved, and sadly still loved, and I shook my head. "No. No other reason."

The Grim Reaper digested my request and glared at me the entire time. His eyes held no recognition, simply boredom and disdain.

"And will I be permitted to dole out the punishment to the Angel of Mercy?" Gideon inquired with a murderous look in his sparkling red eyes.

"Umm… I was kind of hoping I could do that, but I suppose it's up to Clarence Smith."

"John Travolta," Gideon corrected me with a grin replacing his angry frown.

His flirting was a knife to my heart. He didn't remember me—didn't remember our relationship. Didn't remember our love. It meant nothing to him. I meant nothing to him.

"Right," I said with a forced smile. "John Travolta."

"I will come. However, there is a price," he said smoothly.

Shit. No one told me about a payment. I didn't have much money. I suppose I could take out a loan against my house when we got back. I did finally receive Steve's life insurance settlement. But Gideon was the Grim freaking Reaper. A hundred thousand dollars was probably nothing to someone like him.

I nodded stiffly. "Name your price."

"You," he said coldly.

"I'm sorry," I snapped. "I'm not for sale."

"Everyone has a price, Messenger," he said with a wicked grin that I was drawn to even though I wanted to slap it off his beautiful face.

Steve's afterlife was on the line. Lindsay's safety and afterlife were on the line. Tim was at my house hunting vibrators to rehome. I wasn't a casual sex kind of girl—especially with someone I was madly in love with. On the other hand, Birdie had already called me a hooker. Maybe I'd make it come true. Meaningless sex between two consulting adults was no big deal.

Except it was to me.

Hopefully, the Grim Reaper would negotiate.

"I'm not a whore," I said.

"Messenger, everyone is a whore for the right price. However, I wasn't proposing *sex* if that's what you were thinking. Although, I wouldn't be opposed."

My blush came up fast and furious. I felt it rise up from my neck and slap my face. Why in the hell did I think he wanted to have sex? I was a forty-year-old widow wearing a postal uniform and my hands were a bloody mess. I wasn't really sex material. My embarrassment made me want to cry.

I didn't. I let my lady balls take over.

"My bad," I said in a tone that was as cold as his. "What do you want from me?"

"I want to understand how someone so inconsequential could break down my wall."

I wasn't sure how to accomplish that, but it was far better than becoming a whore in the true sense of the word.

"Fine."

"Do you need assistance getting back, Messenger?" he inquired casually.

I really wanted to tell him to shove his assistance up his rude ass, but I hadn't come this far to get lost in Hell.

Sucking back my pride, I nodded. "Yes, please."

"So polite," he muttered with a raised brow.

"Occasionally," I shot back.

His laugh was the last thing I remembered before the world went dark.

CHAPTER FIFTEEN

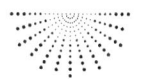

"Oh my God," I screeched as I came to on my sofa and was greeted with every sex toy I owned laid out neatly on my coffee table. "Are you kidding me? This is not what friends do."

"I didn't rehome them," Tim said in his own defense. "I believe your exact words were *do not hide, throw away or destroy my vibrators*. You said nothing about displaying them on the coffee table."

Leaning forward and resting my throbbing head in my bandaged hands, I tried not to laugh. "Tim, this is why you have no friends. You can't do shit like this."

"You should have been more specific," he pointed out.

"Yes, well, this particular scenario didn't occur to me," I said, wondering where Gideon had gone.

He had a house here in town. Maybe he was there. Or possibly he went to have a chat with John Travolta. Whatever. The less I saw of him the better.

I didn't recall a thing about coming out of Lindsay's mind. My body hurt and I was pretty sure my hands were broken, but I wasn't bone tired this time. Considering what I'd been through, I was surprised.

Still staring at the floor, I wondered if my friendship with Tim was going to last. Right now, I had my doubts.

"Is Lindsay here?" I asked. "Is she okay?"

"You've both been here the entire time," Tim said.

"Dude, you are going to have to stop being so literal. You know what I mean," I snapped, massaging my temples.

"So, was that a dick move I just made?" he inquired, truly curious.

I sighed. It would be quite a while before Tim was allowed to commingle in a group. "Yes. That was a dick move."

"I see. So sorry. Lindsay is here and is fine," he said, awkwardly patting the top of my head. "She's presently helping the one with the active middle finger find her missing body parts."

"Please tell me you didn't remove the head from the fridge," I said.

"I did not. I also didn't eat it."

"Mmmkay," I said, gagging. "Didn't realize that was a possibility. You cannot eat my ghosts. Ever. I will kick your ass so hard you won't sit for a year. You feel me?"

"As you wish."

"And since you brought it up, can that actually be done? Eating a ghost?" I asked.

"No. I was making a joke," Tim replied. "It was funnier in my head than when I actually voiced it."

"We're going to need to work on your sense of humor, dude."

"Yes," he agreed. "Congratulations on not dying and bringing Gideon back to this plane."

"Thank you on the not dying part, and how in the heck do you know I was successful?" I asked, thinking I should go share the news with Steve.

"Because I'm standing right here," Gideon said.

My adrenaline shot through the roof and I was sure I screamed. Someone screamed, and it wasn't Tim or Gideon. Therefore, it had to be me. Diving onto the coffee table, I attempted to hide the six vibrators Tim had put out for display. Mortified didn't begin to cover how I felt. Not only had I mistakenly thought the Grim Reaper wanted to have *sex* with me… now he knew no one wanted to have sex with me if my collection of battery-operated boyfriends was anything to go by.

"Yes. Welcome to the umm… earthly plane," I choked out, staring daggers at Tim. Friends did not let friends humiliate themselves. Tim had a very long road ahead of him in the friendship department. Thankfully, Gideon was not in my sightline. I didn't need his pity or to see his amusement right now. "I'm grateful that the Grim Reaper agreed to return even though he has *no clue who I am*."

"What?" Tim asked, confused. "But—"

"But," I said, swiftly cutting him off. "If you would be so kind as to take the Grim Reaper to his house in town, that would be great. That's what a *friend* would do for another *friend*."

Pinning Tim with a stare that threatened bodily harm if he contradicted me, he shrugged and nodded.

"As you wish."

"I'll be staying here," Gideon said flatly. "The Messenger and I have things to discuss."

"Nope," I said, still lying prone on the table, which wasn't exactly a power position. "No can do."

"We have a deal, Messenger," Gideon reminded me.

"We do," I agreed, debating if I should stand up. He'd already seen my stash. I shouldn't be embarrassed about it. There was nothing wrong with a woman taking control of her own pleasure. I just wished Tim hadn't found all of my pleasure devices. "However, you have a house in town. Staying at mine wasn't part of the deal."

"Terms change," Gideon said coldly. "Take them or leave them. I have better things to do anyway."

Standing up, I whipped around and got up in his face. "Are you threatening me?" I demanded as Tim sat down on the couch and got comfortable.

"What do you expect?" Gideon inquired. "I'm not exactly a nice guy."

"You used to be," I muttered as I turned and walked away.

His scent was intoxicating and my desire to touch him was out of control. He could not stay here. I'd already made a fool of myself. I wasn't strong enough not to do it again.

"What was that, Messenger?" he asked.

"Nothing," I snapped, pressing the bridge of my nose and wanting to disappear.

"Tim, you're excused," Gideon said in a curt tone. "Tell the others I've returned."

He remembered the others, yet he had no clue who I was? Shaking my head, I gave up.

"You can stay," I said emotionlessly. I was worn out. I could pretend until after the tribunal was over, and then I would do everything in my power to forget the man who had forgotten me. "You will not harm my squatters, and you will take the guest room on the first floor. Once you have the answers you want from me, you will leave."

Tim stood and walked to the front door. "Just so you know, you've been gone for a week. Very impressive. I didn't think you'd wake up for months."

"I was gone a week?" I shouted as both Gideon and Tim stepped back. "I was only there for a few hours. Three at the most."

"Time runs differently on other planes," Tim reminded me as he took his leave. "And please keep the uniform. It suits you well, friend."

The silence after Tim left was louder than the explosions in Hell.

This was my house. I had lady balls and had just survived a visit to the darkness. The Grim Reaper might insist on staying, but I wasn't going to make it pleasant. I was about to break every Southern rule in the book.

"Kitchen's over there," I said with a dismissive nod as I walked up the stairs. "Eat whatever you can find, but don't mess with the head in the fridge. That stays."

If he answered me, I didn't hear him. I had no desire to hear anything he had to say. The only upside was that after a few days of this bullshit, I'd be over him. Yesterday I would have said that sending Gideon away was the single biggest regret in my life. Three days from now I would hate him.

Win-win.

∼

"He doesn't remember me," I told Steve, playing off that all I wanted to do was sleep for about a year so I could forget about today. I grabbed my phone off the nightstand and checked it. "Holy cow. I have forty messages. Hope the ringing didn't bother you while I was gone."

"Naawwwooo," Steve said, looking concerned. "Oooooaukayah?"

Sitting down on the bed, I kicked off my shoes and cuddled up next to him. "No, I'm not okay," I said, trying to figure out who I was angrier at… me or Gideon. "I'm angry and sad. I'm embarrassed. The fact that he doesn't remember me makes all my insecurities about myself rear up and eat away at my confidence," I told Steve and took a moment to gather my chaotic thoughts. "I still see glimpses of the man I fell in love with, but his mean side is pretty intense. The asshole calls me *Messenger*."

"Dausseeeeee. Ssssoooorrry," Steve said.

"Nothing to be sorry about," I said, caressing his cheek. "The important thing is that Gideon is on this plane and the tribunal can happen."

"Yausssss."

"Steve," I said, realizing we hadn't discussed his death

much after he'd come back. "Do you remember the accident?"

He was quiet for a long moment then sighed. It sounded like a death rattle, but I wasn't disturbed. He was dead. That would never change.

"Naawwwooo," he whispered.

I hoped like hell that wouldn't be a problem when I had to go into his mind and relive it to prove his innocence. People could suppress a traumatic event, but it still had to be somewhere in his memory.

"It's okay," I told him, praying I was correct. "Everything is going to be fine."

"Daisy?" Lindsay said, standing in the doorway of my room sounding terrified and excited at the same time.

"Oh Lindsay," I said, rolling off the bed and approaching her slowly.

She was no longer a decaying corpse of a girl. However, she was still dead. An ethereal and somewhat blinding golden glow surrounded my friend, and her body was restored to what it had been before she'd passed. She was beautiful. Her eyes twinkled and her sweet smile would stay etched in my memories always.

"It's time for you to go," I whispered.

"I can stay if you need me," she said. "I mean, I can take a rain check on this ride and call it back later."

I shook my head and laughed. "Not sure that's the way it works. It's not a taxi."

"I want to go, but I don't want to leave you," she said, sounding so very young.

She shouldn't have died. Lindsay should have had a whole life ahead of her. Instead it had been stolen by greed.

"I'll be fine. I promise," I told her, running my broken hands through the silky golden mist surrounding her. "I may have helped you, but you helped me far more, my friend."

"Will you remember me?" she asked as the light around her intensified.

"Always. I will always remember you, Lindsay."

"The only way a person lives on is in the memories of those who loved them," she said with a serene smile on her lips. "I love you, Daisy. Thank you for loving me too."

As she began to fade away, my tears came quickly. I knew this was the last time I would ever see Lindsay. Endings were hard even when they were beautiful and meant to be.

I stood and watched until the golden light disappeared, taking Lindsay with it. I had no clue how long I stood there. A small grunt from Steve pulled me back to reality.

Walking to the bed, I laid down next to him and whipped off a quick text to Gram to let her know I was home and I was fine. Closing my eyes, I pushed away everything except the smile on Lindsay's face as she faded into the light.

I helped put the smile on her face. Gideon couldn't make me lose my confidence as a woman. I was in charge of that. Confidence in myself as a woman had never been my strong suit, but I would work on it. However, I had confidence in myself as a person—a loyal, loving, good person.

The proof was in Lindsay's smile and all the others who had left before her.

Gideon could screw himself. I certainly had enough devices in the house to make that a reality. I smiled at the absurd thought. I would throw all my vibrators away tomorrow. The fact that Tim had manhandled my electric boyfriends made them useless. Tim's face was now permanently attached to those vibrators.

Was that Tim's dastardly plan? Did he know his cooties on my toys would make me throw them out? I'd save that discussion for another time—a far, far, far distant time. Right now, I wanted to take a long nap next to my best friend.

I knew in my heart that Steve would be leaving me soon too.

CHAPTER SIXTEEN

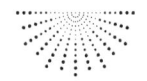

It's perfect.

Gideon loves me and Steve is alive and well. We all dance and laugh as the sun, moon and stars light the sky. I don't think I've ever been so happy. The celebration takes place in a beautiful world I've never visited—cascading flowers in every shade of gold imaginable and rows and rows of cookies made by June. The fireflies wear pink sequined ballgowns while a quartet of puppies play classical music with kazoos.

My dress is scandalous—bright sparkling gold and very sexy. Steve has chosen it to match my eyes. Gideon is very appreciative of the exposed side boob revealed by the low-cut creation. Gram boogies with Bob Barker on a table and looks better than she has in years. Gram hoots and hollers as Bob does a lively can-can number with Dip Doody as his backup dancer.

I laugh until I cry… and then, in slow motion, Gideon

drops to one knee in front of me. The crowd of at least a million guests and ghosts quiets and watches with joyous anticipation. My heart beats so loudly in my chest, I am sure the entire Universe can hear it.

∽

"Daisy?"

"The answer is yes," I muttered sleepily with a smile on my lips.

"Daisy, wake up," the voice insisted.

It wasn't Gideon.

I'd had a dream… or a nightmare depending on how I wanted to look at it.

"Daisy." The voice sounded more urgent now. "You have to wake up. Please."

The voice belonged to Heather. My eyes shot open and my body jack-knifed forward.

"Shit. What day is it?" I asked, glancing wildly around the room.

Steve was fine. He lay peacefully beside me on the bed. It was dark outside and I had no clue how long I'd slept. Heck, for all I knew it had been a week.

"It's Friday," Heather said, pale and agitated.

"Okay." I rubbed my eyes and checked the bedside clock. "I only slept about three hours."

"We need to talk," Heather said.

"You're telling me." Standing up, I took off the postal uniform, stepped into comfy yoga pants and grabbed a sweatshirt then searched for my tennis shoes. "Gideon is back and has no clue who I am. Lindsay went into the light, which made me happy and broke my heart at the same time. Hell is some serious strange and Gideon doesn't know me." I paused and scrunched my nose. "Wait. I said the thing about Gideon twice."

Heather nodded and began to pace the room. "I need to —" she began.

"Hold that thought," I said, cutting her off. "Tim told me I was out for a week even though it only felt like I was gone for a few hours. Is that correct?"

"Yes. That's correct."

"Wow," I said, stuffing the heinous uniform into the dirty laundry basket. I wanted to burn it, but I knew Tim would get his feelings hurt. However, after the vibrator debacle, I wasn't sure I cared about Tim's feelings. "So, the *Grim Reaper* basically ripped my heart out of my chest and tore it to shreds, called me *Messenger,* and saw all my vibrators."

Heather's mouth fell open in confusion.

"Yep. Just so you know, Tim does x-ray and steal mail. He likes to rehome sex toys because he thinks married women shouldn't own vibrators. Can you believe that shit? He housesat for me while I went to Hell and felt the need to rehome all my vibrators to the coffee table. Embarrassing, but whatever. At least my battery-operated boyfriends don't call me Messenger. I will *never* ask Tim to housesit again."

"Okay," Heather said, sitting down heavily on the chair by the bed. "Just so you know, I was here a lot this past week to check on you and keep everyone away."

"God, I didn't even think of that. Thank you," I said.

"That could have been bad. Did Jennifer, Missy or June come over?"

Heather sighed and ran her hands through her hair, making it stand on end. "All of them."

"What did you say?"

"That you had a major migraine and I had it covered," she replied. "June dropped off enough cookies to last a year."

I laughed. Heather didn't.

Odd.

"And umm… about Gideon," I said, chewing on my lower lip. "It's for the best that he doesn't remember me. It clearly wasn't meant to be. I don't want anyone to say anything to him about me… or rather, us. He's an asshole. He was extremely dicky in Hell. And I'm really… you know, fine. I mean, I will be soon. He blackmailed me into staying here and he's treating me like hired help. That will kill my feelings for him dead in about three days… or years. And it doesn't matter anyway. I went to get him for Steve, not me."

"Daisy," Heather said. "You need to stop talking. Please."

"I'm so sorry. What did you want to tell me?" I asked, feeling guilty that I'd talked about myself while Heather was clearly upset.

"Sit down," she said, pointing to the chair next to her.

The tone of her voice made the hair on my neck stand up.

"No," I said, feeling a little panicky. "I'll stand. Is it something about Steve? Did Clarissa come back?"

"No. Not about Steve," Heather said, sounding exhausted.

"Okay," I said slowly. "Then who?"

"Daisy." Heather walked over to me and wrapped her arms around me. "Gram died this morning. I'm so sorry."

My skin went hot then icy cold. My mind raced so fast I couldn't follow my thoughts. My knees buckled and the sound that left my mouth was inhuman. I'd made the same sound a little over a year ago when the police had shown up at my door to tell me Steve had died in a car accident.

"Daisy," Heather said, letting her tears flow as she led me to the chair by the bed and sat me down. "I'm so sorry."

"Has to be a mistake." My side-vision grew gray and it was difficult to suck air into my lungs. "Someone else. Wrong person," I wheezed.

Heather clapped her hands and produced a paper bag out of thin air. "Breathe into this," she insisted, placing the bag over my mouth. "Just breathe, Daisy. I've got you."

Taking several breaths, I calmed down for a moment until the meaning of Heather's words exploded in my head again.

"No, no, no," I cried out, tossing the bag aside. I stood, only to drop to the floor and pull my knees to my chest.

I dealt with death every day. All the time. Death shouldn't shock me or undo me. It was a natural part of life.

But I dealt with the *already dead*. Except for Steve, I hadn't known any of my squatters before they'd died. They hadn't loved me when they'd been alive. They hadn't sacrificed their lives to raise me when my mother had killed herself. They hadn't walked me down the aisle when I'd gotten married. The dead who I helped hadn't bandaged my scrapes and sung me to sleep.

The dead didn't smell like Ivory soap and dime store perfume.

"Was she alone?" I asked in a hollow voice.

"No," Heather said, lying down on the floor next to me. "Jennifer was with her. It was peaceful."

"Did she… umm… did she know?" I asked, despising myself for not being with her.

"I think she did," Heather said, brushing my hair off my tear-drenched face. "She told Jennifer to let you know you were the light of her life."

Gram's message brought on a whole new slew of tears.

"And," Heather said as a tiny smile came to her lips. "Gram said when she got to Heaven, she was going to bang Richard Dawson."

"What about Bob Barker?" I asked, laughing a little through my tears.

"Not dead yet," Heather said, pulling a tissue from her pocket and handing it to me. "Said she'd bang him when he got there."

"Oh my God," I said, holding on to Heather like a lifeline. "I can't think."

"You don't have to," she said, gently pulling me to my feet. "You have friends."

I nodded and glanced over at Steve. He'd heard everything. He'd loved Gram something fierce and she'd loved him right back. Walking over to the bed, I leaned over and kissed his forehead.

"I'll be okay," I whispered. "Not today and not next week, but I will be okay. I promise. Gram would be pissed otherwise. She'd yank my tail in a knot."

"Dausseeeeee, ssssoooorrry," Steve said.

"Me too," I told him as a sob of anguish came over me.

"What the hell is happening in here?" Gideon demanded as he burst into my bedroom.

He took one look at me then turned his fury to Heather. "What did you do to her?" he snarled.

"I did nothing to her," Heather said flatly. "Too bad the same can't be said for you."

"Answer my question," Gideon snapped.

"Get out," Heather said in a voice so icy it made me shiver. "You don't even know who she is. Get the hell out of here. You're not wanted."

"Fuck you," Gideon hissed as he crossed the room, stood next to me and put his hand on my back. "Daisy, what happened? Tell me."

The look in his eyes was one I remembered well. His touch warmed me all over. It was full of love and concern… and destroyed me almost as much as Heather's news.

My eyes narrowed to slits. I shook his hand off. I wanted to scream. "You know me?"

Gideon's chin fell to his chest. He said nothing.

"You know who I am?" I demanded in a shrill voice. "You remember me? Did recognition hit you upside the head just now or did you know all along?"

Gideon stayed silent.

"You know what?" I snapped, standing up and pushing him away. "I deserved your anger. I may have even deserved your hatred for what I did. But do you really think I deserved you turning me into nothing?"

"Daisy, I—" Gideon began.

"No," I shouted. "Just no. You knew my insecurities as a woman… as a person, and you went right for the jugular. I screwed up with you. I've regretted it every second since I sent you away. It was the biggest mistake I'd made in my life."

"Let me explain," he said.

"No. I'm done. Maybe I got what I deserved," I said wearily, yanking on my tennis shoes. "My intention had been to apologize to you. I didn't think you'd accept it or that I even deserved your forgiveness. I've been dealing with a whole lot of impossible lately. I was blind because I couldn't find any other logical explanation. I didn't trust you. I should have asked more questions. I didn't. I'm sorry. The end."

"What I did was wrong too," Gideon said, running his hands through his hair as his lips compressed into a flat line.

"You think?" Heather snapped.

"Heather, I've got this," I told her, glancing over at my friend with a small, grateful smile.

She had my back, but this was my battle.

"How long would you have kept the charade going?" I asked Gideon. I didn't yell. I wasn't mean. I simply wanted to know. "Another day? A week? Forever? What would have made you feel like you'd won? Watching me break?"

"No," he whispered, closing his eyes.

"Trust goes two ways," I said, devoid of all emotion. The world no longer held color for me. It was gray and sad. Too much was happening and my self-preservation mode kicked in. "I didn't trust you. I was wrong. I'm sorry for that. However, you win. I feel nothing. I'm empty."

"Daisy, I'm sorry," Gideon said, approaching me warily. "I was stupid. I was completely thrown when I saw you in the darkness. I wanted to hurt you the way you'd hurt me. I didn't think. I just acted. I wish I could take it all back."

"That's the funny thing," I said, walking straight up to him. "You can't. Heather is right. You aren't wanted here. You should go. And as far as our deal goes, I suppose that was a metaphor of sorts—you wanted to understand how someone so *inconsequential* could break down your wall?"

Gideon shook his head and looked as defeated as I felt.

"It's called love. That's how I broke down your wall. I loved you," I said.

"And you don't anymore?" he questioned, searching my eyes.

"I still do, but I'll get over it. You've helped me tremendously with that. Thank you."

Picking up my purse and sliding my phone into it, I grabbed a wad of tissue and shoved it in the bag as well. I would need it.

"I'm going to the… where is she?" I asked Heather.

"The funeral home," Heather said, staring daggers at Gideon. "Walton's Funeral Home."

"I'm familiar with it." I glanced over at Steve. "Too familiar," I whispered sadly.

"Who's at the funeral home?" Gideon asked, startled.

"Not that it's any of your business," I said, slipping into my coat. "But it's Gram. She died this morning."

"When you were in the darkness?" Gideon asked, pained.

I nodded.

Gideon looked devastated. "I don't know what to say, Daisy."

My name on his lips made my heart sing for the briefest of moments. I knew he wanted to comfort me. The thought was appreciated. The reality was impossible. It was something I couldn't accept.

"I'm going to say goodbye to Gram. When I get back, I want you out of my house."

"As you wish," Gideon replied.

"Heather, can you drive?" I asked. "Not sure I'm up to it."

"Of course," Heather said. "You ready?"

"No." I let the tears roll down my cheeks. "But that's irrelevant right now."

I didn't look back at Gideon as I walked out of the room. I wasn't going to look back ever again.

Only forward from now on. One step at a time. It was that or fall apart like one of my squatters.

Regrettably, I didn't have anyone to glue me back together.

CHAPTER SEVENTEEN

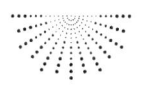

Walton's Funeral Home was formal and very Southern in its décor—full of antiques upholstered in Pepto Bismol pink and lime green silk. Gram had hated it. I wasn't fond of it either, but it was the only game going in our small town. It had been owned and run by the Walton family for generations. The smell of lilac hung in the air and clung to my clothes. Looking down, I realized I was in a sweatshirt and yoga pants. Gram would have pitched a hissy fit if she could see me.

Gram would never know.

I hoped I didn't run into any ghosts. Right now, it was all about me—no one else. I wanted to see Gram one last time and I didn't want interruptions.

Selfish? Maybe. I didn't care. Heather understood completely without me saying a word and waited in the lobby. She was golden to me. I appreciated her more than I could explain.

If I didn't take care of myself to a certain degree, I wouldn't be good for anyone—especially my squatters. I deserved some privacy with the woman who'd loved me more than anyone.

"Right this way," Goober Walton said, leading me down a hallway to a private room.

I was pretty sure Goober's name was Paul, but no one called him that. He was in his mid-forties and had been a few years ahead of me in school. He'd always been a sweet guy. I had a suspicion he was gay, but due to his hellfire-and-brimstone religious upbringing, like Steve, I doubted he'd ever acted on it.

"My condolences on your grandmother's passing, Daisy," Goober said, kindly. "We will take very good care of her for you. She was a wonderful lady."

"Thank you, Goober," I said. "She really is… I mean, was. Do I need to do anything right now?"

Sadly, I was aware of what needed to be done to arrange a funeral. Goober had helped me with Steve's only a year ago.

"There's a packet for you in the room. When you make your choices, let me know. Take your time," he said.

"Thank you," I said again.

"It's my pleasure."

Goober dealt with the dead. I dealt with the dead. Granted, my dead could talk, but…

"Goober, do you like your job?" I asked.

He smiled and nodded. "I do. I'm doing something good for people in a time of great pain and sorrow. I do it for those who have passed and for those who loved them. It's a calling for me, Daisy."

I understood him more than he would ever know. "Goober, you're a special person. Gram always liked you, and I do too."

"Thank you," he said. "The feeling is quite mutual. Give me a call tomorrow when you're ready to make arrangements. I'll leave you to say goodbye now."

Goober turned and quietly walked back down the hall. Behind the closed door in front of me was Gram… kind of. Her body was in there but that was all.

Opening the door, my breath caught in my throat. She was so small and frail, but she was still beautiful.

"Hey, old lady," I whispered as I took a seat next to where she lay. "You picked a bad time to kick the bucket. I still need you."

Gently tucking her hair behind her ears the way she liked it, I made a mental note to tell Goober. Gram liked her ears—said they were perfectly shaped. Her hearing aids were still in. I smiled. As much as she bitched about the *little nuggets*, she did indeed wear them. Slipping them out of her ears, I put them in my purse. Maybe they could be donated. I'd have to check that out.

"I'm carrying a shitty purse and wearing sweats," I told her as I laid my head on her silent chest. "However, the sweatshirt has no holes and only a little splattered paint on the sleeves."

The room was too formal for Gram. She liked cozy and comfortable. It didn't matter. What mattered was that I knew Goober would take good care of her.

"I'm so sorry I wasn't there for you," I told her as my eyes welled up again. "I love you so much. I'm going to miss you forever."

Gram's silence tore through me. I knew I had some voice messages from her saved on my phone. The thought of forgetting what she sounded like scared me. Lindsay's words rang in my ears. *The only way a person lives on is in the memories of those who loved them.* Gram would live on until the day I died.

"So… umm… Hell was weird," I told her, fully aware she couldn't hear me. "I brought Gideon back. That didn't go so well. He's a dick and I hate his guts… except I don't… but I do."

What the heck was I doing?

Who cared?

It was cathartic to lay it out.

"It's a hot mess, Gram. I screwed up bad, and then he hit a home run of screw up with the bases loaded. Bottom line, we're too screwed up for each other. Plus, he is millions of years older than me. And he's a dick."

I laughed and shook my head. Gram didn't appreciate that kind of language. But she was gone, and it made me feel good to say it.

"He's a dick-dick-dick-dick-dick." I slapped my hand over my mouth to stifle my giggles. "I'm sorry, not. I just have the worst taste in men. My husband was gay and my ex-boyfriend is the Grim Reaper. Not sure I could do much worse."

I knew I was making light of the fact that my heart was

broken for so many reasons right now, but I was in survival mode.

Picking up the folder Goober had left, I flipped through the selection of coffins. I hated coffins. When I died, I wanted to be cremated and have my ashes spread on the farm. Steve was the exact opposite. He had wanted to be buried, as did Gram. It felt morbid to me, but I'd followed Steve's wishes, and I would follow Gram's.

"I like the gray one with the silver on it," Gram said. "Goes with my hair."

"Really? It's kind of gaudy," I said, squinting at the picture—then froze.

"I've finally lost it," I muttered. My gaze jerked to Gram, who I was fairly sure was dead.

"Can't believe you walked out of the house lookin' like that. And to a funeral home, no less," she chastised me.

I'd lost my mind for real. I stood up, the brochure slipping from my fingers and falling to the floor. I put my hand on Gram's heart to check for a beat. I quickly thanked a God I was starting to believe in that she hadn't been embalmed yet. Was there a horrible mistake? Was she still alive?

"Gram?" I said, shaking her. "Wake up. I can get you out of here! I'll have a chat with Goober and Heather can drive us home."

"Daisy girl, I'm over here," Gram said from across the room. "Haven't quite got the hang of flyin' yet. Keep bashin' into walls. Hurts worse than listenin' to William Shatner sing."

"What the fu…" I gasped out as I whipped around and

saw Gram hanging upside down over the makeshift altar in the private visitation room.

"You're gettin' a real mouth on you, girlie," Gram said with a laugh as she tried to right herself. "Can you gimme a hand here? I'm kinda stuck."

"Umm… sure," I said. I didn't know whether to cry for joy or laugh. She was dead, but she wasn't gone. I was able to converse with her like I did with Steve when he'd first come back. I chalked that up to our closeness during life. "What are you doing here?"

"Thought I'd hang out for a bit and make sure Goober doesn't put that awful red lipstick on me he seems so fond of. That boy makes every dead woman in town look like a drag queen. Can't be havin' that. I want a nice burnt orange. Better with my skin tone."

"Makes sense," I said, taking her by the feet and spinning her like the wheel on *The Price is Right*.

"Wheeeeeee," she squealed. "Do it again!"

"Okay." I giggled as I spun my tiny Gram like a top. "You're going to get dizzy."

"Lordy at a pig roast on the Fourth of July," she said as she came to a stop with her head and feet where they should be. "Haven't had that much fun in ages."

I stared at her in awe. She was semitransparent, but not decaying at all. But then, she had just died this morning.

"Do you have unfinished business, Gram?"

Anything she wanted or needed, I would do. I didn't care how illegal. If she wanted me to sneak her into Bob Barker's house, I would do it. I wasn't sure *how* I would do it, but I'd figure it out. I was just so happy she was here.

"No, baby girl. I don't," she said, floating awkwardly over to the couch and seating herself. "Tell you what, this furniture is fugly and uncomfortable. Goober needs to get a decorator in here. All the pink and green is givin' me gas."

"I'll let him know. And I'm pretty sure you don't have bodily functions anymore." I was perplexed that she had no unfinished business. "If you don't have a reason to stay, how are you here?"

She scratched her head. "Don't rightly know. I suppose it might be because I know I can be here. Working with the dead all those years taught me a thing or two."

I thought about it. Maybe she was right.

"Can you stay?" I asked, holding my breath.

"You bet I can. I'm not quite ready to go, and you said you needed me," she replied, winking. "I also heard all the bull-honky you spouted."

"I didn't spout bull-honky," I told her with an eye roll.

"You most certainly did," she said, wagging her finger at me. "Never should have hidden all my boyfriends from you over the years."

"You had *boyfriends?*"

"Yep," she said with a grin. "And I feel right bad you never saw a healthy relationship between a man and a woman, Daisy girl."

"Wait," I said, trying to absorb her words. "You had boyfriends? As in plural?"

"I was a looker when I was young—still am," she informed me with a little shimmy that knocked her right off the couch.

Picking her up and placing her back on the couch, I sat

down next to her and put my arm around her so she didn't take another tumble. "Why would you hide that? I don't get it."

"Well, mostly because I had no intention of marryin' any of them," she explained. "We had enough to live down with your mamma doing what she did. We didn't need everybody in town thinking I was a hooker."

"I've got a squatter that you're gonna love," I muttered, digesting the news. "I wish you hadn't hidden anything. I feel bad, like it was my fault."

"Oh, sweetie child, we can't be at fault for the actions of others. Only our own," she said.

"That was kind of profound," I commented with a raised brow.

"Bob Barker said it," she informed me with a cackle of glee.

"Of course, he did."

"Anyhoo, you never saw the good and you never saw the real," Gram told me.

"The real?" I asked, not following.

"Yep, the parts that aren't so pretty. The stuff you gotta work through."

"I turned out fine."

"Did you?" she asked, giving me a look.

"You're saying I *didn't* turn out fine?"

"You turned out perfect, child," Gram said. "But hear me out."

"Okay. Hang on." I crossed the room and locked the door in case Goober popped in. I didn't need him to think I was nuts. I knew I was nuts, but I didn't want it getting out. This freaking town was small and gossip was the most popular hobby. "Speak, old lady."

"If you don't have enough of a foundation to rock, then the first time something goes wrong, the house falls down."

"You lost me," I said.

"You and Gideon weren't together long enough to deal with what you dealt with. Trust takes time, although you do tend to jump the gun and think you know what's goin' on when you don't," she pointed out.

She was correct and I was working on that.

"So, the fact that he made me feel like dirt is fine?" I asked, getting annoyed.

"Nope," she said. "That is not fine at all. Both of you need to yank up your panties and realize it ain't all big prize wheels and houseboats."

I sighed and held Gram close. Her scent was gone, but she was with me. That was all that mattered. And she didn't get it. She hadn't seen what had gone down and there was no way I was going to share the details. Gideon and I might not have had a solid foundation to rock, but what we *had* got decimated in an F5 tornado mostly of my doing. It was gone.

"Want to come home with me?" I asked, resting my chin on the top of her head.

"Well, I'm not goin' back to the nursin' home, so that sounds good to me," she said with a laugh. "You have an extra TV in the guest room, don't you?"

"I do."

"Thank Jesus in a jockstrap—got that one from Jennifer," she informed me with a wink. "I'm gonna need my own TV to watch my shows. Those ghosts only watch reality shows. Drove me nuts."

"You're one of *those ghosts* now," I told her as I gathered up the folder and my crappy bag.

"I'll be damned," Gram said, slapping her knee, missing and falling over. "You're right. Are any of the men single?"

"Oh my God," I choked out as I helped her up. "Are you serious? They're dead, for the love of everything weird."

"So am I, Daisy girl," she reminded me with a grin. "So am I."

I shook my head and realized that one of the worst days of my life hadn't turned out so bad in the end. "Heather's going to crap her pants," I muttered as I unlocked the door and turned out the light.

"Should I sneak up on her?" Gram asked, her eyes wide with excitement.

"Umm… no," I said, taking her ghostly hand in mine. "She's had a rough day too. Let's go hug her."

"Can I do that?" Gram asked, confused. "Won't I just go right through her?"

"Actually, yes," I said. "But it's the thought that counts."

"Amen to that, baby girl. Amen."

CHAPTER EIGHTEEN

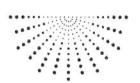

"He shouldn't be here," Heather hissed as she pulled the car to a stop and glared at the man sitting on my front porch swing.

My stomach filled with butterflies. Gideon's raw power and beauty would forever fascinate me. Heather was correct. The Grim Reaper should not be sitting on my front porch framed perfectly in the late afternoon sun, but I was secretly delighted he was.

"Heather, I love you like a daughter, but you need to relax your crack or I'm gonna have to tan your behind, which would be damn hard right now since I'm dead," Gram said, with half of her body in the car and half of it hanging out of the passenger window. "This is Daisy's fight and she needs to take care of business."

Heather sighed and banged her head on the steering wheel. "You love me like a daughter?" she asked, sounding more vulnerable than I'd ever heard her.

"Yep," Gram said, patting her back.

Of course, her hand went right through Heather, but as I'd told Gram earlier, it was the thought that counted.

"You might be a little older than me, but I love you hard," Gram said as Heather laughed.

"*A little older* is an understatement," Heather pointed out. "I love you too, Gram. I'll back off and let Daisy do her thing. However, if Gideon steps out of line again, I'll take his ass out."

"You can do that?" I asked as I watched Gideon squint in surprise when he saw Gram's head pop through the roof.

The motion of the swing was steady and slow. However, I could see the tension in his body. His eyes flashed red and the muscles in his neck were taut. It should have scared the hell out of me—pun intended. Instead, I found it heartbreakingly sexy. I needed my head examined.

"I can't end him," Heather admitted. "But I can make his existence very unpleasant."

"I can do that without your help," I told her. "I believe I already have."

"Gotta build that house before you let the Big Bad Wolf of Life blow it over," Gram announced as she floated awkwardly right through the windshield of the car. "Did y'all see that? I'm magic!"

"She's going to be a handful," Heather said with a laugh.

"Understatement," I shot back as I opened the car door and helped Gram off the hood. "Old lady, you're a hot mess."

"Thank you, Daisy girl," she replied with a whoop of joy as she turned summersaults through the air and landed with a thud at Gideon's feet. "You've got some work to do, boy."

Gideon nodded his head and smiled at Gram. "I'm aware of that."

"And not just you," she said, glancing back over her shoulder and giving me the eye. "Both of you need to get your building permits and some better hardhats. Y'all have been as ridiculous as tits on a bull."

"Okay," Gideon said, shooting me a look of puzzlement.

I couldn't help him. I knew what most of Gram's bizarre analogy meant, but I wasn't sure I could help myself right now, much less the Grim Reaper. Gideon was on his own this evening.

Tomorrow? I wasn't sure. One step at a time.

"Would you like to be more specific?" Gideon asked Gram as she held on to the railing so she wouldn't float away.

"Where would the fun in that be?" Gram inquired.

"A hint?" Gideon asked, observing Gram negotiate her new weightlessness with amusement.

"Fine," Gram huffed, tumbling over the railing and falling into the bushes. "Knocking on the door might be a good ice breaker. Son of a biscuit! Need a little assistance here. Dang near lost my head. Just wouldn't do to meet all my suitors without my noggin."

"Good God, old lady," I muttered with a groan as I pulled her out of the shrubs and helped her up the front porch steps. "I'm not running a dating service."

"Not to worry. I'll handle that," she announced with a squeal of delight as she floated right through the front door.

"I *really* don't want to leave right now," Heather said, leaning on her car and narrowing her eyes at Gideon. "But

Gram is right. This is not my fight. That being said, I'm the backup and I'm armed with weapons that will make you regret your existence for the rest of time."

"Noted," Gideon replied tightly. "Good evening, Heather."

"Remains to be seen," she muttered as she got back into the car and flipped off Gideon. "Daisy, call me if you need me."

"I will," I promised.

We stood in awkward silence as Heather slowly drove away with one last middle finger salute to Gideon.

I wanted to say a million things, but I was terrified.

"Daisy, I—" Gideon began.

I pressed my finger to his lips and shook my head. "We need to talk. A lot," I said, tempted to trace his full bottom lip. "But tonight is not the night. I can barely keep my eyes open and falling asleep on you right now isn't the best way to build a new foundation."

"Is that what Gram was referring to? Starting over?" he asked.

I nodded, afraid if I spoke, I'd suggest making out like teenagers on the swing. That was not the way to earn trust even though my desire for him was making me dizzy.

"Trust," I whispered, pulling my gaze from his sinfully beautiful mouth and raising it to his eyes. "We have to build it before we can put it through an F5 tornado."

"I see," he said with a lopsided grin.

I stared at him. He stared at me. I would've been happy to stay like this for the rest of time. However, the day had kicked my ass and I needed to make sure Gram hadn't started pairing off my squatters.

"Go inside, Daisy," Gideon instructed.

"Umm… okay," I said, confused. Guess he was done staring. I didn't blame him. I was a disaster in my messy outfit.

"Stay by the front door."

"Why?" I asked.

"Because," he replied. "Just do it. Please."

"Okay," I said with a shrug. "Bye, Gideon."

He said nothing. Simply stood there and grinned.

He was nuts, but that wasn't a deal-breaker. I wore the nuts title just as well or better than he did.

Closing the door behind me, I screamed when a rush of magic shot through my body and almost brought me to my knees. Glancing down, I gasped, and then giggled.

Gone were my yoga pants and the paint-splattered sweatshirt. Now, I was wearing the sexy little black dress that I'd worn on our first date. Gideon had clearly not forgotten anything, including the toe-crushing black stiletto heels and the diamonds in my ears and at my neck.

The butterflies in my stomach had now progressed to a herd of clog-dancing baby dinosaurs. I stayed by the door as instructed and waited to see what would happen next.

The knock wasn't loud. It wasn't urgent. It was hesitant and polite. The sound made me tingle from my head to my squished toes.

"Who is it?" I called out, and then smacked myself in the head. I sucked at stuff like this. "Wait. Scrap that. Knock again."

His laugh made me smile. Donna and Karen bounded over and sat at my feet.

"Do not attack him," I whispered. "He's here for me. Cool?"

Donna barked and wagged her tail. Karen turned in a circle and trotted back to the kitchen. Most likely to scrounge for food.

"How do I look?" I asked Donna, who barked her approval.

"You look like a princess," Gram announced with a bevy of squatters floating around her.

"Thank you," I said then narrowed my gaze at her. "Are you guys going to just hang out?"

"You bet your bippy we are," Gram said as the ghosts began to shriek and dance midair. "We're your backup."

"Thought this was my fight," I reminded her.

"We're also nosey," she added with a wink. "You won't even know we're here."

"Doubtful," I muttered and turned back to the door.

When the knock came a second time, I said nothing. I'd already screwed up round one. This time I was going to play it cool, or as cool as I could. Opening the door, I grabbed the frame to steady myself, so I didn't fall like a sack of potatoes at his feet.

Gideon wore a black tux and carried a bouquet of sparkling gold flowers like the ones from my dream. His aura was powerful, but the look of insecurity in his eyes matched mine. My instinct was to reach out and hug him, but I hesitated. I wasn't good at role-playing games, so I waited to follow his lead.

"I'm Gideon," he said, extending his hand.

"I'm Daisy," I replied, biting back the grin threatening to overtake my mouth. I took his hand in mine.

The electricity was real. It shot right up my arm, and I gasped.

"That's one heck of a handshake," I told him with a raised brow.

He nodded and held out the golden bouquet. "Very rare that it happens that way. Once-in-a-lifetime rare. It's lovely to meet you, Daisy."

"The feeling is mutual," I said, taking the flowers. I wanted to jump him. That would be horrifying. Not that I thought he would mind, but it was uncool and unsophisticated. Plus, I was wearing heels. Knowing me, if I went for it, I'd land on my ass in a crumpled pile at his feet. It wasn't the way I wanted to start over. Not to mention, Gram and the squatters were watching. "These are beautiful."

"They're appropriate. Beautiful flowers for a beautiful woman."

"You're doin' great, boy," Gram shouted as the dead chattered and hissed their agreement.

"We have an audience," I said with a wince. "Sorry about that."

"Not a problem," Gideon replied then nodded at Gram.

"Keep goin'," Gram yelled. "Tell her a little about yourself."

"Okay, I'm older than dirt and have a very unusual job," Gideon informed me with a twinkle in his eye.

"Really?" I asked, doing my best not to laugh. "I might

have you beat in the job department, but I'm only forty. How old are you, if I may be so bold as to ask?"

Gideon grinned. "Isn't that a rude question?"

"Only if you're a girl," I replied.

Gideon looked down and shoved his hands into his pockets. "I'm definitely not a girl."

"Definitely not," Gram shouted as the ghosts laughed like it was the funniest joke they'd ever heard.

I clearly had competition as the comedian to the dead…

"Thanks, Gram. I can handle it from here."

"You've got this, Daisy girl," Gram said, flying around the living room like she was wasted. "Alrighty, dead people. Follow me. I'm gonna introduce you to the greatest show in the Universe… *The Price is Right!*"

In a gust of wind that blew my hair around my head, Gram and her posse disappeared.

"Where did they go?" Gideon asked.

"Probably the kitchen," I told him. "There's a TV in there."

"I know," he replied.

He did know. He'd spent a few hours in my kitchen whipping up gourmet meals, including the best pancakes I'd ever eaten. But that was before we'd knocked our metaphorical house down. He would have to earn his way back into the kitchen, and I'd have to earn his trust that he'd be safe and loved.

"So, your age?" I repeated, grinning.

"Let's just say it's in the upper-million range," he replied and waited for a reaction.

I didn't bat an eye. "So, basically, you're telling me you're a cradle robber? Not that forty is cradle material, but you get my drift."

His laugh delighted me, and I wanted to make him laugh again.

"Yes. Yes, you could basically say that. However, there's only one cradle I'm interested in robbing."

"Smooth," I said, leaning on the frame of the door. "Does that line work for you?"

"I have no clue. Did it?" he shot right back, looking at me like I was good enough to eat.

"Umm… yes," I said as I felt a blush crawl up my neck and land on my cheeks. "I'd invite you in, but it's starting to get late, and I think we need to know each other a little better before we take the next step."

"I agree," Gideon replied without hesitation. "You have no issue that I'm the Grim Reaper?"

"Nope," I said. "As long as you don't wear a cheesy black cape and carry a scythe, I'm cool."

He shook his head with amusement. "Noted."

"And you're fine that I live with dead squatters, partake in questionably legal activities to help them and own a Hell Hound?"

"I find that wildly attractive," he replied with a look that made my insides dance with desire.

"Mmkay," I said, backing away so I didn't tackle him and beg him for a kiss. "That's very flattering. I would definitely like to get to know you better."

"That can be arranged. It would be my pleasure. And Daisy… I want you to know, I would have aided you in the tribunal even if our house was beyond repair."

I nodded and wanted to cry. "Thank you. And I'm sorry."

"As am I," he said, growing serious. "You're a first for me, Daisy. I don't know how to do this. There is a fine chance I'll do something very wrong again."

"Look," I said, taking his hand and leading him over to the porch swing. We both sat down. "There's an insanely fine chance that I'm going to screw up too. But Gram is right. We need a foundation to rock. I want that."

Gideon wrapped his strong arms around me and held me close. It felt like home. I could die happy in his arms.

"The tribunal will not be pleasant," he whispered.

"I didn't think it would. Nothing worth it is," I said. "But I'll tell you now, I will win."

"I believe you," he said. "However, the journey will be dangerous. Crossing planes and bringing justice to ills that are millions of years old has not been done."

"Not real encouraging," I muttered, cuddling closer.

"The barrier between worlds may be thin, but not all that lies behind it is savage."

"Meaning what?" I asked, leaning back and searching his face.

"It means I'm on your side. Always, Daisy. No matter what happens with us, I will be on your side."

"Can I jump ahead in the house foundation rules?" I asked, not one to play games.

"Does my opinion matter?" he inquired with a smile.

"Umm… no," I said with a laugh, and then turned serious. "Gideon, I love you. I never fell out of love with you, and I'm not sure I ever could. I was wrong not to trust you and from now on, I promise to talk to you before I make life-altering decisions that require me to go to Hell and drag your ass back."

Gideon sighed and shook his head. Wasn't the reaction I wanted, but…

"It's okay if you don't feel the same," I told him as my chin dropped to my chest. "I get it. I'm not exactly as much of a prize as you are and—"

"Daisy, stop," Gideon insisted, putting his hand under my chin and raising my gaze to his. "You are a prize beyond my wildest dreams. I'm not sure I deserve your love, but I refuse to let it go. I want all of you—your body, your mind, your soul and your love. I want to be seen by someone who makes me feel alive. You make me feel things that I thought were lost. I love you, and there's very little you can do to change that."

"Your declaration was better than mine."

Gideon threw his head back and laughed. "I disagree." He hauled me to my feet. "I want to kiss you."

"Works for me," I replied.

As he lowered his mouth to mine, I forgot how to breathe. His lips gently parted mine, and I felt all of his beautiful words in a physical way. The entire world around us evaporated and we floated on air.

This man had been created to kiss. Suddenly I understood the poems that described kissing as melting. Every inch of me dissolved into him. Gideon stole my breath as his tongue searched my mouth with a ravenous desire. I stole his right back. Right now, I had no clue where I began and he ended. It was perfect.

He slowly pulled back. His eyes were hooded with desire. My body felt like a live wire of need.

"Foundation," he said, closing his eyes and pressing his forehead to mine. "Have to build a foundation first."

"You sure?" I asked, still breathing hard.

"As much as it pains me, and trust me, it *pains* me," he said, referring to the large bulge in his pants. "We are going to say good night now."

"You're right," I agreed.

"Damn, I was hoping you'd fight me on that."

I laughed and shook my head. "Don't tempt me. You going to be okay?" I asked, eyeing the front of his pants with concern.

"After a very long, cold shower, I think I'll survive," he said. "Will I see you tomorrow?"

"Yes. You will definitely see me tomorrow. I think we should lay the concrete slabs first."

Gideon raised a confused brow.

"You know, for the foundation."

"Ahh, yes," he said. "How long do you think it will take to get the bedroom finished?"

The loaded question delighted me.

"Umm… right after the concrete dries?"

"And how long will that take?" he inquired, enjoying the game.

"Depends on the weather."

"Then I shall hope for a sunny day," Gideon said as he stepped off the porch and into the sunset. "Will it freak you out if I transport away?"

"If I said yes, what would you do?"

"Walk home."

"That's about a ten-mile walk," I told him.

He shrugged and grinned. "Worth every step."

"Poof away, Grim Reaper," I said with a wave. "I'll see you tomorrow."

"As you wish, Daisy."

CHAPTER NINETEEN

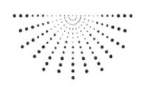

"That right there is *not* workin' for me," Gram said.

"It's pretty bad," I agreed, unsure what to do about it.

We were alone in the visitation room with Gram's body only minutes before the funeral was to begin. Gram was about to birth a cow of a hissy fit, and I didn't blame her.

Staring at the garishly awful bright red lipstick on her lips, I reached into my purse and dug around. I was careful since my hands were still bandaged due to the unattractive scabs. Thankfully, they were no longer swollen and sore.

"I think I have a better color," I muttered.

"He turned me into a dang drag queen," she complained as she zipped around the room in agitation. "If I had a dog that looked like that, I'd shave his butt and make him walk backwards."

"Should we turn you over and expose your ass?" I suggested with a laugh.

"Might be an improvement," Gram grumbled, shaking

her head. "If I wasn't dead, I'd jerk that Goober up by his tighty-whities and cancel his birth certificate."

"That wouldn't go over well," I said, finding a tube in a nice shade of rust at the bottom of my bag. My first repair attempt was iffy. "What the heck? Is this crap painted on?"

Gram examined her face and snorted with disgust. "I have never," she lamented. "Didn't you tell that boy no red lipstick?"

"Yep," I replied, trying to carefully cover the red with the rust. I eyed my handiwork and shrugged. "It's a little better, but I can still see the red. That's some heavy-duty shit."

"I'm gonna haunt his ass," Gram threatened.

"That's just rude, and you will do no such thing," I told her. "Goober is a nice man… with not-so-nice taste in lipstick."

"You'd think a gay man wouldn't make a woman look like a hooker at her own funeral," Gram griped.

"I always wondered about that," I said, putting on one more layer of lipstick.

"What? If I was a hooker or if Goober was gay?"

I rolled my eyes. "Not going to answer that, old lady. You have to behave at the funeral. I won't be able to talk to you. You feel me?"

"Yep," Gram said as she nodded with approval at the lip touch-up. "Not to worry. I brought a friend."

"A friend or *friends*?" I asked, terrified I wouldn't be able to act normally with thirty or so ghosts in attendance. It was difficult enough acting appropriately sad about Gram's death in front of *my* friends.

Bizarrely, both Gram and I were happier now that she

was dead. We were together all the time. She wasn't in pain, and once she'd quit falling off the furniture, she was getting around like she had when she was young. Of course, every TV in the house was permanently set on the game show channel, but it was a small price to pay to still have Gram.

"Only brought one nice fella along to keep me company," she announced with a wink.

"Who?"

"Jimmy Joe Johnson," she replied, putting her hands over her heart and swooning like a schoolgirl. "Always did have a crush on that fine man when he was alive."

"I give up. Which one is Jimmy Joe Johnson?"

There hadn't been a lot of extra time this past week to help my squatters. Having to act like I was in mourning in front of Jennifer, Missy and June while planning Gram's funeral was draining.

However, building a house with Gideon was magical.

The concrete foundation was coming along very nicely and the bedroom was partially finished. Not finished enough to *bang* but getting closer. We were both a little wary of the process, but took a few hours at the end of each day to talk. Gideon had millions of years' worth of stories and I was fascinated by all of them. I felt boring in contrast, but he hung on my every word.

"I do believe you've proclaimed my Jimmy Joe as the Mayor of Squatter Town," Gram said with a giggle.

"*Your* Jimmy Joe?" I asked, hiding the lipstick in the casket for a quick touch-up if needed. I wasn't exactly going to use it again after smearing it on Gram's dead lips.

"Yep. *My* Jimmy Joe," she confirmed.

"The one who cries all the time?" I asked, unable to picture Gram with the poor man who lost his hands daily and sobbed at the drop of a hat.

"He's a sensitive sort," Gram said in his defense. "I like a man who can show his feelings."

"He's certainly cornered that market," I said with a laugh of disbelief. "Gram?"

"Yes, sugar?"

"I've been wondering something. Can you talk with the others now that you're dead?"

"Yep," she said. "It's not as clear as a conversation between you and me, but I can understand them more easily than you can."

"Interesting." I sat down and mulled over what she'd just said. "So, you could help me help them? Faster than me using the Ouija board?"

Gram's eyes lit up and she cartwheeled through the air. "Well, I bet I could," she said, narrowly missing crashing into her own coffin. "The thought of it just dills my pickles. We could be a team of Death Counselors, Daisy girl!"

"I'd still have to use the Ouija board to mimic their handwriting," I said, making a plan in my head of how it could work.

"Yep," Gram agreed, checking out her lips. "That's much better, child. The green eyeshadow is a bit much, but it looks nice with the dress I picked out."

Gram had chosen and approved every detail of her funeral. It was surreal listening to her plan everything from the sermon to the songs. Her last wishes had definitely been met. Well, not the red lips but everything else, including a life-size photo of Bob Barker with Gram in her Sunday best superimposed right next to him. June had it made at the copy shop when I'd suggested it. I'd gotten a strange look from Goober when he saw it, but he covered his reaction quickly and congratulated me on a creative way to honor Gram. Missy had laughed until she'd cried and said that Gram would have loved being with her *boyfriend* for all the town to see.

Little did Missy know it was Gram's idea in the first place. Not exactly proper, but Gram and I weren't exactly proper either.

Jennifer had been devastated by Gram's death. She'd privately shared every moment of Gram's last hours with me. Told me over and over how honored she'd been to be there.

I loved Jennifer so much and wished with all my heart that I was able to tell her the truth. I couldn't. I had no proof to show her. It would be unkind, and she would think I'd snapped. One of the bright spots was that she and Dip Doody were going strong.

Chief Doody, along with my new friend, anti-vibrator Tim, were among the pallbearers. Gram had also chosen Gideon and Candy Vargo. The choice of Candy Vargo was surprising, but Gram had pointed out that the woman would probably commit the sin of wearing pants to the funeral and be the subject of gossip for years to come. Gram wanted to save the hot mess from the vicious biddies in our town. Gram swore it was appropriate for a woman to wear trousers if she had to carry a damn coffin.

Candy had been wildly baffled by the invitation, but

Gram was persuasive. In the end, Candy was honored to be included and relieved she wouldn't have to go out and buy a dress. Of course, I threatened an ass-kicking if she picked her teeth during the funeral. Candy grudgingly agreed. It helped that I carried a little weight after knocking down the tree with my bare hands.

"You ready to be a guest at your own funeral?" I asked Gram with a grin, checking the lipstick on her body one last time.

"Hell to the yes," Gram squealed. "Can't wait to listen in on everybody turning me into some kind of saint. People are ridiculous at funerals. You just make sure they follow my rules."

Her rules, which were relayed through me, were that no one was allowed to cry. Only fun stories were permitted and it was to be a celebration of Gram's life.

"I'll do my best," I said, taking her hand. "Should I tell the story about the time you answered the door buck naked when the Jehovah's Witnesses stopped by?"

"Wait till the reception for that humdinger," Gram suggested with a cackle. "But I don't want you breathing a word that I used canned peaches and margarine instead of butter in my prize winnin' cobbler."

"You did?"

"That's the secret," she whispered. "I'm takin' that one to the grave."

"My lips are sealed," I promised.

"Only thing I'm sad about today is that Steve can't be here," Gram said as we made our way to the chapel area of the funeral home. "Love that boy like a son."

I nodded so it wouldn't look like I was talking to myself if anyone was watching.

Steve had been the happiest of all that Gram was still with us in a roundabout way. They'd spent hours together this week and Steve's speaking had improved a bit. His physical condition had not. If Gram was shocked by his state of decay, she didn't show it or mention it. She fussed on him like she had when he was alive and well.

"I know," I said. "Steve's sad about that too."

"You think he'll be leaving soon?" Gram questioned.

"I do," I said.

The day Steve went into the light would be the last gift I would give to my best friend. The injustice of what Clarissa had done would not stand when challenged. I believed it with every bone in my body. Watching the Angel of Mercy pay for trying to destroy Steve to get to me was what I lived for.

"Will you be able to let him go?" Gram questioned.

I'd let Steve go once and it had devastated me. But his life now was in a horrifying and inhumane limbo. This time, it would break my heart, but I would be happy and at peace with it.

I nodded to Gram so I wouldn't cry. It was against the rules today.

There were some important points to settle before the tribunal could occur. How to bear the burden of proof was among them. Gideon could read the Sumerian in my book perfectly. He'd discovered it was impossible for more than one person to enter the mind of the dead at a time unless it was another Death Counselor. That was kind of out of the question since Gram was deceased.

It was a major issue. While Tim, Gideon, Heather and even Candy Vargo were fine with me reporting what I saw, John Travolta was not. The conflict of interest was insurmountable in his opinion and could derail the result I sought.

It made sense. I didn't like his position and secretly wondered if he was rooting for Clarissa since they were both Angels. It didn't matter. When the truth was out, the Angel of Mercy would go down.

The conundrum was how to get definitive proof. My socially awkward buddy Tim had come up with an idea. I hadn't heard it yet but planned on speaking with him after the reception. Any kind of plan Tim came up with was welcome as long as it didn't include stealing sex toys.

"Everything okay?" Gideon asked, putting his arm around me and covertly nodding at Gram.

It had taken my friends a few days to accept Gideon back into my life. The deciding factor was them seeing how happy I was despite Gram's passing. Jennifer had let Gideon know multiple times that she was banging the chief of police and that he had better watch his step. The Grim Reaper took it all in stride and was impressed by how loyal my girls were. Even Tim had taken Gideon aside and threatened to put a permanent stop on his mail if he screwed up.

I'd tried to explain to everyone that it took two to tango and I was as much at fault, if not more than Gideon. However, no one would hear it. Gideon didn't care. Our house was being built, he knew he was loved and the bedroom was close to completion.

"She's upset about the red lipstick Goober slapped on her," I told him, waving at a few of Gram's neighbors. "I did my best to fix it."

"What color does she want?" Gideon asked, as Goober somberly rolled the casket to the front of the chapel.

"Rusty orange," Gram said, popping her head in between Gideon's and mine. "Can you make that happen?"

"I can," Gideon said, keeping his gaze on the coffin. "Anything else?"

"Can you give me a quickie boob lift and a little more mascara?" she inquired.

"Are you serious?" I asked, almost turning to look at her.

"As a heart attack," Gram said. "Always wanted to get my knockers done. Just didn't have the time."

Gideon bit down on his lip and swallowed back a laugh or a groan. I wasn't sure which. Either one would have been appropriate.

"Okay," he said, eyeing the casket. "Rusty orange lips, perky knockers and more mascara?"

"You got it," Gram answered. "If you can make my girls look like they did when I was twenty, you're gonna earn a bunch of brownie points."

"I'll see what I can do," he said as he moved toward the casket.

"He's a keeper," Gram announced.

"Because he's giving you a postmortem boob job?" I asked, moving my lips as little as possible.

Gram giggled. "Well, that's a nice added bonus, but nope.

That boy's a keeper because you love him and he loves you. Steve is beside himself with joy that it worked out."

"That was his unfinished business," I told her, digging through my purse to find some tissue I could put over my mouth to hide our conversation. "He wanted me to find real love."

The room filled quickly. For the most part everyone was following the rules. Several of the gals from the Gladiola's Ladies Club were horrorstruck at the homage to Gram and Bob Barker, but most laughed with delight.

"Can you believe what Anne Wilson Benang Walters is wearing?" Gram gossiped in my ear. "That woman is eighty-two if she's a day. That is entirely too much cleavage to be showing in public, much less at my funeral. Everybody and their brother can see straight down to the promised land in that travesty. Wonder if Gideon could deflate Anne's knockers?"

"No. Absolutely not. Do *not* even ask him," I hissed. "We are not here to maim anyone. Am I clear? Even someone named Anne Wilson Benang Walters."

"Fine," Gram pouted, and then grinned. "I'm just gonna float around and listen to what people have to say about me. Knock a few heads together if I don't like what I'm hearin'."

"That should go well," I muttered as she zipped away.

"You doing okay, sweetheart?" June asked, approaching with Missy, Jennifer and Heather.

"I am," I said. "And thank you guys for making all the food for the reception. Gram would have loved that."

Actually, Gram had insisted on it.

"It was our pleasure, Daisy," June said, smiling sweetly

and giving me a warm hug. "Charlie will be here any minute. He drove all the food over and set it up."

I smiled and wondered if Charlie would be freaked out if he saw Birdie's head in the fridge. While a human wouldn't be able to see it, Charlie definitely would.

"Penny for your thoughts," Missy said, taking my hand in hers and squeezing.

"Just thinking how much Gram would have liked this party."

I caught Heather out of the corner of my eye trying not to laugh. She'd witnessed Gram insisting on the homage to Bob Barker. I'd almost decked Heather when she'd suggested Gram also pay tribute to Alex Trebek, Pat Sajak and Monty Hall. Thankfully, Gram didn't want any focus pulled from her boyfriend Bob.

"You did such a bang-up job," Missy said, scanning the crowd. "Couldn't have been better if she'd planned it herself."

The irony almost made me laugh. However, catching a glimpse of Gram across the room trying to pull Anne Wilson Benang Walters' low-cut dress to a more demure spot did make me laugh.

"Jesus in a thong," Jennifer said, throwing her little hands in the air. "Gram looks like a million bucks."

"Jennifer," June chastised. "Not exactly what you're supposed to say at a funeral."

"No, it's okay," I said, kissing Jennifer's cheek. "Gram would be delighted."

"I am," Gram shouted over my shoulder, scaring the crap out of me. "Tell Jennifer to keep talkin'. I've missed that gal."

"So… umm… Jennifer," I stuttered, trying to figure out how to phrase Gram's wish without sounding like a whack job. "Let's compliment Gram… and talk about how great she looks."

Missy eyed me a little sideways, but didn't say anything. Yes. I knew it was odd, but I was doing my best to grant all Gram's wishes. It was her day… so to speak.

"Not. A. Problem," Jennifer announced, grabbing my hand and dragging me over to where Gram's body rested.

Gram was right on our tail and whooped with joy.

"Look at those knockers," Jennifer said, to the appalled astonishment of some of the older townswomen paying their respects. "Gram had it going on! Her makeup is divine and the lipstick is perfect. Goober Walton should open up a beauty salon. I'd be there in a hot sec. She looks gorgeous."

"Bullshit," Gram hissed. "Tell her it was Gideon, not Goober."

"Nope," I told Gram as Jennifer glanced over at me.

"You don't think she looks beautiful?" Jennifer asked.

"I do," I said quickly.

"But you said nope," she pointed out.

"I was saying no to umm… Goober running a salon. Because, you know… his… umm… way with a tube of lipstick would be missed here."

"Smooth," Gram said with a giggle as she floated away to cause more trouble.

"I feel you," Jennifer agreed. "Ohhhhh, I almost forgot. Can you believe that shit about that poor gal's brother getting killed by bees? Karma is a real bitch."

"What?" Candy Vargo asked as she stepped up to the

casket to pay her respects to the woman who she could clearly see flying around the chapel like a nutbag. "Somebody call me?"

"No," I said, widening my eyes so it was clear Jennifer knew nothing about the insanity that existed around her.

"Huh." Candy pulled a toothpick out of her pocket, noticed my irate expression and put it back. "My bad. Thought I heard my name."

"Nope," I said, gently pushing Jennifer toward the seats. "It's time to start. Why don't we all sit down?"

"Good plan," Jennifer said, grabbing a seat in the front row. "I just wish Bob Barker had been able to come."

"I'm sorry. What?" I asked, sure I'd heard her wrong.

"I invited him," she told me. "Told him Gram was his biggest fan. Maybe he'll show up at the reception."

Jennifer had always been excellent at stunning me to silence. Today took the cake.

"How did you reach him?" I asked.

"Gram had his address. Gave it to me on her final morning. Told me if she kicked the bucket to invite her boyfriend Bob."

And that's when I laughed. Hard. I knew there were some who thought I was disrespectful, but I didn't care. All of the people who truly mattered to me did not. Especially the woman of honor. Gram's opinion was the only one that mattered today.

"Of course, she had Bob Barker's address," I muttered as Gideon sat down next to me and the celebration of Gram's life began.

"Never seen anything like this," Gideon whispered in my

ear as we watched Gram zip through the mourners and land with a crash on top of her dead body.

I was fairly certain I heard Candy Vargo and Tim laugh. A few other Immortals in attendance gasped. Even John Travolta seemed amused. The man was a strange one, and I wasn't sure he would attend. However, he'd shown up, and chances were good that he would stop by my house for the reception afterward.

I had plans for an impromptu Immortal meeting. The clock was ticking, and the thought of Clarissa getting away with what she'd done was abhorrent. Steve deserved the afterlife he'd earned. And I was going to make sure he got it.

CHAPTER TWENTY

"I just can't believe it," June gushed, fanning herself and blushing. "He looked *so* good in person. Such a dapper man."

I couldn't believe it either. Bob Barker had pulled up in a black limo and stopped in to pay his respects to Gram. He'd flown all the way from California to Georgia and stayed for an entire hour.

"I'm a little shocked too," Jennifer said, coming out of the kitchen with a wipe to clean off the tables now that the food had been put away.

"You wrote him," Missy pointed out, picking up used plates and napkins.

"I know," Jennifer said, flopping down on the couch and petting Donna. "But I sure as hell didn't think he'd show up."

Karen was sound asleep under the coffee table. She'd successfully raided the trashcan three times and was coming down off of a doggy sugar high. I was sure she'd have some house- clearing gas later, but I didn't care. The reception had gone smoothly and Gram was pleased.

"Must have been good *karma*," Candy Vargo said, picking her teeth and winking at me.

I was flabbergasted. I didn't know the Immortal rules for favors done. However, I was fairly sure Candy Vargo didn't do nice things for free. What in the heck had *Karma* done to get Bob Barker to come to a funeral reception on the other side of the country for a woman he didn't know? I decided not to ask. Some things were far better left to the unknown.

"I've asked them to stay after for a meeting," Gideon said quietly.

I was looking forward to it. The time had come. I could feel it.

I smiled and leaned into Gideon for comfort. Exhaustion didn't quite describe how I felt. Thank God for my friends. I could swear the entire town had shown up for the reception. If I had to guess, I'd say thirty percent didn't even know Gram and were nosey. However, it was a sin in the South to come empty-handed to any kind of celebration—especially a funeral.

In other words, I was stocked with pies and casseroles to last into the next year.

"Today was outstanding," Heather said, joining Gideon and me as the last of the crowd made their exit. "Best part was when Gram crashed into the casket."

"Shhh," I said with a laugh. "There are still people here."

"What are we?" Heather inquired playfully.

"We're freaks," I told her. "Do *not* announce it to the town."

"Whoops," Heather said, grinning as she skipped away and helped with the cleanup.

"It really was quite spectacular," Gideon said. "Never saw anything like it. Best funeral I've ever attended."

I laughed. I'd laughed a lot today. "It really was funny."

The squatters adored having a party. They inserted themselves into random conversations all over the house and front porch. It reminded me of the haunted house ride at Disney World. If only the snooty old gals knew that ghosts were sitting on their heads…

And Gram? She went nuts when Bob Barker arrived. I was worried that she'd be devastated he couldn't see her, but she seemed fine. Her new beau, the Mayor of Squatter Town, aka Jimmy Joe Johnson, stayed glued to her side the entire afternoon. He'd only cried three times during the gathering, which was a huge improvement.

"Did everyone agree to stay?" I asked Gideon.

He nodded. "Took a little convincing for John Travolta, but I succeeded."

"Did you call him *John Travolta*?"

"Was tempted, but no," he replied. "Thought I'd save that for when everyone was present."

"Looking forward to it," I said, biting back a giggle.

"As am I."

"Do you always succeed?" I questioned, waving goodbye to Gram's favorite nurse from the home.

Glancing down at me with a sexy and very naughty

expression, Gideon chuckled. "Remains to be seen. I've been working quite hard on the bedroom. How am I doing?"

My stomach fluttered, and I could feel the heat rise in my cheeks. "I think the bedroom will be completed very soon."

"How soon?" he inquired with a raised brow.

"When the paint dries," I said, lightly punching him in the arm.

I was seriously careful about playful hitting now. After the tree debacle, I was wary of my strength. I'd busted three jars of pickles opening them just yesterday. The ghosts thought it was a comedy act and went wild. I did not. Getting to the bottom of why I was turning into the She-Hulk was on my increasingly long to-do list.

"I'll be sure to buy a few industrial fans," he replied then changed subjects. "Where should I tell the Immortals to meet?"

"Let's meet in the kitchen."

"I'll let them know," he said, heading away toward Candy and Tim.

"Okay," June said, looking around the living room and nodding with satisfaction. "Kitchen's all cleaned up and it looks pretty good out here."

"Thank you for everything," I said, giving one of my dearest friends a hug. "Thank you from me and thank you from Gram."

June swiped a few tears away. "I'm going to miss her so much. She was just a hoot."

"Still am," Gram said, floating next to June and touching her lovingly. "Sure wish June could see me."

I nodded. The gesture was a two-fer. Commingling the living with the dead was tricky, especially when Gram was involved.

"No time for crying," June said, leaning on Charlie as he came up behind her and put his arms around the love of his life. "Gram would want us to turn that frown upside down."

"Darn tootin'," Gram said, zooming in circles around June and Charlie.

Charlie covertly winked at Gram and gave his wife a squeeze.

"You sure you're fine riding home with Chief Doody, Jennifer, and Missy?" he asked June.

"Absolutely. Kind of excited to ride in the back of the cruiser, seeing as I've never been arrested before," June said with a grin. "Now Charlie, I want you to help Daisy break down all the tables and chairs. And anyhoo, if I rode home with you, there wouldn't be any room in the car for me and my big bottom once you load it up."

"It's a lovely bottom," Charlie told her as she blushed and fanned herself with her hand.

"You're a keeper, Charlie," she said, giving him another peck on the cheek. "After you get done, make sure Daisy eats something. I didn't see her eat much this afternoon."

June gave me the mom eye then winked.

"Will do," Charlie promised.

"We're out," Missy announced. "I love you, and I know Gram would have loved today."

"Got that right," Gram said, hanging upside down on the ceiling fan.

"I still can't get over her knockers," Jennifer said. "They

were downright perky. That Goober Walton is a genius. I'm gonna make an appointment with him."

"For the love of everything tacky," Gram groused, falling from the ceiling and landing on top of Jennifer's head. "Make sure she doesn't ask Goober for a boob job. That would be a god-dang disaster."

Making use of a two-fer again, I nodded to both women. Gram was correct though. Jennifer needed to stop with the self-improvements. She was awesome as she was.

"You don't need Goober Walton to make you beautiful, Jenny," Dip said. "You're pretty dang perfect in my book right now."

"You just earned yourself a BJ," Jennifer announced to all who were left.

Dip belly laughed and shook his head. "I'll meet you gals at the cruiser when you're ready to go."

"Are you going to marry him?" Missy asked when Dip was out of earshot.

"Nope. Gonna live in sin with that fine man until the day I die," Jennifer said. "Like I told Daisy, I love him way too much to marry him."

"When did you start making so much sense?" Heather asked with a grin. "As I recall, you used to call him Big Dick Dookie the Dunghole."

Jennifer burst into laughter and made a valiant attempt at waggling her eyebrows. The Botox blocked her move. "Yep. Shortened it. Just going by Big Dick Dip now."

"You're just awful," June said, giggling.

"Thank you," Jennifer replied with a thumbs up. "You gals ready?"

"We are," Missy said, giving me one last hug. "Call me if you need to talk."

"I will," I promised as I watched June chastise Jennifer for her TMI comment all the way out of the front door. "And thank you for the book. Heather dropped it off."

"Got one for myself to see what all the fuss was about," Missy said. "Can't read a word of it, dude. Not sure it's going to be helpful. I can search for something else on the Sumerian language written in English if you want me to."

"Nope. It's no big deal," I said, lying through my teeth. "I'll use it as a doorstop."

Missy grinned. "Good thinking."

Heather walked her out, and I wondered if something was happening between them again. I hoped so.

"Full disclosure," Tim said, walking over to me and looking guilty. "I hid your toys."

I'd thrown out the first batch of vibrators and it was looking abundantly clear that I was going to have to toss the two new *toys* I'd ordered.

"Is that what a good friend would do?" I asked, shaking my head.

"Actually, yes," Tim said, rocking from one foot to the other.

"Not following." I crossed my arms over my chest and waited.

Tim glanced around then leaned in close. "Some of those terrible Gladiola women were digging through your drawers. I busted them and took names. They will not be receiving mail for the next six months."

My mouth hung open. People could seriously suck.

"So, to keep them from your filthy secrets, I hid your electronic sin tools."

"Umm… thank you," I choked out with a horrified laugh. "That is exactly what a good friend would do."

Tim preened and rocked even faster. "Thought so. Glad I got it right."

"You did," I told him. I was tempted to hug him, but that might scare him. We'd get to that eventually.

"Is everyone ready to meet?" Gideon asked.

"How long will this take?" Clarence Smith inquired, checking his watch.

"As long as necessary," Gideon replied in a curt tone.

"Of course," Clarence said. "My apologies."

"No fighting… yet," Candy Vargo said, eyeing both Clarence and Gideon. "I say we get started. Now."

~

"Hell's bells," I muttered as I let my head fall forward. The swirling grain in the oak of my kitchen table was far more interesting than the gibberish that was being shouted and echoing throughout the house.

The furious disagreement between the two powerful men made me wish I'd told everyone to go home.

"Just be happy no one is throwing lightning," Candy Vargo whispered, picking her teeth with a toothpick.

I stared at her with my mouth open. I never knew if the woman was serious or just trying to screw with my head. "Is that an actual possibility?"

She winked. "Yep. You wearing rubber soled shoes?"

"No," I hissed under my breath. "I'm wearing my funeral freaking best. Tennis shoes don't exactly go with dress clothes."

Candy shrugged and grinned. Lifting her leg, she showed me her ratty tennis shoes. "I beg to differ."

It was truly horrifying that Candy was the Immortal in charge of karma. She was a hot mess of rude and some serious scary.

"I suppose you could duck," she suggested with a chuckle.

Rolling my eyes, I was tempted to flip her off. However, *tempting* fate wasn't a great plan. "Roger that," I said and turned my attention back to the action I hoped wouldn't take my house down.

The Grim Reaper and the highest-level Angel in existence fighting in a dead language wasn't what I'd envisioned when I'd called the meeting of the Immortals in my kitchen. It had been a heck of a long day with Gram's funeral and over half the town in my home for the reception afterwards.

"You okay, Daisy?" Heather questioned quietly.

I smiled and shrugged. "Not sure I know the meaning of the word anymore."

She gave my hand a quick squeeze and watched as the undecipherable argument grew more heated. With a reassuring glance, she moved to the kitchen counter and observed the disagreement with an emotionless expression on her lovely face. Having Heather here was a blessing.

My head felt like it might explode. Gideon and Clarence had been arguing back and forth in Sumerian for an hour. I couldn't understand a word. The ghosts had gotten bored and wandered away in search of a reality show to watch. Gram had stayed.

Gram had nodded off a few times and fell off of her chair, but in her defense, she'd had a big day. How often did one get to attend one's own funeral as a ghost? Gram's mid-service crash landing on top of her dead body in the casket she'd chosen to match her hair wasn't an everyday occurrence. However, it did make for an excellent story.

"Eat this," Candy Vargo said, slapping down a plate in front of me at the kitchen table while the two men continued to debate. "Those nosey bitches who showed up left enough food to feed an army."

Glancing down, I couldn't quite understand what I was seeing. Candy was clearly as messy with her food as she was with her appearance. Potato salad was piled on top of apple pie. Next to it sat a piece of fried chicken dangerously close to a large helping of banana pudding. The topper was the unidentifiable casserole that had blueberries and ground beef in it.

It was all I could do not to gag.

"Umm… thanks," I said. "Not hungry right now."

"Try that," Candy insisted, pointing her ever-present toothpick at the blueberry beef surprise. "Looks disgusting. I want to know if it tastes as bad as it looks."

I pushed the plate over to her. "Then you try it."

Candy shrugged, removed the toothpick from her mouth and took a bite of the mysterious concoction. "Tastes like baked ass with blueberries," she muttered, swallowing with effort.

I was wildly pleased she didn't spit it back out onto the plate. Candy's manners were iffy at best.

"Can you understand them?" I whispered as I watched Gideon grow angrier and Clarence narrow his eyes in displeasure.

"Yep," she replied, putting her tennis-shoe-clad feet on my kitchen table.

"Nope." I knocked her feet back to the floor. "Tell me what they're saying."

"Can I put my feet back up?" Candy bargained.

"Only if you want to eat the entire blueberry ass casserole," I shot back.

"Spicy," Candy muttered with a laugh and scooted her chair closer to me. "They're arguing about if you can be trusted to tell the truth of what you see in Steve's mind. Clarence believes you're too close to be neutral. The Angel of Mercy stands to lose everything if she's deemed guilty. The Grim Reaper is on your side completely… of course, you're banging him."

"First of all, I'm *not* banging him," I snapped. "And if I was, it's not any of your business. While I do understand you're a badass who could probably incinerate me with a flick of your woefully under-manicured finger, I'd like to remind you that I punched a freaking tree and it fell over."

Candy eyed me until I grew uncomfortable. Unsure if she was going to tear my head off with her bare hands or laugh, I held my breath.

"You've got enormous nards," she stated, raising her brow.

"Lady balls," I corrected her.

"Whatever," Candy said. "It's impressive."

"Thank you," I replied, shaking my head. My Southern manners were ingrained. A rude compliment was still a compliment and required a polite response.

Candy stabbed the baked blueberry ass with her tooth pick and pulled out a fresh one. "So, as I said, Clarence isn't on your side, Death Counselor."

"John Travolta is being a dick," I hissed under my breath. "And Clarissa *is* guilty."

"What you just said is proof of Clarence's issue," Candy pointed out. "You've already damned the Angel of Mercy without proof of guilt. While I hate the bitch, I have to side with Clarence on this."

Shit. She did have a point. I questioned how far I would go to ensure the safety of Steve's afterlife. I would go very far… very, very far.

"The problem is that Gideon has found in the text that it's impossible for another to join a Death Counselor in the mind of the dead," Charlie said quietly.

"Do you agree with John Travolta and Candy that I can't be trusted?" I asked.

Charlie was quiet for a long moment. "Trust is not the issue," Charlie explained. "Much more than you can comprehend is on the line. What I do believe is that your loyalty is with Steve. It muddies the waters."

"There's another way," Tim announced loudly.

Everyone stopped and stared at Tim. God, I hoped my new, socially awkward, vibrator rehoming friend was going to make sense.

"Speak," Gideon said tersely.

"Daisy is a hybrid Angel," Tim said, pointing to my eyes.

That woke Gram up fast. "What in tarnation are you talkin' about?" she demanded. "Her mamma was a human Death Counselor just like me and just like Daisy."

"And her father?" Tim asked.

Gram sighed and shook her head. "I don't know."

"*If* this is true," I said, feeling strange and a little panicky. "What does it have to do with anything?"

"Interesting," Karma said, leaning in and studying my eyes. "I hadn't noticed. Very, very interesting."

"Again. Why?" I demanded. "How does the *possibility* of me being some kind of half-breed freak help get justice for Steve?"

Ignoring my question, Clarence leveled me with a hard look. "What is it that you want? To send your dead husband into the light or to destroy the Angel of Mercy?"

"The Angel of Mercy damned Steve to the darkness out of hatred of me. Her decision can't stand." I snapped. "So to answer your question… it's one and the same."

"Not necessarily," he replied.

"Bullshit," Heather said. "You would let the Angel of Mercy take a plea deal, so to speak? Get away with taking fate into her own hands unchecked? That is *not* how it works."

Clarence brought his fist down on the table in frustration. "Do you have any idea what stripping an Angel could do to the order of the Universe? Do you?" he shouted.

"I do," Gideon said coldly. His eyes turned red and his features sharpened. "I know exactly what happens when an Angel falls."

"With all due respect," Charlie said, nodding at Gideon. "We're not talking about a demotion. We're talking a removal of power, heritage and Immortality."

"Shit," Karma muttered with a laugh. "That would certainly suck."

"Enough," Clarence growled. "*If* the facts are indeed proven against the Angel of Mercy, the punishment shall be doled out and the price will be paid. But…"

"But what?" I asked, feeling like my world was spiraling out of control. Was Clarissa going to get off scot-free?

"But I see no clear way to prove that your husband's death was indeed an accident," he finished, sounding tired.

The room was silent. Gideon's jaw worked a mile a minute and he looked like he wanted to kill Clarence. Heather was furious and pressing her temples. Gram was simply in shock. Candy seemed bored, and Tim…

Tim was grinning.

"I see a way," Tim said.

Tim had just moved to the top of my friend list.

"Out with it, Courier," Charlie demanded, focusing on Tim with interest.

"Blood-related Angels can see into each other's mind by touch," Tim reminded the others.

"This is true," Heather said, getting excited. "It can also be broadcast."

"Meaning?" Gram asked, as befuddled as I was.

"Meaning, an Angel could send—or rather, telecast—what he or she sees to those Immortals within close proximity," Gideon explained.

"Like a TV show?" Gram asked.

"Close enough," Candy confirmed, no longer bored.

"The point?" Clarence asked tersely.

"Daisy was sired by an Angel," Tim explained. "He can be used to show us what Daisy sees in the mind of her husband. We would all relive the death and know the outcome. Daisy's neutrality or lack thereof would no longer be an issue."

My hope died as quickly as it had started. There was a huge hurdle. An impossible hurdle.

"I don't know who my father is," I said flatly. "The plan is not possible."

"Nothing is impossible as long as you believe," Candy reminded me, twirling her toothpick in her fingers.

"While the idea is excellent, the reality is not. I have no idea who he is," I repeated.

"Clarence," Tim said, sounding ominous and cold. "Would you care to join the discussion?"

Everyone watched as Tim stood and walked to the back of the chair where Michael the Archangel was seated.

"I would not," Clarence ground out.

"Would you rather I deliver the news? I am the Courier after all."

Clarence Smith was not a happy man. It was very clear he knew who my father was. It was also clear that he didn't want to give up the information. Hatred for the man who had been so kind to me for years blossomed in my chest and made it difficult to breathe. Was he so taken with Clarissa that he would let her get away with unforgivable crimes?

I'd take a Demon over an Angel any day of the week.

"The conversation is over," Clarence said. "The meeting is done."

"The conversation has just started," Charlie said in a tone that made me want to hide. Charlie's eyes blazed silver and his hands sparked menacingly. "You will reveal the name of Daisy's father, Archangel… or there will be hell to pay. Am I clear?"

The house shook, and I wondered for a brief moment if I would have to find a new place to live. I glanced over at Gideon, but his blood-red gaze was trained on Clarence.

No one knew who my father was other than John Travolta and Tim. That was abundantly clear by the reactions of the rest of them.

"The answer will be displeasing," Clarence said, devoid of emotion.

"I don't care," I said. "I want nothing to do with the man other than using him to save Steve. I'll use him like he used my mother. He is nothing to me other than a sperm donor, a deadbeat asshole, and a means to an end. Period."

"I'm quite sure he'll be relieved to hear that," Tim said with an undecipherable expression on his face. "Clarence, will you make sure to tell him what his daughter said?"

Clarence sat silently, and then genuflected.

"Making the sign of the cross won't save you," Tim said. "Speak now, or I shall."

I was ready to puke. I didn't understand what the heck the holdup was.

"Give me his name," I said. "Tell me where he is. I won't let him know how I found out. Your secret is safe with me."

"Oh, the irony," Tim said with a chuckle as the Archangel's body tensed in fury.

"Shut up!" Clarence roared at Tim then turned his angry gaze on me. "I'm your father."

The next few moments defined the term deafening silence.

The looks exchanged between the Immortals were ones of shock and confusion. Gideon was ready to strangle the Angel.

"Are you fucking kidding me?" I shouted, standing up and not caring that Gram heard me drop an F-bomb. "Are we in a *Star Wars* movie? Is this some kind of sick joke?"

Clarence closed his eyes and shook his head. "It's not a joke. I'm your father."

I heard a thud and turned to see that Gram had passed out. I had no clue until now that a ghost could do that.

"Help her," I directed Candy, who hopped to her feet then sat down on the floor next to Gram. "I'm processing a whole lot of shit right now. The words disgusted and horrified come to mind, as well as hatred and revulsion. You have known me my entire life. My entire fucking life."

"I have," he said, staring at me. "It was for your own good."

"My own good?" I snarled. "That's certainly big of you, John Travolta. Thanks for that, you no-good son of a bitch."

"There is much you don't know," he said.

"Enlighten me," I replied.

The man who claimed to be my father said nothing.

"I'm talking to you," I snapped.

"And I hear you," he replied.

"Then answer me."

Again, he was silent.

I wanted to hit him. I wanted to destroy him. Why hadn't he wanted me? What was so wrong with me that he'd been around me my whole life and never acknowledged me?

My mother had preferred death to me, and my father hadn't wanted me. It was entirely too much to take in.

So, I didn't. I shut that part down. I'd turned out fine without a mother or a father. I'd had Gram, who had loved me enough for a hundred mothers and fathers. I didn't need a father. I didn't want one.

"Your explanation doesn't matter," I said with no emotion in my voice. He wasn't even worthy of my hatred. "You mean nothing to me. All I want from you is to touch me when I go into Steve's mind and share his death memories with the others."

"He is bound by honor and blood to obey your request," Charlie said, still shocked by the revelation.

"Correct," Heather said, coming to my side and placing her hand on my shoulder. "As the Arbitrator, I consent to the request of the daughter of the Archangel Michael. He is bound by the principles of virtue and goodness to aid in the case against the Angel of Mercy."

"His noncompliance shall result in punishment." Gideon stared daggers at Clarence. "By me."

"And me," Karma added, sounding delighted by the prospect.

"Your reply?" Charlie demanded of Clarence.

"As you wish," Clarence said with his gaze pinned on me.

I nodded jerkily at him and held on to my composure only by a thread.

"When shall we begin?" Tim asked, joining Heather at my side.

"Now," Gideon said. "I don't trust him to keep his word."

"My word is good," Clarence growled.

"Then what's the problem?" Gideon shot back.

"There is no problem," he said, sounding old and tired.

"Where is Steve?" Charlie asked.

"Upstairs," I whispered, light-headed and terrified.

Without another word, everyone stood and made their way to the stairs. My heart felt like it was going to explode out of my chest. This is what I had been fighting for and now that it was here, I was almost paralyzed.

Gideon and I were the last to leave the kitchen.

"Remember two things, Daisy," Gideon said as his eyes still blazed red. "One, I love you."

"And two?" I asked.

"The barrier between worlds may be thin, but not all that lies behind it is savage. We will win."

Taking his hand in mine, I slowly led him out of the kitchen and into the violent storm that awaited us.

"Are you ready?" Gideon whispered as we took the steps one at a time… moving forward and not looking back.

"Yes," I said without hesitation. "I am."

The End… for now

MORE IN THE GOOD TO THE LAST DEATH SERIES

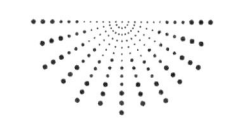

ORDER BOOK THREE NOW!

Midlife's a bumpy journey. The ride is a freaking roller-coaster. The crisis is real.

With my life back to normal--*normal* being a very relative word--one would think I'd catch a break.

One would be very wrong.

With an Angel gunning for me and a Demon in my bed, life couldn't be more complicated. Not to mention, I'm going to have to make a rather *large* life choice.

Do I want to live forever?

Does anyone? Forever is a very long time.

Whatever. I'll think about it tomorrow... or next week... or next month. As long as I have my girlfriends, my dogs, a super-sized case of merlot and my deceased squatters, I'm good to go.

My midlife crisis. My rules. If it doesn't kill me dead first, I plan to have a most excellent midlife crisis.

ROBYN'S BOOK LIST

(IN CORRECT READING ORDER)

HOT DAMNED SERIES
Fashionably Dead
Fashionably Dead Down Under
Hell on Heels
Fashionably Dead in Diapers
A Fashionably Dead Christmas
Fashionably Hotter Than Hell
Fashionably Dead and Wed
Fashionably Fanged
Fashionably Flawed
A Fashionably Dead Diary
Fashionably Forever After
Fashionably Fabulous
A Fashionable Fiasco
Fashionably Fooled
Fashionably Dead and Loving It
Fashionably Dead and Demonic

More coming soon...

SEA SHENANIGANS SERIES
Tallulah's Temptation
Ariel's Antics
Misty's Mayhem
Madison's Mess
Petunia's Pandemonium
Jingle Me Balls

SHIFT HAPPENS SERIES
Ready to Were
Some Were in Time
No Were To Run
Were Me Out
Where We Belong

MAGIC AND MAYHEM SERIES
Switching Hour
Witch Glitch
A Witch in Time
Magically Delicious
A Tale of Two Witches
Three's A Charm
Switching Witches
Your Broom or Mine
The Bad Boys of A$$jacket

HANDCUFFS AND HAPPILY EVER AFTERS SERIES
How Hard Can it Be?

Size Matters
Cop a Feel

If after reading all the above you are still wanting more adventure and zany fun, read *Pirate Dave and His Randy Adventures*, the romance novel budding novelist Rena was helping wicked Evangeline write in *How Hard Can It Be?*

Warning: Pirate Dave Contains Romance Satire, Spoofing, and Pirates with Two Pork Swords.

NOTE FROM THE AUTHOR

If you enjoyed reading *Whose Midlife Crisis Is It Anyway?*, please consider leaving a positive review or rating on the site where you purchased it. Reader reviews help my books continue to be valued by resellers and help new readers make decisions about reading them.

You are the reason I write these stories and I sincerely appreciate each of you!

Many thanks for your support,
~ Robyn Peterman

Want to hear about my new releases?
Visit robynpeterman.com and join my mailing list!

ABOUT ROBYN PETERMAN

Robyn Peterman writes because the people inside her head won't leave her alone until she gives them life on paper. Her addictions include laughing really hard with friends, shoes (the expensive kind), Target, Coke (the drink not the drug LOL) with extra ice in a Yeti cup, bejeweled reading glasses, her kids, her super-hot hubby and collecting stray animals.

A former professional actress with Broadway, film and T.V. credits, she now lives in the South with her family and too many animals to count.

Writing gives her peace and makes her whole, plus having a job where she can work in sweatpants works really well for her.